THE SEASTEAD CHRONICLES

by

STEVEN R. SOUTHARD

Pole to Pole Publishing
Baltimore

Library of Congress Control Number: 2025937132

Table of Contents

I dedicate this book (1) to fellow writer Andy Gudgel, who first told me about seasteads and thought I might be interested; (2) to all submariners with whom I had the honor of serving; and (3) to mariners everywhere, who show us how to live on and under the sea.

THE SEASTEAD CHRONICLES

Arrow of Life

I'm more American than Native American, Samantha Dawnstar thought, *more cowboy than Indian.* She sat in the library area of the Osage Cultural Center, checking her smartphone.

As an Air Force officer, she kept up with military news. Opening a news app, it surprised her to see an article about a Navy destroyer, USS Kinkade, suffering damage in the central South Pacific.

Through the wall she heard the monotonous heart-beat pounding of drums and the ancient chants of hoarse, old men. In the parking lot outside, young men wearing brightly colored Osage apparel prepared for the final night of the *In-lon-shka*, the celebratory Dance of the Eldest Son. The tribe gathered in Pawhuska, Oklahoma every June for the event, and at age twenty-seven, Sam had attended more of them than she cared to recall.

Sam read further in the article. The destroyer had received several radio warnings to stand clear of "the sovereign aquastate of PaCitadel," as had a Chilean merchant ship traversing the area several weeks earlier. Though the merchant ship had heeded the warnings, the destroyer entered the zone, just a patch of open ocean. Two torpedoes came out of nowhere and damaged the ship's sonar and rudder, forcing the warship to leave the area.

Within the cultural center, garish clan symbols, totems, and artwork cluttered all available wall space. Tribe members milled around or chatted in small groups. Some admired or sold crafts. The smells of pemmican, turnips, maize, and squash wafted in from the kitchen.

I hate all this stupid nostalgia, people clinging to a dead culture. Samantha sighed, wishing she could have spent her precious leave doing something more enjoyable. *I just have to be here one more night to please Dad. Tomorrow I can drive back to the airbase and get back to being Captain Dawnstar, U.S. Air Force.* Sam had fifty percent blood quantum; she favored her non-Native mother in appearance, but lacked her mother's interest in Osage cooking and clothing.

In a side room dedicated to tribal youth, her grandfather, Fred Dawnstar, Director of the Cultural Center, sat cross-legged on the floor explaining history to two dozen small children who stared with wide eyes as he spoke and gestured. He wore his showy, multicolored outfit with the large feathered headdress.

"Many ages ago," he told the children, "We Osage were nomads, people who wandered, seeking the best hunting grounds. We settled in vast areas of this country, farming and hunting when we could, fighting other tribes when we had to. The white man came with his stronger weapons and didn't want us living there. He drove us West from our lands to this part of Oklahoma."

Sam shook her head. She'd heard her grandfather's lectures many times before. The news article ended with quoted statements from politicians condemning the unwarranted attacks by the illegal and mysterious "PaCitadel" organization. *Who are these people? Some new terrorist group?*

"What the white man did not know," Sam's grandfather droned on, "was that this land had valuable oil underground. They paid us well for this oil, but they surely would not have settled us here if they'd known about it. We must use our wealth to hold on to our culture. That means our art, music, food, and ceremonies. You must never forget you belong to the Osage Nation.

"Listen, children," Sam's grandfather lowered his voice, leaving his young audience spellbound, "one of our traditions that you'll see later tonight is the shooting of the ceremonial arrows. One arrow is black, the arrow of death. The other is red, the arrow of life. You'll see a brave arch his bow—" he mimed the action, "—and shoot both arrows toward the West. The sun and moon mark the days by moving from East to West, so our ceremony shows how life and death forever follow day and night."

Sam snorted quietly. *I wish he'd quit filling young minds with Stone Age myths.* She spent a few minutes reading and responding to e-mails and social media messages from friends. When she looked up again, her grandfather had finished with the children, dismissed them, and was walking her way. She rose and gave him a hug.

"Thank you for coming, *Mo-sa-ne,*" he said, using her Osage name. "Will you be staying long?"

"No, Grampa. Just through the ceremony tonight. I head back to the base tomorrow."

She recognized the disappointment in his eyes, having seen it often before. "You know I don't go in for all this stuff, Grampa." She waved her hand to indicate the Cultural Center. "We're in the Twenty First Century now. We've got to keep up with the times."

"Some things do not change with the years, *Mo-sa-ne,*" he frowned, "such as a granddaughter showing respect to elders."

She sighed and looked down. "I'm sorry, *Weet-see-koe,*" using the title meaning Grandfather. "I meant no disrespect. But it is my life and I must follow my own path."

"Your own path." He smiled and looked far away. "When you were born, I knew you'd seek a path. That is why, at your naming ceremony, I named you *Mo-sa-ne,* the—"

"The Arrow of life," Sam finished, grimacing. "I know. But Gram—uh, *Weet-see-koe,* that just proves my point. I work at a base that's northeast of here, not west. I fly a bomber, painted black, not exactly meant to be the red bringer of life. The opposite, really."

He gave her a wrinkled smile and for once his sad old eyes gleamed. "Perhaps the day you *earn* your name has not yet come."

"Small radar contact at one o'clock," Soupy said, his voice distorted by the air mask. "I think it's a UAV."

"Come right to course 015 and slow to 0.7," Sam said. "Let's show it a small cross section." Sam sat in the cockpit's Mission Commander seat, just to the right of Second Lieutenant Greg *Soupy* Campbell, the jet's pilot. She barely saw the tiny Unmanned Aerial Vehicle as it flashed past on their right.

"Think it detected us, Warpaint?" Soupy asked.

Sam scowled. As soon as the guys in the squadron had seen her bristle at being reminded of her Native American ancestry, they'd saddled her with a callsign she hated. Still, they might have picked something even worse than Warpaint. "Unlikely, thanks to stealth magic." She scanned the radar display. "Proceed to the—"

"Another UAV, dead ahead."

"Come right to 025. No, further, to 035."

"The UAV launched a missile! It's—"

"Break left. Eject decoys," Sam said. "Probably heat-seeker, so shut down engines. Evasive maneuvers."

Soupy complied with her orders. "Damn, the missile didn't bite on the decoys. It's still closing. Five, four—"

"Punch out!" Sam yelled, reaching for the eject handle.

The cockpit leveled and the view-screens turned black. She heard an irritated male voice say, "Sim complete. Mission failure. Report to the debriefing room ASAP."

Sam sighed, shook her head, and turned to Soupy. "Guess I gooned that up."

"We both did." He took his helmet off. "*Two* armed UAVs. They've never thrown that at us before."

As Sam hopped down the catwalk off the B-2D bomber simulator, she wondered if she'd ever qualify as Mission Commander. She'd never been paired with Soupy before, but their unfamiliarity was no excuse. As implied by the "Anytime, anywhere" motto of Whiteman Air Force Base, she'd have to be ready to fly with anyone.

In the debriefing room, Lieutenant Colonel George Kaster tugged at his mustache, so Sam knew he was angry. "If you're going to be a Mission Commander, Warpaint, you've got to leave the piloting to your pilot."

Behind him, several screens replayed the scenario, each showing different views, while the trainee's voices played from speakers.

"Don't give your pilot courses to fly. That's micro-managing," Kaster went on. "You've got bigger concerns. Both of you have got to learn to deal with UAVs. They're the new threat, and they're getting more potent and devious all the time. In this sim, you only had two. What would you do against a whole swarm?"

Sam bit her lip. "Sir, I tried to avoid detection by—"

"Yeah, by giving up your biggest advantage, your speed. They're smaller and more maneuverable, but they're slow." He sat back in his chair and rubbed his chin. "I know UAVs are tough. The eggheads at the research lab are cooking up some countermeasures, but until those are available, you'll just have to survive with what you've got." He looked at each of them. "All right. Back to the sim. New scenario. And this time, let's see if you can—"

The door opened and a Sergeant leaned in. "Sir, it's all over the news. They're saying one of our subs has been destroyed."

"What?" Colonel Kaster stood and tugged his moustache. "I got a cousin in the sub service. I gotta see this." Sam and her fellow pilot followed him out the door.

In the cafeteria, the rest of the squadron personnel sat before the overhead TV watching a solemn-faced cable news anchor. "— spokesperson announced the Navy has lost communication with the nuclear sub USS Wisconsin and detected explosions in her area of operations. The Wisconsin entered the self-declared aquastate of PaCitadel to enforce freedom of navigation in international waters, following President Gannon's condemnation of the shadowy PaCitadel group three days ago for violating the international Law of the Sea Treaty."

Sam saw Colonel Kaster sigh and wipe his brow. Apparently, his cousin wasn't aboard that sub.

"Who do they think they are?" someone asked.

"Kill 'em all, I say," another aviator chimed in.

"Shut up. There's more," Kaster said.

"—speculate that PaCitadel may represent a secret underwater base, unaffiliated with any known country. Some see a possible connection with billionaire J. Hugh Robard, who disappeared five years ago after speaking to friends about *seasteads,* or sea-based homesteads. Subsequent satellite photos of that area in the central South Pacific showed ships and equipment typical of seafloor mining operations. More on this story as it develops."

"Who do they think they are?"

"You can't *own* the oceans."

"They won't get away with sinking our sub."

Others chimed in with similar thoughts, but Sam stayed silent. *There has to be more than one person on that seastead,* she thought. *What sort of people leave their home on land to live in secret on some undersea base?*

We're at war. Sam felt a creeping feeling of dread as Lieutenant Colonel Kaster spoke and gestured with his laser pointer. She sat with eleven other pilots in the spacious ready room while Kaster pointed to the huge electronic map.

"It's called Operation Seadragon, classified Top Secret. We're sending two birds, a primary and a backup," he said.

Three weeks had elapsed since the sinking of USS Wisconsin and President Gannon's immediate decision to dispatch a naval battlegroup to the area. Spokesmen from the United Nations confirmed they'd received a petition from the aquastate of PaCitadel to join the United Nations, further stoking the President's outrage.

"The target is within your aircraft's range, so we don't anticipate refueling, though tankers will be standing by along your return route, here. The mission calls for a single Bravo Niner Four nuclear bomb to be released from the primary bird, or the backup if the primary is unsuccessful."

Just hours before Kaster's mission briefing, the mysterious PaCitadel people had sunk all six ships in the battlegroup, an aircraft carrier, a cruiser, two destroyers, and two submarines, killing over six thousand crewmen. Radio broadcasts from PaCitadel stated they'd warned the group repeatedly to stay away, and they were recovering survivors who'd be sent home. The President had denounced the attack and called on Congress to declare war on PaCitadel.

"The Air Force is lead for this operation," Kaster said. "We'll make 'em pay for what those criminals did to our Navy."

"Damn straight," someone said.

Two birds of our squadron will rendezvous with four Navy stealth fighters at Waypoint Charlie, here," the colonel went on. "These F-35Cs from the USS John F. Kennedy will escort you from there. When you reach Waypoint Delta, here, you'll receive either the authorization code for weapon release, or the stand-down code," Kaster continued. As a reminder, the JACCIE system has been installed on both birds."

Sam nodded, recalling her training. The JAmming and Code Cracking Intelligence Engine was an artificial intelligence computer designed to analyze enemy transmissions and movements, to detect patterns and exploit them. Sam wasn't sure she could trust an experimental system that had never been tested under combat conditions. But it was the best they had.

Lieutenant Colonel Kaster looked around the silent room. "Here are your assignments. The primary bird will be Spirit of Phoenix. Captain Radcliff, you're Mission Commander and Lieutenant Lu is your pilot."

Two guys Sam knew as Ratfink and Lugnut cheered and high-fived each other, while others moaned in disappointment.

Kaster tugged his mustache and scowled at all of them. "This isn't a training flight, guys. Keep it professional. The backup bird is Spirit of Columbus. Captain Dawnstar, you're M.C. and Lieutenant Campbell's your pilot."

Beside her, Soupy pumped his fist and smiled at Sam. "Just backup," he said, "but at least we'll be flying, huh?"

"Yeah." She gave him a half-smile, but hoped the President knew what he was doing. *Maybe these PaCitadel people shouldn't have built a base in the ocean, but so far all they've done is defend their declared borders.*

Kaster clicked off the map and turned the room lighting up. "Take-off is in two hours. Let's not let our country down. This briefing is over. Good luck."

Sam and Soupy had agreed to take turns napping during the eleven-hour flight to the drop point, but Sam found sleep impossible. She couldn't shake off the enormity of their mission, to release a nuclear weapon for just the third time in history. As a Mission Commander of a bomber, she'd long known there was a chance this could happen. She'd imagined, if it came to that, she'd be dropping weapons on some indisputably evil country to end a war and save American lives. Destroying PaCitadel wouldn't be like that at all. Still, being in the backup plane gave her some comfort, and emotional distance from the responsibility.

The two bombers had slowed to join up with their escorts, Navy fighter jets from the Carrier, but now cruised at Mach 0.85. Sam's Spirit of Columbus trailed the Spirit of Phoenix while the F-35Cs occupied the corners of a diamond surrounding them.

"I'm picking up a weak air search radar at eleven o'clock," Soupy spoke loudly and tapped her arm. He looked like a gigantic insect in his face mask with its projecting air hose.

"I'm awake, Soup." Sam leaned forward to squint at her radar display. "Small image. Probable UAV. Maintain formation."

A minute later they flashed past the barely visible speck on their left.

"Yeah, it saw us." Soupy pointed to the new display console bolted to their panel. "JACCIE's working on it."

Blinking lights indicated the JACCIE system had detected increasing radio comms from, and to, the UAV just after the jets passed it. The computer's analysis of the coded transmissions had begun, but had so far only achieved a seven percent confidence level, displayed in red.

That fancy gadget is a piece of junk. "At this rate," Sam said, "JACCIE will crack their codes sometime next wee—"

"Unidentified aircraft," a voice said. "You are entering the sovereign aquastate of PaCitadel." The stern male voice, speaking in English, sounded from their radio speakers and came over Channel 70, the international distress frequency. "Reverse course within five minutes, or you'll force us to defend ourselves. You have five minutes."

Sam said nothing, and Soupy stayed silent as well. *We're the avenger here, so why do I feel like the aggressor?* All six jets remained in their diamond array. The pilots had been told to expect warnings. The illegal PaCitadel target had sent similar radio transmissions to all of the previous ships.

"Coming up on Waypoint Delta," Sam said. Her weapon status showed green, so the B-94 nuclear bomb sat ready in their weapons bay, all its systems nominal.

"...and our EAM is coming through right now," Soupy said. "Running it through crypto."

Sam stared at her heads-up display, watching the Emergency Action Message get decoded. *Please, please, let it be a stand-down order.*

"Unidentified aircraft, you now have four minutes. You have entered the sovereign—"

"Turn that off," Sam said.

Soupy silenced the PaCitadel warning. "Decoding complete." He let out a whistle and read the message aloud. "You are directed to release one B-94 unit from primary or backup aircraft at coordinates 34°57' South and 150°30' West on direct orders from C-in-C." He let out a low whistle. "Let's see…yeah, those coordinates match what we got in the briefing." He looked at her, stone-faced and dead serious. "Do you concur, Mission Commander?"

She double-checked. Yes, the stated latitude and longitude coincided with the location they'd been given for PaCitadel, and the computer had correctly decoded the message. She gulped. "I concur. Entering coordinates into weapon…coordinates entered. I'm inserting my arming key."

Soupy said, "I'm inserting *my* arming key. Ready to arm on your command."

She and Soupy had practiced this many times in the last few weeks, but it felt different now, and he wasn't just Soupy any more. He was Second Lieutenant Gregory Campbell, and his voice, though professional, held a tone of tension and fear.

"Arm on zero." She kept her voice even. "Three, two, one, zero." She turned her key counter-clockwise just as Campbell did the same with his.

A green light came on. She looked at Campbell, trying to stay expressionless, though her heart jackhammered. "Weapon is armed."

"Ten miles to the drop poi—" Soupy froze. "Holy crap. They just popped up out of nowhere. A dozen, no, two dozen UAVs. A *swarm.*"

Recalling her failure in the simulator, Sam said, "Punch through. Let the fighters deal with 'em."

Letting her pilot focus on the situation ahead, she watched the radar picture of the melee in their six, far behind them.

Their escort fighters shot down several UAVs, but some of the unmanned craft struck back. One by one, the blips representing Navy jets winked out. Sam could only hope the occupants had been able to bail out.

"More UAVs ahead." Soupy swerved right to avoid them.

"Oh, God, they got the primary." Sam gasped as Spirit of Phoenix erupted in flames just after ejection seats popped free.

"Did they drop their nuke?"

"No." She refocused forward and set her jaw. "It's up to us now. We're on our own."

"Ten seconds to target." Soupy jinked left to avoid a cluster of UAVs.

"Opening bay doors."

A staccato, metallic rattle resounded around her.

"Damn robots are slinging triple-A at us!" Soupy yelled.

"Stay on course." Sam could only hope the anti-aircraft ammunition hadn't penetrated their shielding and hit something vital.

Green lights shifted to yellow, then red all over their consoles.

"What the—?" Soupy cried. "They really roughed us up. I'm losing systems left and right."

They'd reached Waypoint Delta on their chart. Biting her lip, Sam pressed a button, releasing the nuclear bomb. "Bomb's away."

A wisp of smoke wafted from somewhere and began clouding the cockpit. "Slow down," she said. "Do you still have control?" Designed for stealth, B-2 bombers were inherently unstable and required computer assistance to fly. *If that computer's damaged…*

"Barely." His clenched hand turned white as he gripped the joystick. "It's bucking me."

"Keep it together and get us out of here. I've got other problems." Sam watched the radar in horror as four UAVs sped toward the bomb she'd just dropped and shot at it. She knew what Colonel Kaster would say: "Plane busted, mission failure, sim complete. Report to the debriefing room." In desperation, she scanned through the thickening smoke at the hundreds of red blinking indicators in the cabin. *Doesn't anything in this flying deathtrap still work?*

Steady green lights caught her eye. JACCIE. That jury-rigged, bolt-on magic box still functioned, somehow. Its confidence level clicked up to sixty-three percent as she watched. The lab scientists had said to wait for eighty percent to depend on it. *I can't wait that long.* The UAVs would soon fire on her descending bomb or ram it, and render it useless. Had the machine hacked the UAV transmissions or not?

"Come on, JACCIE," Sam coaxed as she keyed in the command to direct all UAVs to break off their attack and dive into the ocean."

Green lights flickered to indicate the box was transmitting her orders.

Great Spirit Wa-kon-tah, I've never asked you for anything. Please, please let this work.

Through the cloud of smoke, her radar screen showed the UAVs had stopped shooting and were dropping fast.

Seconds later her screen showed her bomb and the chasing UAVs had splashed. *I guess sixty-three percent was just good enough this time.* She looked up and smiled. *Thank you, Wa-kon-tah.*

"Bend the throttles off, Soupy," she said, knowing the bomb would take some time to descend to its preset explosion depth. "Get us high and far from here."

He fought the controls. "Any faster and she'll shake apart. We'd be Spirit of Colum*bust*. Look at the bright side; we're flying faster than either of us could swim."

Sam smiled at his summation of their alternatives, but sobered when she thought of the other pilots shot down and floating in rafts. Using the only radio that still worked, she reported their position to U.S. Indo-Pacific Command, though it distressed her to know rescuers would never reach them in time. She turned to Soupy. "Prevailing wind's from the west. Try to head more that way to get upwind of the fallout. I'll see what I can do about this smoke."

She located a seam between two adjoining panels through which smoke leaked in. With the fire extinguisher, she hit it with foam until the vapor cloud lessened. With so many systems offline, the aircraft had automatically shut down nonessential functions, so she manually redirected power from her weapons system to ventilation.

Half the lights in the cockpit winked out, including the radar displays. It felt like trainers had shut down the simulator, but they weren't in a sim.

"EMP," Sam said, as a few panel lights blinked and came back, proving that at least some of their electronics had been hardened against electromagnetic pulses. Several miles behind her, she knew, the B-94 nuclear warhead had reached its target depth and detonated. It must have sent a titanic column of water skyward, an immense white pillar of spray, which then collapsed. From its base, a circular wall of water would be expanding outward from that point toward every direction of the compass.

And everyone on that submerged seastead just died. Sam fought to stay focused despite a rising wave of horror and despair.

"Well, the pulse didn't crash *all* our electronics," Soupy said. "Let's hope the shock wave—"

A giant hammer struck the jet from behind. Sam's head slammed back into the headrest. She felt a momentary disorientation, then shook her head. The plane careened through the air, buffeted by the turbulence.

"Lost number two," Soupy strained at the controls and was able to bring the bomber back to steady flight. "We're leaking fuel, down to one engine, and we've got more stuff broken than working on this crate. But at least we're still alive for the moment."

"Can you get us to Hickam?"

He took his time, then said, "Yeah, probably, but the landing won't win any prizes if I can't get the gear down."

"Head that way, then. I've never been to Hawaii." Sam smiled. "And may I say, Lieutenant Campbell, you sure have the golden hands."

"Maybe, but it'll be *your* name in the history books, Captain Dawnstar. First nuclear weapon dropped in eighty years."

She frowned. "Let's not talk about that, okay?"

"Why the hell not? It's the mission these bombers were built for, and you're the first one who got to—"

"These bombers were built so no one would ever have to do this. And I killed those people only because our leaders didn't want them living there. All the seasteaders wanted was to be left alone." She felt her cheeks flush with shame. "I've done something worse, far worse, than what was done to my ancestors."

After a silence, Soupy spoke quietly. "We were ordered to do it, Sam."

"Like an arrow from a bow, huh? No. When an archer shoots, the arrow has no choice, no responsibility, and no regrets. But I had a choice; I can't dodge the responsibility; and I'm going to regret this as long as I live."

Next to a bookshelf in the Cultural Center, Sam waited with new-found patience for her grandfather to finish. His back to her, he sat cross-legged on the floor, telling a group of children an Osage legend.

"...and ever since that day," Fred Dawnstar said, "we of the Osage Nation have revered the spider for its patience, and because it builds its own house and lets the world come to it. That is why you see the spider image in much of Osage art."

Sam longed to surprise her grandfather with news of her permanent return to the reservation in Pawhuska. After a rough landing on a Hickam Air Force Base runway, Sam had returned to Whiteman Air Force Base in Missouri and submitted her resignation from the service. The bureaucrats had taken their time processing it, but her paperwork had gone through, and she'd driven back to Oklahoma. She knew she couldn't continue in the Air Force, but wasn't sure if she'd ever fit in with her tribe.

She thought of buying a traditional fringed deerskin dress, leggings, and moccasins, but wasn't quite ready to wear Osage garb. For now, she just wanted to learn more about the culture she'd long rejected.

As her grandfather dismissed the children and stood up, Sam rushed to him.

"*Weet-see-koe*, I've come home." She hugged him.

He broke the embrace to look her in the eyes and smile. He appeared weaker than the last time she'd seen him. He'd lost weight and developed a twitch in his left eye. "It's wonderful to see you," he said, his gravelly voice hoarser than before. "Welcome home, *Mo-sa-ne*."

Sam looked down. "*Weet-see-koe*, I must ask you to give me a new name. *Mo-sa-ne* doesn't fit me."

"What do you mean?"

"You know I dropped the bomb and destroyed that seastead, don't you? I was the black arrow of death, not the red arrow of life."

He looked at her quizzically, then smiled. "You haven't heard, have you?" From within his buckskin tunic he pulled out a smartphone. "You've got to keep up with the times." He fumbled to activate a news app, then handed her the phone. "Watch and listen."

The video showed a female newscaster behind a desk. "Reaction to the unilateral bombing of PaCitadel has been swift. Many in Congress are calling to impeach President Gannon and remove him from office. Meanwhile, the United Nations has convened a Fourth Conference on the Law of the Sea. Countries around the world are pressuring to amend the treaty to allow seasteads and the formation of nations at sea, so-called aquastates. Some experts believe this could usher in a large-scale movement of humanity to the seas, and the colonization of the oceans."

Sam looked into her grandfather's tired, brown eyes.

"So, you see," he said, "Life and death forever follow day and night. You flew west, and in a manner of speaking, you brought life. I gave you the name *Mo-sa-ne*, and now," he smiled, "you've earned it."

Islas Aurora

Lican Nagashima keyed her microphone. "Bridge, it's a Seaquake! Tell everyone to brace—"

The small research vessel Juan de Alderete shuddered, its hull creaking and moaning. Lican and the other Search Lab technicians leaned forward like passengers in a braking car. She grabbed the edge of an electronics cabinet to steady herself. She heard the belated warning go out over the ship's PA system. Falling objects thudded and crashed in other compartments.

She shook her head. *Should have known how fast that pressure wave would travel. Should've used the PA myself. A more competent geologist would have known that.*

"Search Lab, this is the bridge," spoke the voice from a bulkhead-mounted speaker. "Report if your equipment suffered any damage. Also, should we can expect more seaquakes?"

Lican recognized the voice of Fernándo de Mendoza, senior engineer for the EmPetró Company. On this voyage, even the ship's captain took orders from Mendoza. *Asked about the equipment, not the people.*

"We're okay, and there's no apparent damage to the gear. Running diagnostics now," Lican said. "And yes, aftershocks are likely. We'll keep a watch on the seismometer, and we'll go straight over the PA with a warning next time."

"Understood, Search Lab. Maybe that shake-up opened up a lead for us, no?"

"I don't see any so far, but you'll know the moment I do. Lab out." Lican gritted her teeth and shut her eyes to keep from voicing her frustration in front of the technicians. *Fool! Does Mendoza think I'd fail to report if I found petroleum?*

Looking over the detection and analysis equipment in the lab, she knew much of it would appear magical to a non-geologist. Still, despite all the technology, interpreting the data could seem like some mystical art.

Two weeks here without a single lead, Lican thought, *and Mendoza nagging me the whole time. I'm not right for this. They should have sent Pedro.*

Inexperienced geologists rarely went on such expeditions. Just before departure, Pedro González, the company's best oil-finder, had taken ill. Of the three other seasoned geologists, one had planned a vacation, another had to attend a daughter's wedding, and a third was out of the country presenting a technical paper at an international geology symposium.

"Don't worry," Pedro had told her. Even from the hospital bed he looked imposing on the phone—bushy eyebrows and mustache, mad-scientist style gray hair. "You can handle this. You're ready. Remember your training. Give them your best estimate about the presence of oil and the stability of the seafloor. In any case, Mendoza makes the decision about whether to drill, not you. I have confidence in you." His words had comforted Lican by lifting imagined responsibility from her shoulders. *Just make your observations and let Mendoza make the decisions.*

Undulating up and down in a chaotic, eternal rhythm, waves stretched to the horizon in all directions. The evening after the seaquake, Lican stood on the vessel's portside deck. Her technicians could continue the search without her for awhile. She gazed around and pondered the sea beneath dark, low-hanging cumulous clouds. To her, the ocean's surface resembled the land, but moved much faster. Mountains, valleys, plains, and cliffs moved in a different timescale but in the same way, subject to forces unseen and powerful. Pedro had always said, "the Earth is ever-changing." She felt puny and weak in the presence of such vast, invisible energies.

The advancing waves gave the illusion of rapid motion, but Lican knew Juan de Alderete crawled with deliberate slowness along its back-and-forth search path, six hundred nautical miles off the southern Argentine coast.

Two miles to the west, a larger research ship with PetRoyal company logos and a British flag motored at a stately speed along its own search pattern. She guessed those English geologists had more experience and more advanced survey equipment. Likely they even used satellite imagery to guide their explorations, imagery capable of detecting oil sheens. If oil lay beneath this ocean, the British searchers would find it first.

Earlier that day, the captain of the English ship radioed an arrogant warning to the Juan de Alderete, stating that any petroleum found by either vessel would belong to the United Kingdom. Therefore, they urged the Argentines to clear the area so as not to interfere with PetRoyal's search. Lican had admired the *Alderete's* captain, Huenu Chihuailaf, for ignoring the warning.

Lican didn't hate the British as did so many of her fellow Argentines. The war over the Malvinas had occurred before she was born. Many of her countrymen might despise the nation that had defeated them, but Lican felt respectful envy for their superior equipment and expertise.

Only a few years earlier these two companies would have claimed equal rights to whatever petroleum they found, and would have sought an international court's permission to set up oil rigs. But the seasteading phenomenon changed all that.

A billionaire had erected an oceanic habitat in the South Pacific and declared ownership of a large sector of ocean. The United States sent warships to enforce the policy of open seas trade routes, but the seasteaders defended their *aquastate* . Finally, the U.S. dropped a nuclear bomb on the undersea community, leaving a vast radioactive zone, unsafe for any ships to enter. Universal condemnation followed, forcing the U.S. President to resign and world leaders to reconsider the concept of international waters. The UN created the term *aquastate* for countries with no land at all.

Pundits predicted a resulting 'rush to own the oceans,' but careful investors made it more like a tentative stroll. The expense of constructing seasteads dissuaded all but the wealthiest countries, companies, and billionaires. In theory, a UN World Court could resolve disputes about aquastate boundary claims, but in practice the guiding principle became, 'you own what you can defend.'

Lican turned her gaze to the British vessel. The PetRoyal company owned several oil rigs, as did EmPetró, over the known oil deposits nearer the continent. As yet, the World Court had not resolved the claims of either company over those disputed zones. For the moment, neither side had deployed warships to settle the issue. The British craft's captain could bluster all he wanted, but without a naval vessel nearby, his assertion of ownership meant little.

If the English detected petroleum first, Lican would know it from their ship's behavior as they tightened their search pattern. She'd asked the Alderete's radar operator to inform her of changes in the other vessel's movements, but so far it continued its established patterns.

Thunder sounded from the east, and Lican looked in that direction. An odd sort of thunder, it sounded like a deep, rumbling explosion. She saw, or imagined she saw, a vast and distant column of water leap skyward, then collapse.

"Brace yourselves!" the PA speaker crackled with the voice of the lab's seismograph technician. "Seaquake!"

Lican rushed toward the lab, holding handrails as she went. She had just entered a side door into the ship's interior when the shockwave hit.

The craft pitched up by the bow and heeled over to starboard, flinging Lican sideways, her shoulder striking the bulkhead. A crewman slid on his back down the inclined central passageway, screaming as he went. Crashes and bangs resounded throughout the vessel. The lights flickered twice, but remained on.

When the ship steadied, Lican ignored her bruised shoulder and attended to the fallen crewman. After ensuring he was uninjured and could walk on his own, she continued to the Search Lab.

She stood in the lab's doorway, taking in the scene. All the technicians scrambled about on hands and knees, cleaning up paper, pens, and shattered tea cups. None of them looked hurt, but then they *did* have the earliest forewarning of anyone aboard, Lican thought.

"All compartments, report damage." The captain's voice sounded calm but concerned. Lican waited her turn, then kept her report succinct.

"Lican, please come to the bridge," the captain said when she'd finished.

It relieved Lican to see that the bridge crew had suffered only bumps and bruises. Captain Chihuailaf stood listening to a headset, shaking his head as a crewman updated the damage status board. Despite the serious situation, he managed to smile and nod at her as she entered. *If anyone can get this ship through a seaquake, you can,* Lican thought as she smiled back. The salty old *Mapuche* Indian would have a few more gray hairs from this accident, she suspected.

Fernándo de Mendoza scowled at the damage board. Piercing eyes glared from a face of rugged features, set off by a thin black mustache and wavy, black hair. *With a breastplate, helmet, and goatee,* Lican thought, *he could be a Spanish Conquistador.* As the senior engineer on this mission, perhaps he *was* a modern conquistador, out to conquer the new landscape while seeking a darker kind of gold.

"No leads yet," she answered the question he always asked her first.

"Not a single sniff?" he asked in his usual gruff tone.

"Nothing. The noise of the seaquakes themselves gave us a good acoustic picture of the area, and there are no petroleum-bearing formations beneath us. But I'm seeing some odd readings east of here."

"We're wasting our time in this sector." Mendoza moved over to the navigation display. "We must search elsewhere."

"Was that the last of the quakes, Lican?" Captain Chihuailaf held the headset microphone away from his mouth as he spoke to her.

"I wish I could say, Captain." She hated to disappoint him with a non-answer, but then had an idea. "May I radio the geologist on the PetRoyal ship? If we compared readings, I could better calculate the epicenter and—"

"We will *not*," Mendoza clenched his fists, "cooperate with the British under any circumstances."

"That British ship stopped searching here," the young radar operator piped up, trying to be helpful. "They turned south five minutes ago and picked up speed."

"We should head south also and search there next," Mendoza said, staring at the screen.

Chihuailaf shook his head. "The engine room just reported significant damage, Señor. The port rudder is inoperable. There's a major leak in the starboard shaft seal, and one of the starboard diesel's engine mounts sheared. Also—"

"Details are *your* problem," Mendoza snapped. "How does all that affect our search?"

"We have electrical power, but no propulsion."

"How long to fix it?"

"Working the crew all night..." the captain ran a hand through his bristly gray hair, "we should have half speed by mid-morning tomorrow."

"Damn!" Mendoza pounded a bulkhead. "Those British dogs will be a half day ahead in the search."

* * *

Lican stood alone at the ship's fantail, staring into a dark sky and the scattered reflections of stars on the water. Gone now were the clouds that had menaced the afternoon sky. *Good to take a break from Mendoza's arrogance.* How could he be angry at her for the lack of petroleum in the area? He probably thought she was too incompetent to interpret her readings correctly. But how could she give him more confidence in her abilities, when she lacked that confidence herself?

Motion and light to the south caught her eye. A wispy ribbon of greenish light shimmered and moved, folding, twisting, and undulating across the sky. Red and green flowing strips of brilliance joined it, dancing together in a silent, ghostly symphony of colors and ethereal wonder.

Lican smiled and thought of another Aurora Australis she'd enjoyed on a quiet summer night many years earlier. A little girl, she sat between her mother and father outside their home watching the heavenly lights in awe. They passed around the traditional *yerba maté*, a strong green tea served in a calabash gourd. This night marked the first time she drank from their shared gourd, no longer needing her mother to prepare a separate portion with sugar.

"What are those pretty lights?" she had asked.

Her father, born and educated in Japan, gave her an explanation heavy with complex words like "magnetic fields" and "solar wind." Her mother, a Mapuche Indian reared in the pampas, told her it was a sign that *Ngen-kürüf,* the spirit owner of the wind, looked with favor on their land. Each parent gently chastised the other for explaining it the wrong way.

"Just remember this, Lican," her father tried to sum up. "When you grow up, always seek to attain greater knowledge. That is the most honorable goal of life."

"Knowledge is fine," said her mother, "but always respect the land. Remember the spirits look with kindness on the land that sustains and enriches our people."

Grasping the rail on the Juan de Alderete, Lican Nagashima laughed aloud in memory of that long-ago event. "Knowledge and land," she said. "And I became a geologist!"

Well, the company's least knowledgeable geologist, and right now I'm very far from land.

The bridge crew must detest this inactivity, she thought. The helmsman, radar operator, navigation assistant, and bridge officer stood at their posts with glazed expressions. Waiting had bred boredom, which led to oppressive melancholy. Gone was their normal atmosphere of teamwork and conversation. *Their moods and thoughts drift like our damaged ship*, Lican thought, *without purpose.* Lacking propulsion, the ship rocked in the choppy sea, a victim of the ocean's whims.

Mendoza drummed his fingers on the navigation console, waiting for the captain to return. "You're certain the instruments show no deposits?" Mendoza asked Lican.

"I'm certain. As we float east in this current, however, the sensors are scanning new, un-searched swaths. My technicians will tell us if they find anything."

"Can they interpret readings as well as you?"

Is he praising me for my expertise or criticizing me for my absence from the lab? "No, but they call more false alarms than I do. There is no chance they would miss something."

That quieted him. Five minutes passed as the ship rolled and Mendoza's fingers drummed.

The captain walked in. Unshaven, with baggy circles under his eyes and grease stains on his EmPetró overalls, he had stayed awake with his crew to help them repair the stricken ship.

He nodded at Mendoza. "We can make half speed, señor, but we must return to Río Gallegos to complete the repairs."

"No," the engineer folded his arms. "We have supplies for four more weeks. We'll keep searching for oil." He tapped the navigation display. "Head south. Search this sector here."

Chihuailaf shut his eyes, sighed, then opened them. "As you wish, señor."

He gave the helmsman his orders, and they heard a single diesel engine throb to life. Lican saw the weary smile on the captain's face as he heard the sound, but worry remained in his eyes.

"Seaquake! Brace yourselves!" The seismograph technician's panicked voice rang over the speakers.

Everyone on the bridge groaned and reached to grab a support.

An unearthly rumbling noise sounded, drowning the ship's engine. The sound went on and on, like rolling thunder, or an Andean landslide.

"Great Spirit help us," murmured the Mapuche captain. "Rudder amidships. Steady as she goes. Take this one off the port bow."

A series of shock waves struck the ship, each milder than the previous single waves. The Juan de Alderete heeled over sharply with each wave but returned and rolled the other way. At any moment, Lican thought, a sudden jolt or a snap-roll could sink the weakened ship. Instead, the roaring noise went on for ten minutes, accompanied by waves with such lengthy troughs and crests that the boat could ride them without suffering damage.

The noise and waves died out, and those on the bridge relaxed their grip on railings and stanchions.

"Three new radar contacts, Captain," said the radar operator.

"The British are back," Mendoza growled, "with warship escorts this time."

"Not ships, señor. These contacts are much too large."

"What's the range and bearing to the closest?" Chihuailaf asked. "Which way are these contacts bound?"

"They're stationary, Captain. The nearest bears zero eight five, range nine nautical miles. And they're growing."

"Growing?"

The radar operator looked up from his scope. "They look like... like islands."

"That's crazy," Mendoza said, his eyes on the navigation display computer. "There are no islands here, and islands do not grow."

"Unless they are rising from the sea." Chihuailaf's tired face held a far-away look. The captain stared out the bridge window toward the east.

Lican looked too, and saw no evidence of the volcanic plumes that always accompany island formation.

The captain snapped his fingers and went to the navigation screen, drawing his finger along latitude and longitude lines. "Three islands...between the Malvinas and South Georgia...it could be..." Chihuailaf turned to Lican. "Have you heard of the Aurora Islands?"

Lican started to shake her head and then remembered something old—a story, a legend, a disproved myth. She'd read of them somewhere, a passing reference. "I think so." Seating herself at a console, she called up "Aurora Islands" on a search engine, and summarized aloud what she read.

"Three legendary islands located near fifty-three degrees south and forty-eight degrees west."

The captain checked the navigation display and nodded.

She read on. "First sighted by the crew of the Aurora in 1762, then by four other ship's crews in the late eighteenth century. Surveyed by Captain Bustamente of the Spanish ship Atrevida in 1794. They went unseen by three ships seeking them between 1819 and 1822. The last two reported sightings occurred in 1856 and 1892, after which they were never seen again, and were deleted from nautical charts."

"Very interesting to someone, I'm sure," Mendoza said. "Proceed to the southern search sector."

Lican stared at the engineer in amazement. "But we *must* go to these islands! Think of—"

"*Must*? We *must*?" Mendoza snarled. "*I* decide what this ship must do, and I say we go south."

Lican wondered how she could change his mind. He thought only of oil, but her instruments had shown none. "The upheaval of the islands might have uncovered previously hidden petroleum seams," she said. "I propose we visit the nearest one while the ship circumnavigates it, performing geological surveys. If there's oil there, we'll find it before anyone else. If we do, it's much easier to erect a derrick on land than out at sea, no?"

Mendoza's eyes narrowed. *Unaccustomed to having his authority questioned*, Lican thought. She felt intimidated by his towering stature, his intense glaring eyes, and his aura of command. *Oh, Pedro, you should be here, not me.*

She tried an argument no conquistador could resist. "Think of it, señor. *New land.* Unseen by anyone for over a century, and we're aboard the closest ship."

A hint of a spark came to his eyes, then they clouded.

"We've endured three seaquakes in two days," Mendoza said, his eyes boring into her like oil rig drill bits into the seafloor. "You said more aftershocks could happen. Our ship is damaged. And you wish us to move *closer* to the seaquake site?"

Lican noted Mendoza's sly abuse of logic. To him, the ship's propulsion systems were sufficient to accommodate his searches for oil, but too weakened for her island explorations.

"Captain," the radar operator said, "all three islands have stopped growing."

"In my judgment," Lican seized on the new development, "the seafloor stresses have relaxed in this region. I don't believe there will be more quakes."

Mendoza turned to her, his eyes narrowed in suspicion. "Another seaquake might sink the ship. Are you willing to stake your professional reputation on this belief of yours?"

More than anything, she had to see at least one of these new islands, and would tell him whatever was necessary to get to them. She looked him in the eyes. "Yes. What's more, if another seaquake happens, I'll resign from the company." *God, what have I said?*

Mendoza blinked and his eyebrows shot up. "You're that certain?"

She met his gaze. Fear and doubt raged within her, but she tried to sound resolute. "I am."

Mendoza smoothed his mustache with his fingers. "It would put the ship's safety in jeopardy." He turned to Chihuailaf. "Captain? Are you willing to risk this?"

Lican's heart sank. Mendoza's emphasis on the words "safety," "jeopardy," and "risk" would give any captain pause, particularly one who had spent all night repairing his ship.

Huenu Chihuailaf smiled. "I still recommend heading back to Río Gallegos for repairs, but if that is not an option, I trust Dr. Nagashima. We're out here to discover, señor. Let's do that."

Mendoza looked from Chihuailaf to Lican, then grunted. "Very well. Captain, head for the nearest island and equip a small party to go ashore. We'll survey that one island for one day. If we find no oil, then we'll move to the southern sector."

Tension on the bridge seemed to melt away. Although Lican felt gratitude for the captain, she felt drained, empty, and alone. For so long she had loved thinking about the vast and mysterious energies at work within the earth. Now, with one hasty statement, she'd granted them another power—to ruin her career with a single aftershock.

"*That's* your geology kit?" Mendoza said as the launch's outboard motor purred behind him. Lican returned her small hammer, pick, and folding shovel to her backpack, along with her notebook.

Lican smiled at the engineer. "Geologists managed to get by before magnetometers, seismographs, and gravimeters." She silently thanked Pedro González for teaching her the old techniques. "I'll be able to tell enough to know whether we have to lug all the electronics ashore later."

It amazed Lican that the captain had opted to join them, leaving the first mate in charge of the ship. Moreover, Chihuailaf must be exhausted after getting no sleep. *But he looks as excited as I must appear right now. New land! Just like me, he wouldn't dare miss this.*

From the ship, the island had looked low and rounded, a smooth arc above the distant horizon. It had wavered like a mirage in the heat haze, as insubstantial as the wispy tendrils of cirrus clouds far above. As they approached in the motor launch, the island became distinct and real.

Smooth, gray-brown rocks formed the shore, leading up to a strip of green grass. Beyond that, a palm forest covered the rounded central hill that crowned the dome-shaped island.

"Welcome to the southernmost of the Aurora Islands," Chihuailaf said, a measure of awe in his voice.

"It doesn't make sense," Mendoza said. "This island rose from the sea just this morning. How can it have trees and grass?"

No one aboard the boat had an answer. A series of whoops and screeches pierced the humid air, further deepening the mystery.

"We should have brought weapons," said Mendoza.

A sword and musket, conquistador? Lican thought, smiling as she clicked several camera shots with her smartphone.

"Pull in over there," the captain ordered, pointing out a spot where the rocky slope appeared more gradual.

When the craft's keel scraped bottom, they all disembarked and assisted in hauling the craft partway up on shore. Lican picked up one of the gray-brown stones and tapped it with her hammer. *Coarse-grained glaucophane schist*, she thought, *metamorphic and not carbonaceous. Not oil rock.*

"Lican! Come here!" Chihuailaf called.

She glanced up and saw the men had advanced as a group toward the forest. She made her way among the rocks, noticing a few crabs scuttling along.

"This isn't grass, and those aren't palm trees," the captain said from where he and the others stood in the field of green.

As Lican neared them, she stepped into thick, moist moss. A

chorus of croaking noises sounded from within, and as Lican moved through the moss, slimy frogs with long legs hopped out of her way.

"Did you ever see trees like that?" Chihuailaf asked as she joined the men.

Up close, the trees lost their resemblance to palms. In place of stiff, jutting leaves, the foliage of these trees drooped in long, bulbous tendrils toward the ground. Green fronds hung from most, but red and brown dangled from others. Whether these trees held fruits or coconuts, Lican could not see.

"I'm no botanist," Lican said, "but those look weird. Like some kind of...seaweed tree." She snapped a few photos.

The chattering and squawking noises intensified, and Lican caught occasional glimpses of movement high in the trees' foliage.

"Did your pick-axe strike oil yet?" Mendoza addressed Lican, but kept glancing around him after each new noise.

Always he doubts my abilities, she thought. "I'll need to collect more samples from other locations, but so far, no petroleum signs." She knew the conquistador was disinclined to linger too long exploring the island's mysteries. "I'll start collecting right away."

The voices in the trees grew louder and a few tiny, pale faces peeked from the foliage.

"Monkeys!" Lican smiled up at them, but wondered how they had come to be there.

Some of the creatures scampered down the hanging leaf fronds to the ground, but all stayed back behind the tree line.

The tallest of them reached only a third of Lican's height. Their light gray, almost white, coloration made Lican wonder if they represented an albino variety. They danced, gestured, and jabbered, but it seemed more an expression of curiosity and interest than a threatening display.

One of the monkeys emerged from the trees onto the mossy strip. His little eyes darted from person to person, and he inched forward in a tentative, jerky manner with his tail flicking back and forth.

On an impulse, Lican slowly knelt down to be nearer the animal's height. From her backpack she removed a plastic-wrapped *empanada* she'd intended to eat later. She unwrapped it and held out the papaya-stuffed pastry treat.

"Come on," she said in a gentle tone. "Come here, *pichi*." She spoke the term her mother's Mapuche people used meaning "small boy."

After a series of cautious approaches and fearful retreats, the monkey finally snatched and nibbled the food. Another minute later the little fellow had perched on her shoulder with apparent intention to stay.

"I'll call you Pichi," she told the animal. It seemed odd to Lican that he lacked hair, fur, or fuzz. His hide felt smooth and leathery.

"I hope you brought more," Mendoza grumbled. "Now you'll have to feed all his relatives."

That set Pichi chattering with great vigor at Mendoza in such a comic manner that all the others laughed.

They walked together into the forest, and the rest of the monkey troop kept their distance. Lican tried a few times to set Pichi on the ground and urge him to return to his family, but each time he scampered back up to her shoulder.

"You've made a life-long friend," Chihuailaf said.

The terrain inclined upward as they approached the island's central hill. Every so often Lican bent down to collect a representative stone, examine it, make notes, and place it in a numbered plastic bag, then into her backpack. Perhaps thinking it a game, Pichi began bringing her stones to examine. She patted and rubbed his bald head each time. She took frequent pictures of the scenery.

"We're past the summit," the captain said after a half hour's walk. He'd kept in periodic contact with the ship using a hand-held radio. The ship had used his signal to track their progress across the island. The Juan de Alderete had completed a circumnavigation and now waited at the morning's departure point for their return. Lican's technicians had reported a complete absence of petroleum leads. To her relief, no further seismic disturbances had occurred.

"Speed up the pace," Mendoza said, lengthening his great stride. "We've wasted a day here, and we must search the southern sector."

Baring his teeth, Pichi yapped at the engineer.

"Lican, you said someone surveyed these islands?" The captain started walking more rapidly, then stumbled, the first evidence that his lack of sleep was catching up. "How come they didn't report the strange monkeys and trees?"

Lican tried to recall what she'd read of the Auroras. "I don't think he actually made a landing. Bustamente called the islands 'cold, dark, and snow-covered,' or something like that. He must have arrived in winter." She clicked her phone's camera once more. "We're probably the first people to set foot here, Captain."

"Please, call me Huenu," he smiled. "Have you noticed what's missing here? No birds. No insects. And without insects, what do those frogs eat?"

Her mind swirled with the strangeness of it all, each new discovery adding to her confusion, denying her any theories to connect the observed facts together. "Mystery upon mystery," Lican replied.

"This is not a debate." Mendoza's eyes blazed. "My decision is final."

Standing before him on the Juan de Alderete's bridge, Lican struggled to keep composed. After returning to the ship, she'd wasted ten minutes arguing and pleading, unable to convince the senior engineer they should explore the remaining two islands. The helm's compass needle pointed south and all three of the Aurora Islands waned with the growing distance in the ship's wake.

She fumed, having run out of ways to persuade him. She had lost. *He can't see the importance of this discovery. This goes beyond oil; this could shake the foundations of geology.*

"Señor," Lican grasped for a way to salvage something from the situation. "May I send a scientific report of what we found to members of the Argentine Society of Geographical Studies? I believe we must get the news out quickly. And securely; I'll have the captain encrypt the report before transmitting."

Mendoza gave a dismissive wave of his hand. "Send a report to your scientist friends." He turned toward the navigation display, then stopped. "However, I must approve it first."

Be thankful you got that much, Lican reminded herself, to keep her anger from flaring again. "Yes, señor. You'll see my report soon."

"You're more of a bother than you're worth." Lican giggled as Pichi flailed inside one of her T-shirts, trying to put it on. While she struggled to write her report, the monkey had opened every drawer and closet in her cabin and examined every item.

Pichi chattered and his head poked out of one of the T-shirt's arms. "I'm trying to work," Lican said. "Don't you *ever* sleep?" Pichi gave her a wide-mouthed grin.

You're one of the island's biggest enigmas, Lican thought as she stared at him. On the computer screen, her report delved into the unknown, or surmised, geographical aspects of the Aurora Islands. The three landmasses sat atop the boundary between two tectonic plates—the minor Scotia plate to the south, and the huge South American plate to the north, a lateral transform boundary moving in a sinistral direction. Lican's report proposed that these features were not normal islands at all.

Islands like Surtsey are thrust up from the sea and others like Tebua Tarawa sink beneath it. But, her report conjectured, the Auroras may represent a new type of formation, a formation unique on Earth—intermittent islands. She speculated that these features rose and fell periodically due to a novel type of interaction of the edge structures of two neighboring plates. Her report compared it to corrugated roof panels forced to slide their ridged surfaces against each other. Such an interaction could explain the various appearances and disappearances of the Auroras. Pedro González had told her the Earth is ever-changing, but he never said the change could be *cyclic*.

Oscillating islands would lead, she inferred, to flora and fauna capable of surviving periodic shifts between water and land. Most likely the islands never sank too deeply for plants to receive light or for animals to surface to breathe. The moss, crabs, frogs, and the curious seaweed trees in her report's photographs had adapted to an amphibian existence. But monkeys? Pichi looked strange with his smooth, gray skin, but—

Pichi had extracted himself from her shirt, and now gazed at the glowing computer monitor, cocking his head. One of his hands reached out, fingers splayed, to touch the screen. Lican blinked, then grabbed his hand and turned it back and forth in her own. "Webbed hands and feet. You're part amphibian!"

"Seaquake!" The technician said, staring at his screen. Don't panic, though, it's a mild one."

Sitting behind him in the Search Lab, Lican made the announcement for the whole ship just to be on the safe side.

The vessel experienced a slight pitching, only a little more pronounced than the normal ocean waves. In moments, Mendoza's voice sounded from the speaker. "Lican Nagashima, report to the bridge."

She hurried through the corridor and up the stairs, dreading what the summons might mean. Two hours earlier, Mendoza had reviewed her report. He just skimmed it, perhaps looking for any adverse mention of his own name. He had approved the report for release to the Geological Society, and Huenu promptly transmitted it.

She arrived at the bridge to find Huenu looking tired and dejected. Mendoza actually smiled as she entered, but then turned serious.

"Do you remember," Mendoza asked her, "saying you would resign if there were any more seaquakes?"

"Yes," Lican said, her heart sinking, "but this one was so mild, it barely registered." *If I hadn't announced it, nobody would have known.*

"Still," Mendoza went on, "though this gives me no pleasure—"

I bet, Lican thought.

"—I must hold you to your agreement."

Hanging her head and shutting her eyes, Lican let a pang of anger and sadness wash through her. *I made the promise*, she thought. *In a rash moment of overconfidence, I assumed scientific knowledge I did not possess. Losing my job is the consequence.* She gathered her composure and looked up at Mendoza. "I understand, señor. Effective immediately, I resign from EmPetró."

"Accepted," Mendoza nodded.

Lican turned to leave the bridge. *Cry in your cabin*, she told herself. *Give him no further reason to gloat.*

"Message coming in, Captain," said the radio operator through the bridge speaker. He added in an awed voice, "It's from the CEO!"

"Standby for transmission," stated the words on the big screen in the Juan de Alderete's conference room. Wearing EmPetró company overalls, all senior personnel occupied chairs around the table. Lican stood against a bulkhead, wearing a plain T-shirt and slacks. Fernándo de Mendoza sat with a pad in front of him, pen poised. Captain Huenu Chihuailaf kept nodding off in his seat.

The company CEO had radioed for the ship to prepare for a video conference. As an ex-employee, Lican would not have attended, but the CEO had requested her presence by name. Mendoza had scowled upon hearing that.

The message vanished from the screen, replaced by a split-screen view of two scenes. In one, a group of men in business suits sat around an elegant conference table bearing the company logo. In the other—

"Pedro!" Lican gasped.

The smiling face of EmPetró's senior geologist stared from a hospital bed. Dr. González's eyes looked tired and sunken, but twinkled. He nodded and gave a slight wave.

"Good afternoon," from the conference room, an overweight, bald man wearing glasses began the meeting. "I am Vasco Álvarez."

Lican recognized the CEO from his picture in the company lobby and the quarterly reports.

"I'll dispense with introductions, except to say we are pleased to be joined by Economic Minister Estaban Torres."

Everyone in the ship's conference room gasped at the presence of an Argentine cabinet minister, while the handsome man with well-groomed hair and a wide smile just nodded.

"We also have a quorum of the Board of Directors, and Senior Geologist, Dr. Pedro González," Álvarez said. "Now then, to business. Where is Lican Nagashima?"

Lican took a half step forward. "Here, señor." Her voice quavered a little.

Álvarez smiled. "Your report caused quite a stir here, young lady. Dr. González told us the Nagashima Oscillation Effect is a most unusual phenomenon."

"The what?" Lican asked.

"My protégé did not name the effect," Pedro said. "I did, with the concurrence of my colleagues in the Argentine Society of Geophysical Studies. She discovered an interaction previously unknown to geology."

"I must break in at this point," Minister Torres said. "This is no longer a commercial concern about oil, nor just a scientific discovery. It has become political. Geologist Nagashima, how much longer can we keep your discovery secret?"

"Secret?" Lican almost laughed. "Señor, the nearby PetRoyal vessel certainly has detected the Auroras on radar. They will, I suspect, be upset that they missed the initial discovery by a few hours. The islands are also detectable by space satellites. This will be world news in hours." She surprised herself by her boldness in addressing this powerful man.

But Torres appeared unperturbed. "In that case, I need to address Captain—" a staff member whispered in his ear, "—Chihuailaf."

"Yes, señor," Huenu said, snapping to alertness.

"Captain, the Argentine government hereby assumes temporary ownership of your vessel. I order you to plant the flag of Argentina on all three islands as soon as possible to establish our claim. Do this before the British get there."

"Immediately it will be done, señor." Huenu saluted in military style and left the room.

"I'll file our claim with the U.N. after this meeting," Torres said as he made notes on a pad. "Very good. That should conclude—"

"Excuse me, Señor Minister, but that will not be enough." Everyone turned to face Lican. She found herself growing more accustomed to speaking to the powerful. "We'll need warships to defend the claim, and permanent island-based fortifications. You should build a base on each island, research stations with military capabilities. These bases must be built to survive sudden and prolonged submergence. Señor, you only own what you can defend."

Torres stared at her, then smiled. "They told me you are the ship's geologist."

No, I'm currently between jobs, Lican felt like saying. She glanced at Mendoza and saw him point to her, then to the EmPetró logo on the chest of his coveralls. He nodded, a faint smile on his face. She had her job back. And she'd won some respect from the conquistador. "Yes, señor, I am."

"Perhaps you've a flair for politics as well," Torres continued. He made a note and rubbed his chin as if musing aloud. "To build three permanent bases, as you suggest, will require someone who can oversee a unique design and construction project. I need a bold leader with untiring drive, passion, and energy. Lican Nagashima?" He stared straight at her.

"You're asking me who *I'd* recommend?" She gaped at him.

Torres frowned and shook his head. "Not at all." The frown softened into his wide, all-encompassing smile. "I'm asking if you'll *do* it."

Lican's knees almost buckled. In the first shock of his statement, her mind went blank. *Me? Design and build a trio of armed research stations? I'll need a good engineer.* She looked at Mendoza, whose face held none of its former arrogance. *Perhaps I could work with him, if he could stand working for me.* "I'll do it, señor."

"Very well," Estaban Torres said. "I'll urge the defense minister to have warships guarding each island within three days. As for you, Dr. Nagashima, you are now assigned to my staff. Send me your project plan, schedule, and budget estimate by the end of this week." He turned to the EmPetró CEO. "I think we all have work to do."

"Thank you, Minister Torres," said Vasco Álvarez. "Meeting adjourned."

Lican felt drained, almost unable to stand.

The EmPetró conference room vanished from the screen, but the view of Pedro González's hospital bed remained and expanded to fill the screen.

Pedro smiled from ear to ear. "Before you left, Lican, I said you could handle the assignment, and that I had confidence in you." He shook his head. "Never did I imagine you'd turn the science of geology on its ear and become an assistant to a cabinet minister!"

"Well, Pedro, I guess the Earth *is* ever-changing," Lican said, "and so are people."

A Green Isle in the Sea

*C**hief Engineer Jeri Calistus bit her lip. She could tell from* the jostling screen view how hard her brother strained to hold his submersible steady. "Get out of there *now*, Trey!"

"Just another couple of meters, Trey said, "and I'll get you a better view." The transmitted image could have been taken from inside a washing machine, with its agitated chaos, its sheets of bubbles streaming first in one direction, then another.

From out of the maelstrom loomed a vast metal surface.

"You're too close to the spar! Back away!" Jeri shouted.

"I'm backing now," Trey said. "Did you get enough to study in slow-mo?"

"It's enough," Jeri replied without knowing, or caring. "Just clear the area before—"

The screen image shook as if an earthquake had struck. She heard a thump over the speakers.

"Oh, great Gaia! Something hit me!" Trey sounded annoyed, not panicked.

Jeri gulped and shut her eyes, struggling to maintain a professional tone. "What's wrong, Trey?"

"Lost buoyancy. I think the impact ripped off my syntactic and gashed a hole in my ballast tank. Dropping keel weights...now."

Jeri shook her head and regretted once again her decision to allow her younger brother out on this run. Unable to blow water ballast, and missing his lightweight syntactic foam, Trey's only remaining option was to release the lead keel weights to keep his submersible from plunging downward.

"Keel weights away...No effect. I'm still sinking," Trey said. "Mother Earth! Got a crack in my bubble—"

Jeri could imagine him gritting his teeth, as he always did when confronting a problem.

"—and I've got a ten meter per minute descent rate."

"What's the bubble leakage? Maybe it will slow and seal." Jeri began to worry. When undamaged, the submersible could survive well beyond the three-thousand-meter ocean depth in their vicinity. However, a crack in its acrylic bubble window could cause it to implode at a much shallower depth.

Jeri hoped that the compressive forces of the sea could press the edges of the crack together and seal it. But with the sea, hope was never enough.

"Maybe half a liter a minute now," Trey said, "but getting worse."

The finality and resignation in his voice brought tears to Jeri's eye. The weight of it all came crashing in. The chief engineer of GreenSea, she'd ordered every precaution taken to prepare the massive seastead for the oncoming hurricane. When the huge habitat disk had started swaying in the blasting winds, she'd needed to know the condition of the spar welds. Would they hold?

To find out, she wanted to send the robotic Unmanned Underwater Vehicles. However, one UUV had been down for maintenance, and the other struck a wave generator float and sank right after launch. It seemed to Jeri that all equipment on the seastead had been built by low bidders, and assembled by disgruntled workers on Monday mornings or late Friday afternoons. Her only remaining option had been to send the seastead's single manned submersible and its best pilot, her little brother.

As far back as Jeri could remember, Trey had never quite fit in. Picking fights in school, disrespecting authority, hacking into secure data networks—he'd always needed her to bail him out of his troubles. She'd always helped him because something about his rebel nature, his devilish smile, made a secret part of her wish she could emulate him. But someone had to be the responsible, respectful one.

For a moment, Jeri stopped focusing on Trey and his problem. Around her, in GreenSea's Damage Repair Central, a dozen of her staff labored to get an accurate picture of the seastead's status in the midst of the hurricane, and direct the repair teams. On wall screens, the views shook as gale winds buffeted the seastead's external cameras. One solar panel ripped loose and blew away as she watched. Spray from twenty-five-meter waves whipped across the habitat's smooth upper surface.

"Chief, another wavegen float just snapped," reported Bret, the assistant chief engineer.

Jeri looked over at the young, blond man sitting at his console nearby. "Nothing we can do about that now." *You've learned so much, so quickly. Hope you're ready for the worst day GreenSea's ever had.* Keeping the systems functional on the four-year-old seastead challenged them enough on the best days. As a woman of fifty-seven, Jeri hoped she was ready for this too.

The wave generator extracted electricity from the movement of house-sized floats in the water. Wind turbines and solar panels also contributed to the seastead's power grid. But now Hurricane Jove snapped float rods, bent turbine blades, and peeled solar panels off. Likely one of the wavegen floats had struck and damaged Trey's submersible, Jeri realized.

She touched her headset earphone. "Trey, do you have propulsion? Can you land on the observation lounge?" The lounge looked like a donut encircling the cylindrical spar that supported GreenSea. Ringed with acrylic ports, the observation lounge offered a panoramic view of the sea. Moreover, it could ride up and down the spar for sightseeing at various depths. Before Jove struck, Jeri had evacuated the lounge and locked it at one hundred meters.

"I'll try," Trey said, "but it'll be tricky."

"Good luck," Jeri whispered into the mike.

"The Guide wants to talk to you," Bret looked up from his console to her.

Jeri nodded to him and an image of Guide Ross Munbar appeared on her screen. A completely bald head surmounted a face full of deep wrinkles. His inset eyes seemed even more tired and shifty than usual, Jeri thought.

"Need a quick status report, Jeri. How is it holding up?" Ross Munbar had been the driving force in the creation of GreenSea. How he'd managed to wheedle funding from the shoestring budgets of hundreds of environmental groups had mystified the world. Yet he'd overcome all obstacles through unstoppable determination and created the world's only seastead based on environmental principles, a solarpunk dream come true.

She glanced at the status screen. "Four wavegen floats wrecked; two wind turbines toppled; a quarter of the solar cells blown away. I think we're facing total loss of power soon, Guide. Our windward side is getting pounded, and I'm expecting damage reports from there any moment." She sighed, "and the submersible's in danger. It's leaking and can't gain buoyancy."

"If anyone can hold GreenSea together, it's you, Jeri." He gave her a transient smile. "What can I do?"

You ask me now? Two days earlier, with Jove on its way, she'd recommended reballasting the anchor cans and moving GreenSea farther north along the Mid-Atlantic Ridge, out of the danger path. But Ross had refused, saying they couldn't miss an observation of the Sei whale migrations. *Now you want to help?* "Send the distress calls, please, Guide. We've got to consider total evacuation. If you could get some rescue ships on the way, I'll keep the 'stead intact as long as possible."

Like everyone at GreenSea, Jeri called Ross Munbar by his title—Guide. The founders of the Aquarius aquastate and its sole seastead had distrusted authority but couldn't abide total anarchy. They'd settled on a single, elected executive, but endowed the office with the least authoritative name they could think of.

A flash of annoyance crossed Ross Munbar's face.

I stepped on his turf, Jeri thought.

"Leave the distress calls to me. And Jeri," his eyes narrowed with what might have been the weight of command, "save my 'stead. Guide out." His image vanished.

A muffled crash sounded, coming from somewhere above her.

"Another wind turbine down," Bret said.

Jeri massaged her temples. Those turbines were supposed to be designed to survive hurricanes. Yet even in moderate winds they required frequent maintenance. "Put out the word. I want all huggers who aren't on damage repair teams to evacuate the upper levels beneath the turbines. Also evacuate all windward rim compartments."

"Got it, Chief." Bret grabbed the PA mike. "All huggers..."

"Jeri, you there?" Trey's voice sounded strained in her earpiece. "I'm trying to land on the lounge now."

On her monitor, the image relayed from the submersible showed a section of the spar swaying and drifting out of view, then back in.

"Control's erratic," Trey said, "Must be a short in the thruster power circuits."

Come on, Trey, Jeri silently urged.

"Chief, you need to see this," Bret said with an urgent tone, pointing at his monitor.

"Whatever it is, handle it," Jeri glanced at Bret, then back to her own screen.

With a loud, metallic creaking noise, the room slowly tilted to leeward, then straightened back.

Jeri shook her head. "Great Mother Earth! We're going to lose the 'stead. Tell everyone who isn't repairing damage to muster in the lower leeward compartments." She sighed, reaching inside for the courage to voice the dreaded, but necessary decision. "Prepare to evacuate GreenSea."

"On it, Chief." Bret said.

"Can't you hold this spar steady?" Trey asked, evidently struggling with the submersible's controls. "I'd like to kill the guy who designed a curved roof for the observation lounge."

"Can you thrust onto it?" Jeri gripped the handset mike in both hands.

"Trying, sis. Thrusters keep cutting out."

"Chief, need your help here," Bret looked confused and stressed. "All wavegen floats are gone. We're down to forty percent of the solar panels, and....there went another wind turbine. External cams on the windward sector are all knocked out, but before they went I saw side panels being ripped off the habitat. And," Bret stopped to take a breath, "you *need* to see these pics."

"Did you shut off all nonessential switchboards?"

"They're off," he nodded, "but—"

"Just prep everyone to evacuate."

Bret raised one hand and pressed the other to his earphone. "Chief, it's the Guide. He wants—"

"*You* give him the damned status report. Tell him why we're evacuating. Ask him when those rescue ships are arriving," Jeri snapped. "I'm busy."

Trey's voice sounded loud over the speakers. "Gaia damn it all, I just slipped off!"

"No!" Jeri shouted. The submersible's forward cam showed the spar moving away. "Oh, Trey, Trey..." Jeri thought about the tiny submersible drifting down into the vast depths with a cracked acrylic bubble. He had run out of options. "Let me locate Cara."

A pause. "No, don't," Trey said quietly. "The clinic's probably full of patients now and she's needed there more. Just tell her...sis, tell her that I loved her; that I want her to marry again." His voice choked a little. "Tell her I went without pain."

"I'll tell her, Trey." Tears rolled down Jeri's face. "I'll stay on this circuit with you. I'll stay with you until..."

"Chief, I've *got* to show you—"

"Not now, Bret. Deal with it."

A new window opened on her screen, an image, a grainy close-up view. "What *is* that?"

"It's what I've been trying to show you," Bret said. "We processed the video taken by Trey—the views of the upper spar welds. We had to filter and clean up the images, but—"

"That's the sloppiest welding job I've ever seen," Jeri stared in disbelief. "Nonlinear, non-continuous. Arc splatter everywhere. Look at the crack along that seam! Was this welded by a drunk?"

"Those," Bret said, "are the welds holding GreenSea together."

"How did they pass the testing and the inspections? How did AquaTech let this happen?" Jeri shook her head but couldn't take her eyes from the image. Like nearly all modern seasteads, GreenSea had been built by AquaTech Manufacturing. Known for solid, sound designs, all the company's construction projects held up under severe conditions.

"Sis, I don't know if this is relevant," Trey's voice came over the open circuit over the sound of spraying water, "but it may tie in."

Jeri's thoughts returned to her doomed brother in the descending submersible. "Go ahead, Trey."

"Access the Whale-Song server, GreenSea admin directory." His voice sounded oddly serene. "Are you there?"

Jeri clicked her computer mouse. "Yes."

"Open up sub-directory 'Guide Munbar,' and find the file named 'Miscellaneous.' Open it."

The Guide's private file! "It's asking for—"

"The password is 'Ross Munbar' spelled backwards, with vowels capitalized and consonants small."

"Now it's asking some security questions."

"The answers are 'green,' 'martini,' 'Buckminster Fuller,' and 'snail darter.'"

"How in Gaia's name did you—"

"Never mind that. Look at the file. Seemed like routine stuff when I found it, hardly worth securing, but I think it might relate to those bad welds."

Jeri's eyes widened as she scanned the file. Letters, invoices, welding records, hand-written financial transactions...

"Oh, Great Mother! This is unbelievable, Trey. Thank you!" Her thoughts snapped back to his predicament. "What's your depth? And how's the bubble leakage?"

"Passing eight hundred meters," Trey answered. "The leak's really spraying in now. I'm staying out of its way."

Jeri heard the high-pitched whistling sound whenever Trey keyed his microphone. She pictured a narrow sheet of water under immense pressure lancing into the submersible's tiny, spherical hull. At his current depth, it could probably cut through bone.

"Passing nine hundred. Got some major hull creaking now. Guess it's time I said good—"

A brief, audible scratch sounded over the speaker.

"Trey?" Jeri pressed the earphone to her head. "Trey!"

Damage Repair Central stayed silent for several seconds after Jeri's head slumped to the console. She shook with sobs. After a time, the quiet murmurs of people speaking over their headsets resumed.

"I'm sorry, Jeri," Bret touched her shoulder.

The entire seastead swayed again to a greater angle than before, and finally righted itself.

All the lights went out. Jeri wiped tears from her eyes and looked around the darkness of D. R. Central. Like fireflies, the foreheads and forearms of her staff members began glowing as they activated their bioluminescent tattoos. Then a third of the lights came back on.

"Emergency battery backup is working," Bret said, "but I don't know how long the habitat disk will stay attached to the spar."

"Tell all huggers," Jeri said, gulping back her sorrow over Trey, "including all damage parties and the clinic, to move to lower leeward compartments and evacuate GreenSea as soon as rescue ships arrive." She raised her voice to fill the room. "That includes all of you. Clear out!"

She turned back to Bret. "What's our casualty count?"

"Fifteen dead," Bret's voice softened, "including Trey, and 136 wounded. Numbers keep going up," Bret said.

His console buzzed. "The Guide wants status again."

"Tell the Guide," Jeri took off her headset and stood up, "I'm coming to see him."

Guide Ross Munbar's large office usually contained a view of the sea through wide windows. Jeri had ordered two days earlier that the protective steel plating be slid over all windows. That left the imitation mahogany desk, and Ross Munbar himself, as the room's most imposing features.

On a corner of his desk stood a gleaming titanium model of GreenSea, half a meter high. Beautiful in form and symmetry, the model stood on three cylindrical ballast cans. Three struts led upward and merged to form the slender spar. Partway up the spar rested the windowed donut, the observation lounge. Atop the spar sat the disk-shaped habitat, which, in the real seastead, projected fifteen meters above the sea's surface. Wavegen floats hung under the habitat. The disk's upper surface divided like a peace symbol into four regions, the two smaller sectors containing a heliport and crop farm, and the larger sectors holding solar panels and wind turbines. Jeri had always loved that model.

"Why aren't you at D. R. Central, trying to save GreenSea?" Munbar asked.

With an effort, Jeri kept her voice calm and measured. "GreenSea is lost. I'm trying to save the remaining twelve hundred people."

"Mother Earth!" Munbar pounded a fist on the desk. "I told you to save GreenSea!"

"Which one? You mean the AquaTech Mark III seastead that I thought I was chief engineer of? Or do you mean the actual GreenSea, manufactured from substandard parts, welded by incompetents, and inspected by bribed officials?"

Munbar studied her, but his expression gave up nothing. "So, you know."

Jeri paced the office, ranting at the walls. "Good Gaia! It all fits together now. My predecessor quit but never said why. Every day it's a constant battle to keep brand-new equipment running. And when I tried to investigate the defects, AquaTech wouldn't respond to my calls or emails."

"They never received them. Your correspondence never left GreenSea," Munbar said flatly. "And phone calls to any AquaTech number got routed to a null line. Please sit down."

When she did, he stood and paced as she had, but in the opposite direction. "You can't possibly appreciate the difficulties I faced in creating GreenSea. I had nowhere near enough funding to buy a standard AquaTech product. So, I bought AquaTech's plans. And, yes, I substituted some materials; I hired less-skilled construction laborers; and I convinced the inspectors to look elsewhere. It's true, I took calculated risks; I cut corners. But I *built* GreenSea! I built it when nobody thought I could and fought to make it nearly self-sufficient. It's a gleaming monument to an idea, an ecological dream of how the whole world should live. It's 'a green isle in the sea,' as Poe put it in one of his poems. They sneered at us tree-huggers, sneered at *me*. But I proved them all wrong."

With a sound of grinding, tearing metal, the habitat disk shuddered and leaned over ten degrees to leeward and stayed there. Munbar staggered and returned to sit, with effort, in his desk chair.

Jeri stood. "GreenSea's spar is about to snap, Mr. Munbar. Once the habitat disk falls into the sea, I don't know how long it will stay afloat. I've ordered an all-hugger evacuation to the rescue ships. Please tell me they'll arrive soon."

"Yes, well, as to that," Guide Ross Munbar stroked his chin, "several neighboring 'stead's offered rescue services, but I told them we needed no assistance. We'll make our stand here, saving GreenSea no matter what sacrifices we must make."

"Ms. Calistus," the detective looked at her intently and placed a plastic-wrapped object on the table between them. "Do you recognize this?"

"Yes." Jeri sat opposite the man. Though they were alone in the small, bare room, she knew others outside could see and hear them. "It's the titanium model of GreenSea."

"Correct. We found your fingerprints on it. Now then, everybody knows you led the effort to keep GreenSea's habitat disk together during Hurricane Jove until all those remaining aboard were rescued. But for this investigation, please tell me what you know about Guide Ross Munbar being bludgeoned to death with that model."

Gazelle's Last Run

*T*he robotic shark nosed around the whale-shaped submarine. The sub's captain, César "Gazelle" Guzmán, flipped a switch and the Ballena Sabia emitted a mournful series of low moans and throbbing pulses, a pre-recorded blue whale song.

He worried the robot might see through the disguise and identify *Ballena Sabia* as an unauthorized sub. If so, the shark would broadcast a long-range wailing tone to alert other sharks and manned Coast Guard subs. If the manned subs found them, the rules for dealing with suspected smuggling vessels were clear—shoot to kill.

The shark still hung close, apparently not fooled.

"Captain, there's a problem," a voice whispered in his headset, the youthful voice of Lorca, the mech on watch back aft. He'd followed the rule about keeping his voice low when in U.S. waters.

"Not now, Lorca; I'm trying to evade a pesky shark." Guzmán scowled in annoyance at the interruption. No doubt the greenhorn mech was magnifying some minor anomaly into a crisis. *As I did on my own first run, decades ago.*

When the shark sniffed at his port side again, he started a leisurely right turn to the north. At this time of year, blues migrate north, unfortunately for Guzmán, since his goal lay to the west.

"It's the hydrogen pressure. The gauge is reading low."

"I've no time now for this, Lorca," Guzmán snapped. "We're using up hydrogen all the time, so the gauge *always* reads lower." Hydrogen-oxygen fuel cells powered the Ballena Sabia and she stored the two gases under high pressure within large carbon-composite flasks. The shark continued exploring, listening.

"I've taken that into account, Captain. The pressure's too low even after I factor in the fuel cell usage." Lorca's voice betrayed his annoyance at being treated like a rookie.

Time for our whale to breathe, Guzmán thought, when the randomizing timer light came on. He pulled back on the control stick and the submarine lunged to the surface. The gazelle tattoo on his right bicep, inked in bioluminescent green against his brown skin, seemed to speed along like the submarine itself. The gold cross on a chain around his neck glinted in the red instrument panel lighting.

As the submarine broached the waves, automated pumps shot a plume of water skyward. To any observer, it would look like a whale spouting. The pumps stopped and ventilation fans whirred, bringing fresh air into the submarine. These inhalations and exhalations alternated.

If valid, Lorca's reported hydrogen leak could be serious, Guzmán knew. Taken to the extreme, enough hydrogen in the sub's atmosphere could render any small electrical spark explosive. "Lorca, what is the pressure now, and what do your calculations say it should be?"

"Fifty megapascals now, but it should only be down to fifty-three."

A noticeable difference. Unlikely to be just gauge error, but Lorca's calculations were probably wrong. Guzmán felt like telling Lorca to have the other, more experienced mech, Salazar, look into the discrepancy during his watch. But it was important to express confidence in the youthful crewman. "Continue to monitor it, Lorca, and watch the ship's atmosphere readouts for increased hydrogen levels. Keep me informed."

"Aye, Captain."

For the moment, Guzmán shelved the matter. The shark still hounded him. He had updated his navigation fix and refreshed the sub's air. The randomizing timer light signaled the normal whale surface breathing duration, so Guzmán submerged the sub. Another activation of the whale's song gave him an updated active sonar picture that told him the shark stayed close behind and above his tail flukes.

Without warning, the shark suddenly yelled its warning into the sea. The piercing cry hurt Guzmán's ears and he yanked his headset off.

"Damn!" he shouted, angry and puzzled. *How had it pegged us?* That had never happened to him before. He pushed the throttle to flank speed and turned right again, heading to the east. *Might as well make them think we're fleeing for home.*

Five minutes later, the shark ceased its loud alarm and turned away. *Finally*, Guzmán sighed, knowing the unmanned underwater vehicle was nearly out of power and headed for its recharging station. But he knew it had sent its alert to Coast Guard subs and other UUVs, imperiling his men and his mission.

Guzmán throttled back to slow speed and felt a hand on his shoulder. He turned to see the serious face and intense gaze of Canepa, his first mate.

"Here to relieve you, Captain," Canepa said, speaking in his rapid monotone. "Did we get snapped up?"

Guzmán grunted, then relayed the current situation and gave his orders. "Head west using the GRD maneuver. If you pick up a shark, revert to blue whale behavior."

"Aye, Captain, I'll take the watch now," Canepa whispered.

Guzmán kept one hand steadying the control yoke as he unbuckled and slid out of the command chair, careful to ensure the sheathed knife at his belt didn't snag on anything. Canepa squirmed into the vacated spot and gripped the yoke.

Starting the Gliding Rise-and-Dive maneuver, Canepa toggled the switch to take on more ballast water, letting them glide forward and downward like a glider in air. Once the sub reached its depth limit, he would force water from the ballast bladder, allowing the sub to rise and glide forward as well. Though not something practiced by whales, the procedure had the advantage of total silence.

"One more thing," Guzmán whispered to his first mate. "Lorca reported a problem with hydrogen pressure. Have Salazar check it out."

"Yes, Captain," Canepa responded without looking. His eyes darted about, taking in every instrument on the panel.

"Canepa," Guzmán touched the man's shoulder to get him to look up. "Call me if you get in trouble. I mean it."

"Of course, Captain," Canepa said.

Guzmán didn't have full confidence in Canepa yet. The first mate had come highly recommended and appeared capable, but he seemed high-strung for this whale-sub trade, perhaps not truly ready to man the forward watch-station. *How will he react in a crisis*?

A wise captain balances experience levels within his watch-standing schedules, and Guzmán had paired Canepa as pilot up forward with Salazar at the aft watch-station. Guzmán had sailed for eighteen runs with that old mech. Salazar could fix anything aboard the ship and had earned Guzmán's full measure of trust. If Canepa screwed things up, Salazar could either unscrew it, or at least wake his captain up.

Guzmán made his way aft through the passageway, ducking his head due to the low overhead. Restrained by nylon netting, tall piles of greenish-brown plastic cargo bags lined both sides of the narrow corridor. More bags lay beneath the temporary plywood flooring on which he walked. The sub carried as much cargo as a real blue whale carried blubber, about fifty metric tons.

Six hours on watch, six hours off watch, all the way from the New Chiapas Seastead to the U.S. coast. If all went well, their seven-day mission would end in two more days.

He walked aft through the mech spaces, checking on the hydrogen-oxygen fuel cells and the electrically-stimulated artificial bio-sym muscles that powered the mighty tail flukes. The entire mech space oscillated up and down in reaction to the tail's motion. Guzmán hadn't felt the movement when forward due to the two watertight joints in the hull that allowed the sub to bend like a real whale. He stopped at the mech station.

"Everything in order, old friend?" Guzmán smiled to see Salazar seated at the mech workbench, repairing a small valve. Salazar's whisper, like his usual voice, sounded rough and gravely. "First time getting pegged by a shark, no?" His eyes glinted as the laugh lines deepened.

"News travels fast on this ship."

Salazar shook his head and pointed to a bulkhead. "Heard it through the hull."

"Well, we're running silent now. Perhaps we can clear the area before more sharks start sniffing around. Don't worry; we'll deliver the goods, just like we always have."

Salazar gazed at the instrument panel showing the status of the fuel cells, propulsion and steering muscles, and auxiliary equipment. "Yes, Skipper, like always," he said.

Guzmán scanned the gauges himself and noted hydrogen pressure was down to forty-eight megapascals.

Salazar followed his gaze. "Lorca told me he thinks the pressure's low. I'll check his calculations. That's probably where he made his mistake."

The captain nodded and turned to go.

"Don't worry, Skipper. I'll keep the hydrogen flowing if you'll keep the sharks away."

Guzmán looked back to see Salazar's wink and grin. "I'll do my best, old friend."

When he returned to the Ballena Sabia's amidships area, he found Lorca eating a pre-packaged *matambre*. Guzman used to enjoy these loaves of steak, onions, and green peppers but had tired of the monotony. The young mech sat on a plastic cargo bag, and ate off a makeshift table made from a plywood board atop more cargo bags. *The cargo is everywhere*, thought Guzmán.

"Want a *matambre*, Captain?" Lorca whispered.

"Gracias, no. I'll get myself a bowl of gazpacho."

"Don't you get sick of eating only cold food?"

Guzmán shrugged. The ship had neither stove nor microwave. *The most sophisticated electronics for the mission, but none for crew comfort.* "It's only for two more days."

Guzmán questioned Lorca about the events of the watch and, after finishing his meal, he reached for a deck of cards. "A game of *Conquian*, perhaps?"

Lorca nodded and cleared the food away. "May I ask you a personal question, Captain?"

"Of course," Guzmán shuffled the cards.

"Why a gazelle?" Lorca was staring at Guzmán's tattoo.

Guzmán smiled and dealt the cards. "On the African savanna, the gazelle must avoid being eaten by the lion, no? The gazelle is born to that job, bred for it. And the lion is bred to chase down and kill the gazelle. Through evolution, better gazelles make better lions, and vice versa. So it is with us in our underwater savanna. We smugglers are the gazelle, always on the run from our lion, the U.S. Coast Guard. You understand this, Lorca?"

"Yes, Captain," but then the young man frowned. "With gazelles and lions, it's a matter of speed. Not so with us."

"Long ago, smuggling was a matter of speed, too." Guzmán said, smiling as he recalled his grandfather's stories. "The analogy is not as good now, but the point is to always get better, think of things that the adversary has not, improve your evasion techniques even as the Coast Guard improves detection methods. Now then, let us play a few hands before we sleep."

As their game progressed, Guzmán recalled when he'd been the youthful learner listening to an aged teacher. He'd grown up in

Columbia, at that time solely a land country, before the first seasteads. His grandfather had shown ten-year-old César Guzmán a gazelle tattoo on *his* right bicep, blurred and faded with age. He'd told exciting tales of smuggling cocaine up the Pacific coast to California. He and his men sailed crude, low-slung submersible vessels. Diesel engines fouled their air, deafened their hearing, and left a sooty, oily sheen on every interior surface.

Those primitive boats did their best to avoid sophisticated satellite sensors, fast surface ships, and advanced military submarines. Somehow, most of the smugglers got through. Guzmán never tired of hearing of his grandfather's exploits and close escapes.

"It's in our blood, boy," the old man had told him. "My own grandfather smuggled rum by speedboat from the Bahamas to Florida during the U.S. alcohol prohibition. And *his* grandfather smuggled whiskey in Scotland."

"All grandfathers?" young Guzmán asked.

"That's right. The calling to smuggle skips generations in our family."

"But *Abuelo*," Guzmán asked, realizing that the odd profession would pass from his grandfather to him. "Why did you smuggle? Isn't it illegal?"

His grandfather laughed. "When a government likes a product, it's *trade*. When it doesn't, it's smuggling. By their own laws, governments create smugglers."

"But aren't they trying to protect people from bad things?"

"That's what your parents would say." Guzmán's grandfather lit a cigar. "But who is so smart he can decide what is bad for everyone else? How is a country free if it tells people what they may put in their own bodies, and what they may not? If people do not own their bodies, are they not slaves?"

Despite his years in the trade, Guzmán himself still felt twinges of guilt when he thought about the thousands of lives ruined by drugs, but it helped to recall the words of his grandfather: "People will want drugs and will pay for them whether legal or not, whether they're smuggled by me or by someone else."

As he grew to manhood, Guzmán found himself drawn to the trade, not by money, but by excitement. He loved the chase, taking his chances with everything on the line, even the risk of death. Perhaps that most of all. He felt the gazelle's thrill at evading the lion's jaws one more time.

"Captain, I can't shake them." Canepa's voice came over the speaker near Guzmán's head. The captain roused himself from his brief sleep and slid from his bunk. He raced forward along the passageway, stooping and keeping his gait stable in case the sub lurched.

"Sorry to wake you, Captain," Canepa whispered over his shoulder at Guzmán's approach. "A very determined pair of sharks back there."

Guzmán saw the two UUVs on the sonar screen, both behind and above them. "How did they get us?"

"Their active sonar. As soon as the first one showed up, I started playing whale again—surfacing, singing, feeding at krill swarms, migrating north."

Had the Americans improved their sharks, pushing the lion to the next evolutionary stage in its eternal race with the gazelle? "Only one screams at a time," Guzmán said. "They're taking turns."

"I think so too, Captain," Canepa said. "When one is out of power, the other will scream and a new, fresh shark will arrive."

How can we escape? They're programmed to keep after us until a Coast Guard sub arrives to torpedo us. Guzmán scowled, cursing the cartel for sending them out in a whale-sub without weapons of its own. To them, cargo was more important than weapons.

Should I abort the mission and return home? He'd never done that before, and hated the thought of it now, especially since they'd come so close to the coast. He tucked his cross into his T-shirt. *No, I've come this far—we'll press on.*

"I'll take the watch now, Canepa."

"But, Captain," the first mate looked up at him. "It's early, and I only woke you to ask for guidance."

"That's fine. I'll take it. Get some rest."

"Another thing," Canepa said. "Salazar reported no hydrogen pressure drop on his watch at all. Also, no increase in hydrogen levels in the ship's air."

"So, this happens only when Lorca's on watch, or—"

"Or the kid's mistaken," Canepa finished. "Reading the gauge wrong, perhaps?"

"Hmm." Guzmán settled into the chair and donned the headset. He didn't think the young mech would misread a pressure gauge, but he knew he could depend on Salazar. "Let's allow our two mechs to sort out the truth, eh? Sleep now."

"Aye, Captain." Canepa walked aft.

As his first mate left, Guzmán considered the sharks again. His whale-song sonar system gave him a continuous update of their locations. He watched their movements as they swam around the *Ballena Sabia*, noting their patterns. One screamed while remaining behind and slightly above his submarine. Its annoying wail made it hard to think. The other roamed all over the exterior of his ship. *Like some mechanical dog nipping at our heels.*

Guzmán smiled as the comparison gave him an idea. He flipped a switch so he could speak to all three crewmen over their headsets. "Stand by for violent maneuvers," he whispered.

He waited until the nipping shark swam into the right position. Toggling a switch from auto to manual, he grabbed a lever and jerked it. The starboard pectoral fin slapped hard against the UUV, cleaving it in two. Guzmán yanked two levers and the pectorals swiveled, acting as a brake to slow the ship. With one more sudden pull on a third lever, the powerful tail fluke slapped up hard against the remaining shark. Its wailing call ceased and it stopped, no longer following him.

Not typical cetacean behavior. He smiled. *Ballena Sabia, you are indeed a wise whale. Today, wiser than a whale.* He patted the instrument panel with affection, then positioned the fins and flukes to GRD mode again and left them there. Now the ship could glide without a sound.

"Secure from violent maneuvers," he told his crew. *This run might just be successful after all.*

Abuelo would have enjoyed that little stunt, he thought, allowing himself another grin. His grandfather had pulled far crazier ploys in his day. Despite the odds, no matter the obstacles, he'd always gotten his cargo of cocaine through.

Times changed, and the drugs of choice changed too, Guzmán thought. Now he and his crew smuggled *gass,* an extract of sargassum seaweed. When one of the ethnic subcultures of old Mexico had founded the seasteading aquastate of New Chiapas in the middle of the Northern Atlantic, gass was unknown. After the drug's discovery, that country found itself in the midst of a floating, ever-replenishing gold mine—the Sargasso Sea. Cartels moved in, merged, took over the government, and now sold the drug to an eager and growing market.

Euphoric, non-addictive, and free of morning-after side effects, gass seemed the perfect drug, though its long-term effects remained unknown. Even aboard a submarine surrounded by the stuff, Guzmán forbade his crew from using it while on a mission. He'd never used gass himself.

The Ballena Sabia had glided down close to its depth limit, so Guzmán pressed buttons to squeeze water from the ballast bladder, and repositioned the fins and flukes for their angled ascent. *Not much farther to the first rendezvous point.*

The gold cross on his neck chain tugged on his chest hairs, so he pulled the pendant out and let it rest on the outside of his shirt. He frowned, thinking of his parents, who had given him the cross at his confirmation. *If only I could forget that last day I saw them.* But the decade-old memory would not fade.

"If you want to smuggle, then get out," his father had said, pointing at the door. "No smuggler sets foot in my house. Not my father, and—if you choose to follow him—not you either."

Seventeen-year-old César Guzmán had looked at his mother, who stood by his father with tears running down. Her down-turned lips moved, but she said nothing.

Guzmán had looked at them both one last time, then walked from the house without a word, and without looking back. He'd lived with that decision ever since, the hardest one of his life.

"Damn!" Guzmán yanked off the headset as the piercing alarm of a shark blasted from somewhere close. He hadn't seen it on the passive sonar screen. *We're completely silent.* He gritted his teeth. *How did it hear us?*

Guzmán put the tail flukes back in motion and resumed blue whale behavior. He turned off the exterior audio and donned the headset again.

"—tain, are you there? It's Lorca. We still have a hydrogen problem."

"Not now, Lorca, I'm busy." Guzmán steered the sub to the north. Lorca must have relieved Salazar on mech watch, he realized.

"But Captain—"

"Lorca, is the hydrogen level going up in the ship's atmosphere?" He was getting tired of the conflicting reports he was getting from Lorca and Salazar.

"No, Captain."

"You're a qualified mech. Think like one. If we're losing hydrogen, and it's not going inside, then—" Guzmán paused. If they were leaking hydrogen bubbles out to the sea, a shark wouldn't need to *hear* them—it could sniff them out by the bubble stream. "Check the outboard hydrogen charging valve. Ensure it's shut."

"I checked that first, Captain. It's shut." Irritation filled Lorca's voice, but not quite to the level of disrespect.

"Then do a hand-over-hand inspection of that system's piping," Guzmán growled. "You understand, Lorca? Hand-over-hand. Every centimeter." The shark lingered behind and slightly above the Ballena Sabia. *Right where it should be, if we're leaking hydrogen*, Guzmán thought. He waited for an opportunity to swat this one with his tail flukes.

His active whale-song sonar now picked up more contacts as they neared the American coast. Just behind him swam the shark, blaring its alarm. To the west, two surface ships steamed in the distance. Off his starboard beam lay some large, indistinct biologic contacts.

Another object materialized in front of him, at close range. Guzmán froze. A U.S. Coast Guard sub. *Must have just risen above the sound layer, summoned by that dammed shark.*

He swerved the sub to the right and played a blue whale's 'B call,' the deep, sad moan. The big contacts in that direction were separating on the screen.

"This is the American Coast Guard submarine *Defender*," the voice came over the underwater telephone speakers, speaking in Spanish. "To the unauthorized submarine off my port bow, you are trespassing in U.S. waters. Stop your vessel immediately and come to the surface. Comply or we will launch weapons."

Guzmán increased speed and continued heading toward the shallow-swimming biologic contacts. *Gracias a Dios! A pod of blue whales!*

The small group had paused in their migration so the cow mothers could suckle their young. Guzmán slowed as he neared them, playing what he hoped was a whale greeting from his hydrophones. *The Coast Guard won't shoot if they risk harming a real whale.*

The Defender slowed some distance from the pod and waited. Guzmán's blood turned icy as he heard the American sub open its torpedo tube outer doors.

Guzmán did his best to imitate the behavior of the whales around him. He swam among them, keeping close to their huge flanks. He surfaced with them to spout, welcoming the fresh air after their long submergence.

The *Defender's* sonar operators might have lost track of the imitation whale, but the real whales hadn't. They shied away from the Ballena Sabia. Cows shielded their calves from the newcomer, and the bull circled the submarine as if sizing it up for a challenge.

"I don't want your females, amigo," Guzmán murmured. "Just play along with me for a little while, please." He tried to stay in the midst of the pod, but it started to scatter.

Praying that the *Defender's* sonar operators had lost him amid the group, Guzmán dove his sub down farther into the depths. With a feeling of relief, he noted the sharp change in seawater temperature as he went deeper. The sudden coolness meant a distinct division between two water layers. All sound would bend downward away from that layer depth. *Ah, Defender; maybe the same layer that hid you earlier will cloak my Ballena Sabia now.* As the seabed drew closer, he leveled off and turned to the west. Little by little he increased speed until they flew along, only a few hundred meters over an ocean floor marked by rounded furrows.

Guzmán patted his tattoo. *Perhaps the gazelle has escaped the lion one more time*, he thought, and smiled.

"Captain, I found it!" Lorca's excited outburst almost rose above a whisper.

"Found what?" Guzmán still guided the sub just above the bottom at high speed. He'd been at it for four hours and knew Canepa would relieve him soon. He suspected the *Defender's* captain had figured out his ploy and would be no more than one hour behind them.

"I did the hand-over-hand inspection and found a bypass line installed around the external hydrogen charging valve."

"What?"

"It was well hidden," Lorca said. "Very thin piping, meant to leak hydrogen to the sea slowly through a narrow orifice."

"Have you fixed it?"

"Yes. I cut the line and sealed both ends as best I could, Captain. We're no longer leaking gas overboard, but my sealing job won't hold for long. We'll get some minor leaking of hydrogen inboard and a little seawater, that's all."

"Good work, Lorca," Guzmán said. "A little internal leakage won't hurt us much. Who could have done this?"

"I don't know, Captain. It had to be an expert. The line was sized to leak very slowly—I barely picked up the pressure drop. And the damned thing was tricky to find. I had to tear off piping insulation to see it. Maybe someone at the subyard did it during the boat's last refit?"

If we get back home, I will hunt down the guilty saboteur bastard and kill him myself. "Thank you, Lorca. You may have saved us all. When Salazar takes the watch, have him monitor the piping and apply more sealant."

"Aye, Captain, I see him coming now." Lorca sounded pleased with the praise he'd earned.

Guzmán concentrated on piloting the sub, sailing low over heavily silted ridged mounds.

Sharks, Coast Guard subs, and now subyard sabotage. My parents were right about this career. Last run for this gazelle. My family's smuggling history shall end with me. If I have a grandson, he won't do this.

The hand on Guzmán's shoulder felt welcome.

"Here to relieve you, Captain," Canepa said. "You had an eventful watch."

Guzmán turned to find the first mate looking over his shoulder at the log.

"You evaded three sharks *and* a C.G. sub, all in six hours? When are you going to tell me your secrets, Captain?"

Guzmán looked at Canepa, who stood smiling behind him. *Could you have sabotaged the hydrogen charging line? If you did it, you'll know from my log that Lorca has undone your damage. What will you try next? What do I know of you, really?*

Canepa's smile vanished under Guzmán's prolonged gaze. He looked curious, even worried.

Guzmán made a quick decision. *For now, I'll trust you, I'll but check on you more frequently.* "Sorry, I was lost in thought for a moment. You can learn what I did from the log. In the meantime, run at full speed for the rendezvous point. Let me know if the Coast Guard shows up."

"Aye, Captain," Canepa said. "I'll take the watch." They switched places.

The voice of Salazar came over Guzmán's headset. "There's been an accident back here. Lorca is injured. Send the skipper."

"On my way," Guzmán said. He rushed off.

Guzmán grabbed a first aid kit as he passed by the amidships living quarters, knowing that there was already an identical kit in the engine room. He sped through the narrow corridor between towering stacks of gass cargo. He entered the mech spaces, now pitching up and down rapidly with the sub's high speed.

He found Salazar kneeling over Lorca, who lay on the deck face up. Blood coated his shirt from his chest to his left side. The medical kit sat open beside the young man.

"He cut himself badly, Skipper," Salazar said in his gravelly voice.

Guzmán knelt near Lorca opposite Salazar. He bent over to examine the wound.

He leaned back just in time to avoid the knife that slashed horizontally at chest level. Some sixth sense had warned him—perhaps the fact that Salazar had not been trying to stop Lorca's bleeding.

Salazar stood, knees flexed, blood still dripping from the knife in his hand.

Guzmán stood also and backed away in the cramped space, pulling his own knife as he did so. "You, Salazar?" *My most trusted shipmate?* His glance flicked between Salazar's eyes to his knife hand. "You sabotaged our ship? Why?"

"The Americans pay well." Salazar stepped forward and jabbed, but Guzmán leaned away.

"You fool." Guzmán searched for places to step and for escape paths. "You led them right to us, but if they attack, you'll die with us and can't spend your money."

"Wrong, *Skipper*," Salazar spat the title out as if cursing. He lunged again, but Guzmán parried, pushing the arm aside. "That's part of the deal I made. Their torpedoes are set to disable our tail flukes only, so we can't escape. They'll come aboard and arrest you, put you and Canepa in jail. But for me—every hooker I can find." He smiled as he rocked back and forth, his eyes flicking between Guzmán's knife and face.

"But Lorca found out, didn't he? Spoiled your plan, eh?" *Bad place for a knife fight*, Guzmán thought. *Too cramped, surrounded by machinery, and Lorca's body on the deck between us.*

"Lorca shouldn't have found my bypass line." Salazar started circling the body, forcing Guzmán to do the same. "When he said he'd already told you, I knew I couldn't bribe him to join me. I had to kill him." Salazar leaned forward to jab the knife and then slashed upward.

Guzmán backed out of the way. Despite his fatigue, he felt alert, his senses keen. He knew only one of them would leave the engineering space alive. If Salazar won, he'd kill Canepa next. He watched for Salazar's eyes to glance away, then lunged.

Quick as lightening, the mech grabbed Guzmán's knife wrist in his free hand and jabbed his own knife at the captain's chest. Guzmán turned sideways but the blade sliced his right bicep, slashing across the gazelle tattoo.

He grabbed Salazar's right wrist and twisted it hard.

The mech winced but retained his knife. He advanced, stepping on Lorca's chest and pushing forward. Locked together, the two men staggered and Guzmán backed into a valve, its hand-wheel pressing against his shoulder blades. Each man fought to free his knife hand, while tightening his grip on the other's.

Salazar leaned close, his face just centimeters from Guzmán's. He scowled and spat. "All those years," he said. "All those runs, with you taking the larger share of pay. You thought yourself better than me. But you were wrong."

"You could have captained your own ship," Guzmán said. "I would have recommended you. You'd be earning a captain's share."

His body exploded with pain as Salazar kneed him in the groin. His knees started to buckle. He struggled to maintain his grip on the mech's knife hand. Knowing he had to buy time until the pain died, he gave Salazar a vicious head butt.

Salazar let go and stumbled backward. He lost balance as the tail's motion caused the room to drop. He stepped on Lorca's face and fell backward on the deck.

Guzmán bent over, unable to press his advantage until the agony subsided. He breathed hard and kept an eye on Salazar as the man scrambled to his feet.

Still in pain, Guzmán backed into the narrow passageway that led forward. Guzmán found he could now stand straight once more. He felt his right arm and his hand came away bloody.

Salazar charged at him like a bull.

Guzmán ducked down as the mech swung his blade sideways. Struck by a sudden notion, the captain flipped open a quick release latch at knee level on the starboard side, a lever used by stevedores during unloading. He stood and ran forward, calling to Canepa. "Hard left! Turn hard left now!"

As he ran, the deck tilted down to the left and cargo netting gave way on the right. The plastic bags of gass lining that side of the corridor slid and tumbled over. Hundreds of twenty-kilogram bags cascaded down, throwing off the sub's balance and tilting it more, so more bags kept falling.

Guzmán ran, but the collapsing wall mashed him hard against the left side of the corridor. He'd stayed ahead of the bulk of the avalanche and his upper body remained free. "Steady up, Canepa! Shift ballast to regain trim."

The sub slowly righted itself. Guzmán struggled to wriggle free, but his injured right arm provided little help. Clambering over the fallen cargo, he looked back. A single hand remained visible and unmoving, the forearm twisted and bent at a wrong angle. A bloody knife lay on a cargo bag nearby. Salazar's bare palm faced Guzmán as if in final farewell.

"Adios, old sea-dog," Guzmán said. "You'll earn no pay from *either* side on this run." *And neither will poor Lorca, a far better man than you.*

Holding his bleeding right bicep, Guzmán made his way forward.

"What in God's name happened back there, Captain?"

Guzmán filled in Canepa and thanked him for the timely response to his course change order.

"I'll take over now," he said.

"Captain, you're hurt. I should stay on watch here."

Guzmán shook his head. "You must be our mech for the rest of the run. It's just you and me now."

Canepa nodded and unsnapped the restraining harness. "We're at the first rendezvous point. When I slowed, I picked up the American on passive. He's coming this way."

"Any sign he detected us?"

"No. He's at flank speed and can't hear a thing. Even going that fast, he's an hour away."

"Very well. Let me know when you're in position back there. Strap yourself in for violent maneuvers."

"Aye, Captain." Canepa looked like he wanted to ask a question, but instead left to go aft.

Guzmán noted the sea bottom in this part of the continental shelf showed the same rounded furrows he'd seen earlier. They had a soft, almost fuzzy appearance. He squeezed some water from a ballast bladder so the whale-sub could drift upward a few dozen meters.

Canepa's voice sounded in his headset. "I'm ready, Captain. I also tied Lorca's body securely. Such a shame about him."

"Yes, a good man," Guzmán agreed. "Brace yourself."

He checked the passive sonar. Behind them, the Defender still raced at top speed. He pushed the control stick forward and guided the

Ballena Sabia on a slanting course downward at high speed. He started leveling as he neared the bottom, but they still struck hard.

All lighting failed, but the emergency lanterns soon came on, emitting their red glow. "Are you all right back there, Canepa?"

"Yes, Captain. What on Earth—"

"Can you get me power to the fins and flukes?"

"One moment…Yes, the last fuel cell might hold together for a little bit."

"That's fine. Check the ship for leaks and plug them."

Guzmán flapped the flukes and the port fin, but found the starboard one too damaged to move. Finally, all the power gave out. He leaned back in his seat and removed his headset. He unstrapped and worked his way aft, checking for leaks. Dust hung in the air, lit up red in the eerie glow of the emergency lanterns.

He met Canepa amidships. The first mate looked exhausted. "I found one leak. It's sealed."

"Good," Guzmán said. "Have a seat. I've bottomed our sub in an area of thick mud and silt, then flapped the flukes to bury us more. Silt is probably still raining down on us. After it settles, we will look like just another furrow on the seabed."

Canepa managed a smile. "I never would have thought of that. It's hard enough to think like a whale."

"Don't just think like a whale," Guzmán tapped his temple. "Think like a smuggler. Or," he looked at his glowing green tattoo, now marred with a streak of red, "like a gazelle."

Canepa nodded. "So we wait here and hope the Americans don't find us?"

"Right. We wait until they get tired of looking and leave. Then we'll take the batteries from an emergency lantern to power the acoustic transmitter. We'll signal the calf to link up and unload us and our cargo. It will take several trips."

Calves were midget subs designed to look and sound like young blue whales. Once signaled, they'd came from shore to hook up with cargo whale-subs like Ballena Sabia and offload portions of cargo. This usually happened at each of several secret rendezvous points along the coast.

"For our Ballena, this is her final stop," Guzmán patted a bulkhead. "Once the cargo is off, we'll flood her and leave her here."

They sat for several minutes as the total silence of the depths washed over them. Finally, Canepa looked at Guzmán. "Captain, I'd be honored if you'd take me with you on your next run."

Guzmán thought that over. *Should I stop now, as I vowed, and break the generational chain of smuggling in my family?* Then he thought about the Americans, whose laws made trading gass a crime in the first place, whose Coast Guard still hunted him, and who'd turned Salazar against him, killing Lorca in the process.

"No, Canepa, this is my last run," he said. "It's time I settled down and started working on having a grandson."

Canepa chuckled. "You mean a *son.*"

Guzmán's tattoo glowed in the darkness. "Well, that's first, of course." He realized he'd lost his cross and neck chain in the fight with Salazar. "But after that, a grandson."

First Flow of the Tide

Dillon didn't hate the blue-green boy. He just couldn't see him as a potential son-in-law.

"I knew you wouldn't get it." His daughter, Cass, glared at him, then nudged her food into a different pattern on her plate. "You never do."

"That's not fair, Cass," said Trid. "We are trying to understand." She reached a hand toward her daughter, but let it rest on the kitchen table.

Dillon wasn't trying, and he knew his wife's attempt to reconcile wouldn't work.

"You're not," said Cass, "especially not Dad. I wanted you to be up-bubble about my engagement, but you're both down on it, down on him." Her lower lip trembled, but her eyes glowered.

Neither Dillon nor Trid had voiced direct opposition, but Cass had correctly sensed the undercurrent. She always did.

"We only want the best for you," Dillon said. His eyes were drawn for a moment to a multicolored fish swimming past the kitchen porthole. "Marriage is—" He looked at his wife for assistance in finishing the thought, but she gave none, "—a big commitment."

"Hardly, Dad. Cass rolled her eyes. "Such an ichthyosaur. It's just a five-year contract."

Dillon winced. He hadn't favored contract marriages when they moved to the seastead of Templemere, in Kernaria. He and Astrid had wed when marriage meant something deeper, and longer.

"Besides," Cass went on, "I do know what's best for me. I love him. It's no froth off me if you hate him 'cause you aren't marrying him." The strain of the fight showed in her wavering voice and tear-filled eyes. Her strawberry-blond hair and hazel eyes had always seemed to Dillon to be a strange blend of her Scandinavian and Gaelic ancestry.

"We don't hate him," Trid said.

"He's a fine young man," Dillon forced himself to say. Except for his bluish-green skin, he didn't add. "We've known his family for years." People within their small seastead knew almost everyone else.

"It's his religion, I know," Cass shook her head and slammed her fork down hard. "You just can't flow with it."

"Well, you've got to admit," Dillon tried to word it with care, "their beliefs are unconventional."

"You don't know anything about them!" Cass said, pushing away her plate. "You always told me to think critically, find things out for myself instead of believing what 'everybody' says, blub, blub, blub. I guess that was all a lie. But you're not open-minded when it's something that matters to me." She stood up. "Maybe if you tried to understand them, you'd like Rio, and then maybe you'd stop giving me flotz and jetz. I'm going pelagic."

The module hatch slammed as Cass departed.

"Flotz and jetz? Pelagic?" Dillon looked at Trid.

"Crap, I think, and pelagic means out." Trid sighed. "We could have handled that better."

She means *I* could have. Dillon shook his head. "She was such a fun little girl. Now it looks like we created a monster."

"We created an adult," Trid smiled and gathered the dinner plates. "Wasn't that the point all along?"

Dillon cleared the table of remaining items and folded it into a wall panel. "Yeah, I know. But she wants to marry an Oceanist. After we raised her to be a good atheist."

Trid paused while loading the dishwasher. "It is a different way of thinking, but—"

"It's a bizarre cult!" Dillon said. "Those loons get their skin permanently dyed. They worship a water god. They give themselves *aqua names.* Now we're supposed to call Merc by this new name? Rio? And we named our daughter Cass, not Brooke."

"Still, Cass has a point," Trid faced him. "You and I don't know much about Oceanism. We're condemning that whole sect out of ignorance."

"Wait a minute," Dillon backed up a step and cocked his head. "What are you suggesting?"

Dillon sat in a plastic seat, his body submerged up to his neck in seawater. Within this seastead module, he could see forty other people's heads sticking up from the water. About half of them had blue or green skin, though he found it hard to tell in this light. Around them all, through transparent walls, they looked out on scenes of the sea. Blacktip reef sharks cruised through a school of mullet. Adult humpback whales cavorted with their young. An illusion, Dillon knew. The images played from large TV screens. In reality this seastead module connected with hundreds of other cylindrical modules that would have obscured an actual exterior view. Sounds of the sea reached his ears—the clicking and crackling of shrimp, and eerie humpback songs. Dillon understood the need to hear the ocean sounds, but did they have to pipe in the ethereal synthesizer music, too?

How did I let Trid talk me into this? Dillon looked at her head sticking up from the water next to him. We should wear our swimsuits, she'd said, go to an Oceanist Temple and get the full experience, not watch on video. Great.

She squeezed his hand; he rolled his eyes.

The music swelled to a crescendo and the holographic image of a starfish, its arms quivering, hovered before him, and similar ghostly starfish floated before them all. The symbol of Oceanism.

"Hail, fellow Oceanists!" A deep voice came from hidden speakers.

"Hail to you!" responded many of those in the assemblage, and Dillon heard more voices sounding from the speakers.

"We welcome our visitors this day as well," the voice continued. The starfish faded and the image of a man's head appeared. He, too, sat up to his neck in water. Beside his image floated the words "High Priest Ford Broadwater." His skin bore a dark blue coloring, though hair and beard were of a lighter hue. His eyes gazed with fathomless intensity, and his smile welcomed all. "I'll be conducting today's worship hour. Let us begin in song."

Though the notes and lyrics appeared before him in holographic form, Dillon didn't join in the hymn. He couldn't read music and didn't know the tune.

Only three years had passed since Dillon had first heard of Oceanism. Since then, the new religion had spread like a spiritual tsunami throughout all seasteading aquastates. Its strange practices had earned some unfavorable press, yet more and more people joined its ranks. Led by a high priest and five pentapriests, the sect conducted worship gatherings remotely by TV and webcast.

The song seemed uplifting enough, flowing smoothly without sudden jumps, and swelling to an emotional crescendo at the end.

"Very inspiring," said Ford Broadwater. "I'll now summarize the first flow of the Tide."

The Tide, Dillon recalled from his research, was the holy book of Oceanists, and they referred to its divisions as flows.

"Oceanus created Thalassa as a watery world. Water surrounds land, dominates it in three-to-one proportion. Oceanus created life in the water, for seawater is the fluid of life. By its very nature, life requires action, motion. It could never have arisen on the static, dry land. Clearly the seas and oceans are the rightful place of all life."

As Broadwater spoke, screens and holograms displayed images supporting his sermon. Scenes of the Earth from space showed the watery planet. *These Oceanists rename everything*, Dillon thought. *Earth is now Thalassa?* Other images showed single-cell life dividing and swimming about in water. Later scenes contrasted moving water with stationary land.

"Some life on Thalassa lost its way, left its rightful home. Some life went to live upon the land and in the sky."

Dillon started to get inklings about Broadwater's creation story, and guessed where it was going.

"Eons passed, and sentient human life began on land. Humans were lost, confused, and fearful, all because they had formed on land, not in life's rightful place. Throughout history, they sought answers to questions about the deeper meaning of life. No answer, no religious teaching, completely satisfied. Why have all other human religions fallen short? Because they all approach the question from a land-based perspective."

Throughout his sermon, holographic and screen images, scenes, and icons accompanied Broadwater's words. From time to time, his head would be visible, lifting a blue eyebrow, smiling at some terrestrial human foible. Dillon grew more and more uncomfortable with the aim and accuracy of the sermon. Oceanism's founders, he knew, had seized corroborative facts and discarded contrary ones to form their strange views. Still, others in this room appeared to listen in earnest, apparently ready to believe. *How can so many people be taken in like this? How can my daughter be one of them?*

"For reasons beyond their understanding, our ancestors felt drawn to the seas. They felt compelled somehow to fish, to swim, to travel by boat and ship. Even today a huge majority of land-dwelling humans live close to the sea. Deep down, we all sense life's rightful place; we know where we belong.

"For most people, the ocean seemed a scary and dangerous place to visit, not a place to live. But one man, chosen by Oceanus, dared to chart a course for others to follow—"

No, thought Dillon, *they've made the guy a saint?*

"J. Hugh Robard, founder of the first seastead, a demi-god among men who..."

Broadwater talked on, but Dillon's thoughts drifted back to when he and Astrid had fallen in love. She'd wanted to live on Robard's undersea habitat, PaCitadel. Over Dillon's objections, she'd gone. The United States considered PaCitadel a rogue state, in violation of international treaties. Tensions escalated until the U.S. destroyed the seastead with a nuclear bomb. To Dillon's intense relief, Trid had not yet arrived at PaCitadel due to a flight delay. Twenty-five years later, a five hundred nautical mile diameter radiation zone surrounded the site.

"...a holy site," Broadwater said, as three-dimensional holographic images of the bombing's tidal waves played on screens. "In his folly, mankind forever scarred this sacred circle of Oceanus' realm. We will eternally mark July 29th as a day of holy reflection and remembrance for the innocent victims..."

A lucky thing Trid wasn't one of those victims, Dillon thought. So much had happened to them since. In a world-wide reaction of shame and sympathy, land nations had accepted seasteads and aquastates as legal entities. After their marriage, Trid had convinced Dillon they could build a life for themselves on a seastead, and they'd chosen Templemere. Her diplomatic training and talents found ready employment in a new nation struggling to establish itself. Dillon's skills in war-gaming and tactical military analysis had found no demand, however, so he'd become a docking officer, ensuring the safe arrival and departure of submarines from the 'stead. *Not glamorous*, he mused, *but it pays.*

The worship hour continued with two more songs and a period of private meditation amid gentle sea-sounds. After a few closing words from Ford Broadwater, he raised his hands from the water.

With surprise and a stifled gasp, Dillon saw webbed fingers on Broadwater's hands. The thin membrane of apparent skin matched the blue of his other features. *A medical procedure*, Dillon thought. They're trying to separate themselves from land humans as much as possible.

"Swim forth, Oceanists!" Broadwater said. "Let the Tide abide! Let the Flow show!"

His image vanished, as did all the TV screen scenes. Normal lighting returned and worshippers stood and filed out with quiet murmurs. Bypassing the contribution kiosk, Dillon went to the men's shower room, washed off the seawater, dried, donned his clothes, and met Trid at the temple entrance.

Together they made their way through the seastead toward their living module. Templemere consisted of hundreds of modules, each one a steel cylinder ten meters in diameter and twenty or thirty meters long. Some modules stood vertically but most lay horizontally, each one connected to others by transit tubes. "A senseless scattering of straws and sausages," some wag had joked, but this modular design formed the basis of all submerged seasteads.

Within these modules lived twenty-three thousand people. As with all seasteads, volume became the main constraint. Like submariners, seasteaders lived in confined spaces between curved bulkheads, enduring close contact with others and minimal privacy.

Dillon and Trid did not speak about the worship hour until they reached their own living module apartment and closed the hatch. They did not find their twenty-one-year-old daughter at home, and suspected she'd gone out with her fiancé, Merc. She might even have attended the worship event, Dillon thought, though he had not seen her there.

"Well?" he asked Trid.

"They are quite strange," she said, looking at him for his reaction.

"Those kooks are worse than I thought," Dillon said, unfolding a couple of chairs while Trid poured coffee. "They're trying to create a whole new artificial race of people, and feeding them pseudoscientific hooey."

"I can understand the appeal, though," Trid brought over their cups and sat down.

That's my Trid, always ready for anything. "Sure, to an impressionable mind, someone confused about her place in this new world. Oceanists give them a new name, a new skin color, and a packaged explanation of life. Like all religions, you pay your money and they'll save your eternal soul."

"What do we do about Cass and Merc?" Trid asked, looking at him over her cup rim as she sipped. "I mean, it's just a five-year marriage contract."

"Long enough," Dillon sighed. "After five years we won't recognize our blue-skinned, web-fingered Ca—I mean *Brooke*."

"She loves him," Trid pointed out. "She's old enough. I don't see what we can do."

Trid's not with me on this. She doesn't see what wackos the Oceanists are. "We can refuse to pay for the wedding."

Trid laughed. "You think that would stop them?"

"We can talk her out of it, explain the mistake she's making," Dillon said, then drank from his mug.

"Like you talked me out of going to PaCitadel?" Trid smiled at him. "She's got a lot of me in her, you know."

No, Cass is different. Not impulsive or adventurous. Sensitive and passionate, yes, and stubborn. "My shift starts in ten minutes." He set his mug on the table and stood, "but I know I can get through to her. I'll talk her out of making this mistake."

"Argonaut, this is the Templemere Dockmaster," Dillon spoke into the acoustic underwater phone. "Comms check, over." On his console sat a small stuffed narwhal, loved by Cass as a toddler. Dillon squeezed it for good luck, and the whale's horn fell off. "Damn." He tried to stick the horn back on without success.

He sat within a docking tube sticking out from beneath one of the seastead modules, a cantilevered boom with its suspended end supported by guy cables. Soon, this tube, three meters in diameter and ten long, would serve as the entry point from the next arriving submarine to the seastead.

No submarine of Argonaut's size had ever docked at Templemere before, so they'd called Dillon, as the most experienced dockmaster on the staff, to bring the sub in.

"Templemere Dockmaster, this is Argonaut, I read you loud and clear. How do you read me? Over."

Hesitancy in his voice, and he's using complete sentences, Dillon thought. Not good. This guy hasn't docked before. "Read you same. Are you neutral, over?"

A submarine at speed could tolerate being somewhat heavy or light because operators could compensate with control surfaces or the angle of the sub itself. However, when stationary—as it would be when docked—the sub had to be neutrally buoyant.

"Yes, we're neutrally buoyant, over."

"Good. Come to all stop. Sending tug-bots to position you. Out."

In response to his keyed commands, a dozen unmanned underwater vehicles sped out in a swarm toward the submarine. These robotic tugs would guide the Argonaut into place so its upper midships hatch could mate with the lower hatch of the docking tube.

"Dad, can we talk to you?" Cass paused at the bottom of the ladder leading down from the rest of the seastead. Higher up, her boyfriend still clung to the ladder as if unsure whether to descend. Lit from two different angles, Merc's skin hue appeared turquoise here, teal there.

Wrong color for human skin. "It's not a great time, Cass. I'm busy docking a sub, but if you both sit over there," he pointed to a row of seats, "I'll listen as best I can while I'm working." He would have preferred to talk to Cass alone, but perhaps it was better they deal with this together.

They sat, holding hands.

Cass took a deep breath. "Dad, I know you don't like the idea, but we came to tell you we're getting married." She stopped, watching him, clearly waiting for his reaction.

Dillon tamped down his irritation and checked his screens to confirm Argonaut was drawing closer at a stately pace, led by the tug-bots. "Cass, Merc, I do have concerns about this, since you're both making big decisions that will impact your whole lives. Even a five-year marriage contract is a big commitment, and so is a commitment to a religion. Do you think you're ready for these commitments, Merc?"

"Yes, Mr. O'Neill, I am." Merc's teal face held an earnest expression.

At least he still answers to 'Merc.' "How long have you been an Oceanist?"

Cass rolled her eyes and shook her head.

"Five months," Merc answered, and Dillon caught the comforting hand squeeze that Merc gave Cass as he said it.

He returned his attention to the screen. The tug-bots had brought the huge sub almost into place and now nudged it upward at a pace that seemed slower than coral growth.

"Are your parents also Oceanists?" he asked.

"Not yet. I'm hoping they'll convert."

Cass shot him angry glares throughout the interrogation, but Dillon pressed on. "How do they feel about you becoming an Oceanist?"

Merc looked away for a moment, appearing to ponder the question. "Down-bubble at first, but they're coping."

"Your skin operation, when did you get that done?"

"Dad!" Cass said.

Merc lifted a blue hand and smiled at it, evidently still enjoying the novelty. "Last month. We call it the Immersion."

If I keep questioning him, Dillon thought, *I'll uncover something Cass doesn't know about that cult, something she dislikes.* "Was it painful?"

"Not really," Merc shook his head.

Shame. Dillon felt a slight shudder as the submarine contacted the bottom outer edge of the docking tube. While the tug-bots scurried to attach mooring cables fixing the submarine to the seastead, Dillon pressed a key to pump water from the short adapter trunk between the docking tube hatch and the submarine's hatch. He heard gurgling water, and turned off the pump when the "Trunk Drained" indicator lit.

"Merc, I understand you want to enter the Oceanist priesthood?"

"That's right."

"They let Oceanist priests get married?"

Merc chuckled. "They *encourage* it, even if just for one contract term."

Frowning at a reading on his panel, right next to the broken-horned narwhal, Dillon spoke to the sub. "Argonaut, mooring cable tension's at the high spec. Okay to equalize and open, but suggest you pump out a half tonne to lighten and get neutral, over."

"Acknowledged, Dockmaster. We're pumping out a half tonne now. Out."

Dillon left his seat and walked to the end of the docking tube and stood above the hatch. He looked at the young couple.

"Tell me, Merc, what are Oceanist weddings like?" *Maybe their rites are really weird.* He reached down and rotated the handwheel to open the hatch.

"Well, first of all," Merc said, "everyone wears swimsuits and they all stand neck-deep in—"

A loud, metallic creaking noise drowned out his voice. The docking tube itself tilted downward a fraction, and three loud explosions resounded in the tube like gun-shots.

Dillon tried to turn the hatch handwheel shut, but a pillar of high-pressure water blasted from the opening, flinging the hatch cover back against the end of the tube.

Oh, God, mooring cables snapped. He glanced at Cass. "Run! Get out!"

With a pressure of 900 kilopascals behind it, the sea roared in. *Stupid sub must have flooded their tanks instead of pumping.* Staggering through the cold and rising torrent, Dillon paused at his console, typing commands and throwing switches. *Can't let the whole 'stead flood.* In the corner of his eye he saw a flash of movement at the ladder—Merc pushing Cass up the ladder and through the opening.

Rising seawater shorted his console's circuits and every screen blanked. His ears popped as the inflow squeezed the remaining air in the docking tube. He gulped and waggled his jaw to equalize pressure.

Water swirled higher, then stopped. *Damn, hand hurts. Get to the ladder.* At least the upper hatch was shut, protecting the 'stead. A blue-green figure clung to the rungs, blood trickling from one ear, his face contorted in a grimace, his eyes wide with fear.

Dillon grasped the ladder beside Merc and grasped his shoulder. "Thanks for saving my daughter. I've shut both hatches, stabilized the pressure. You'll be okay. They'll come get us."

"H-how can they do that, Mr. O'Neill?" Merc's teeth chattered. "The pressure's so high in here."

Wrapping his arms around Merc, sharing some warmth between aquamarine and pale skin, Dillon said, "They'll pump the water out, and slowly match the pressure before opening the hatch."

As he said it, he heard a whooshing sound and the water level visibly receded, with an accompanying decrease in air pressure.

"It's working!" Merc smiled. "They're gonna save us."

His eye on the lowering water level, Dillon shook his head. "Aw, fluke. Their pump's on high speed." In their haste to save him from drowning, they were drawing a vacuum in the tiny space. Already he found it harder to breathe. "Hook your arms in the ladder, son. You don't want to fall in the water when you pass out." He did likewise, panting, while watching Cass' hornless stuffed narwhal float by. "We may...only have...a few sec—"

He heard himself breathing. A machine beeped nearby.

Dillon opened his eyes. He lay on an unfamiliar bed and couldn't move. Two meters to his right stood another occupied bed, the face above the pillow a profile in turquoise. *Kid's got odd-colored skin, and bizarre beliefs,* he thought, *but I was wrong about him.*

A young male nurse wearing a clean purple smock leaned over Dillon and looked in his eyes. "Ah, Mr. O'Neill. You're up." He kept his voice low.

"Wh-where's Cass? Is my daughter all right?"

The nurse smiled. "She's fine. Completely unharmed."

Dillon sighed. "How about him?" He looked over at the sleeping figure to the right and felt a pang of regret and shame. *Yeah, I was way wrong about him. There are things more important than appearance, and religion.*

"He'll be okay. He just needs his sleep now. He's had a mild concussion, lots of bumps and bruises. Like you, he's also suffering from decompression sickness. You'll both have to stay here in the hyperbaric oxygen therapy chamber for several hours."

Dillon's eyes drifted shut but he forced them open again. "I feel so groggy. What's your name?"

"Call me Jex, Mr. O'Neill. You're groggy because of the painkillers. Don't worry, you'll be okay. Except for your right hand. It was smashed in the accident."

Dillon found he couldn't move his hand. He looked down but only saw a shortened limb covered in gauze.

"The restraints are for your own good," Jex said. "Your hand was beyond recovery: they had to amputate. Once you're out of recompression, you'll go into surgery and the doctors will attach a new one."

After trying to imagine getting a new hand, Dillon said, "Leave the fingers unwebbed, please, and don't give me a blue or green one."

The nurse looked confused, but then chuckled. "Of course, Mr. O'Neill. You know, you're quite a hero. Everyone in Templemere has seen the video by now."

Dillon frowned. "What?"

"Oh, yes. It shows you standing at that control panel, pushing buttons with your left hand while the water's gushing and surging around you. They say you saved the whole 'stead. All of us."

Shaking his head, Dillon said, "Can I talk to my wife and daughter, please?"

"Yes, I can arrange that." Jex looked over where Merc still slept. "But please keep the noise down."

Dillon faded in and out of consciousness for the next three minutes. In the background, he heard the nurse trying to put the videocall through. Dillon smiled when the screen lit up, showing the anxious faces of the two women he loved most. With the kitchen cabinet visible behind them, he guessed they sat in their own living module.

"Dad!" Cass burst out. "How do you feel?"

"I could make some off-handed comment," Dillon said, looking at his stump. "In fact, that's all I can do."

Trid looked at Cass. "They didn't amputate his sense of humor. Unfortunately."

"I heard that," Dillon said with a smile.

"Well, did you hear that you're all over the news?" Trid asked. "We've spent all morning refusing interview requests. You're the hero of the day."

Dillon shook his head. "Want to see a *real* hero?" he asked and looked to his right, "it's that guy in the next bed. I saw him out of the corner of my eye. When the wall of water came, he shielded you, scooped you up, and carried you to the ladder."

"It all happened so fast," Cass started to sob, "I was scared."

"I saw him push you through the upper hatch just before I closed it remotely," Dillon said. "It was like one motion, instinctive. Without having time to think about it, he did exactly what I would have done." He looked back at Cass, who was trying to dry her eyes. "It's obvious to me now that his love for you is deep and strong." Dillon felt his own eyes welling up. "Rio would do anything for you, Brooke."

The young woman burst into tears all over again at the mention of her Oceanist name. "Dad, you called me—"

"You've chosen a fine fiancée, Brooke. I wish you every success in your marriage."

"Thank you, Dad," Brooke managed to choke out between sobs.

Trid hugged her and mouthed the words, "I love you," at Dillon.

He winked back as a tear trickled down his own cheek.

"Um, Dad?" Brooke sniffled and wiped her nose with her hand. "Do you think you might someday become an Oceanist yourself?"

Dillon tried to laugh, but it hurt. "Don't push it."

Voyage of the Zalicaprice

*A*s the world's wealthiest man stared at her, *Zalika Harrison* saw shock and consternation reflected in those round irises, in the eyes that had defined and encompassed her life. "Absolutely not," he said. "It's ridiculous."

Their game always started that way. Twenty-two-year-old Zalika gave a slight shrug. "Dad," she said, "I want to do it." *That ought to be enough.*

"Come on, Zalika." Shambe Harrison frowned and set his drink on the table. A robot servant refilled it. "This isn't like one of your weekend jaunts, or that dive in the Mariana Trench. You're talking about traveling around the world, submerged, and alone."

"Exactly, Dad," Zalika said. "It's never been done."

"There are reasons it's never been done," he looked over at his current wife, as if to ask her to supply those reasons.

Zalika looked at Wanda, relieved to find her staring at her dinner plate in silence. *That's right, you better keep quiet. You're practically my own age, and this is between Dad and me.*

"It's dangerous, for one thing," her father said. "The rest of the world is not like Quebrada." He gestured around their spacious and lavish dining room, as if the sweep of his hand could summarize the whole undersea habitat as a single, protected enclave in a harsh world.

"I've traveled. It's not that bad." Zalika didn't need to remind him that she'd just returned from trips to Le Plongeo, Templemere, and Cunardia.

"Small subs aren't designed for round-the-world voyages," her father said, shaking his head. "There could be mechanical problems..."

"Don't you stand behind your products?" Zalika asked the CEO of the largest submarine manufacturer.

He frowned. "Of course I do. It's just that—"

"And haven't you said I'm the best sub pilot you've ever known?"

Her father grunted. "Yes, I said that. I just think that you're not...not the one to do it. You're not suited for it. You wouldn't finish the journey."

Zalika smiled inside. If he'd resorted to that argument, she'd won. "What do you mean?" She kept her voice full of innocence.

"You don't commit to anything." Her father ticked off items on his fingers. You wanted to race a sub in the Quebrada Regatta, so I sponsored you, and you quit halfway through. Then, you..."

Every time he ran through *The List*, Zalika knew from experience, she had to listen to the whole thing. But when he got to the end, shook his head, sighed, and said, "Ah, Zalika," that was always the point where he gave in.

"...and next, you wanted to join the Oceanists—remember that? You had that so-called Immersion operation to change your skin green. Three months later you dropped that religion and said you wanted to know what it would be like to be white. So, I paid for another skin operation. A couple of months later you wanted to be black again. That's three skin jobs in one year!" He sighed. "Ah, Zalika."

Bingo.

The young man climbed down the ladder into her submarine. She watched his eyes widen at its cramped interior, colored in dusty pink with amber trim. He stuck out his hand. "Pleased to meet you, Zalika. I'm Neb Douglas from *This Minute*."

"Neb?"

"Yeah." He grinned. "Short for Nebuchadnezzar, like the Babylonian kings. Hoping to get my own ziggurat someday. Shall we get started?"

"Sure." She pushed a button, and a table and two benches unfolded from the bulkhead.

They sat. As he fumbled with the box that held his humming-cam, Zalika tried to decide how much she'd hate this reporter. She had wanted big, open press conferences at the beginning and at each stop, but her father insisted on granting exclusive rights to just one news service. It unnerved her that she didn't always get her way. At least make it *Celeb* or even *Gush*, she'd begged. Those zines showed flattering video clips of her, and the write-ups were up-bubble, always praising her new hairstyles and outfits. But he'd said it had to be *This Minute*, what he called a reputable zine. Reputable? None of her friends read *This Minute*. That mag always made her out to be some spoiled rich girl. And they sent this guy. Neb seemed starstruck, she judged from his faltering voice and the butterfingered way he handled his cam. *Still, that's not odd. It's just that he's so young—barely my age.*

"Are you ready?"

She nodded.

"Cam on," he said. The humming-cam's whisper-quiet wings started fluttering and its red light blinked. He placed it midway between them, just above eye level, and let it hover there.

"This is Neb Douglas reporting. Today, on April 13th, I'm with Zalika Harrison, international celebrity and daughter of multi-billionaire Shambe Harrison, of Harrison Undersea Enterprises. She plans to be the first person to travel around the world alone, submerged. My first question, Zalika, is…why?"

"It's just something new for me," she said, and the humming-cam turned in mid-air at the sound of her voice. "I guess it's new for everybody," she giggled. "No, really, it's the adventure of the thing."

"And good publicity for Harrison Undersea," Neb added.

Snarky, aren't you? "Harrison Undersea needs no publicity from me. The world's best subs sell themselves."

"Okay. Tell me about this sub that you're planning to take on the journey."

"It's a modified Model 600B Harrison family-sized sub."

"Modified? How?"

"Extra fuel and food for longer range. They also replaced the AI computer with an old-style response-only, non-initiative one. Otherwise, someone might claim I wouldn't really be alone."

"Did you give your sub a name?"

She nodded. "Zalicaprice. I like the sound of the word *caprice*, and I combined it with my name."

"Caprice—is that what this trip is, a sudden change of your mind, on impulse?"

Trying to make me sound flighty? Won't work. "This is a serious voyage, one that's never been done. And I get to name my sub whatever I want."

"What is your planned route around the world?"

"I'll travel west, avoiding the more troublesome aquastates and stopping only at seasteads with underwater docking capability. I plan to pass through both the Suez and Panama Canals submerged, instead of taking the longer trips around the southern capes."

"Meanwhile," Neb looked at the humming-cam rather than at her. "I'll be flying ahead to your next planned stops all along the way, for occasional interviews en route. Is that all right?"

"That's fine." Zalika nodded and forced a smile. *Can't say I'm looking forward to that.*

"How long do you expect your circumnavigation to take?"

"About four months, I guess. However long it takes, I'll be the fastest."

"When do you leave Quebrada?"

"Tomorrow, right after your techs check out the sub."

"Thanks for mentioning that. It's important for our audience to know that *This Minute* will be providing independent confirmation of

Zalika Harrison's history-making journey. We'll check her sub's data logs at each stop to ensure she's stayed submerged. And we'll scan the sub before she leaves to verify she has no artificial intelligences systems aboard—or stowaways!" He looked at her and smiled. "I imagine there are lots of people who'd like to stow away with Zalika Harrison for four months!"

She laughed. "I know one, at least. My Dad said he wanted to go, or even do the trip by himself." She turned so the humming-cam could catch her best profile. "But he has a company to run."

Neb wrapped up the interview, wishing Zalika good luck and signing off. She still felt irked about not getting the zine of her choice. *Maybe I'll start my own mag*, she thought, *after I get back from this jaunt. Still, Neb himself wasn't too bad for a reporter. Not as nice to me as he could have been, but not negative either. I can settle for that.*

"Dear Diary," Zalika spoke to her sub's computer while her words displayed as text on its screen beneath a camera image of her. "Day six. Remember when I told you Dad left three books on board? Not normal ebooks, but old-fashioned printed books, made from dead trees, not electrons. Dad can be such a trilobite sometimes. I finished 'em. Well, okay, I can't lie to you—I skimmed 'em, but I got the gist."

She glanced around her holographic displays to ensure all was well. Still in Penrhyn waters, depth fifty meters, course two six zero, speed fifteen knots. No submerged contacts, and only distant merchant ships on the surface.

Zalika looked over at the books lying on her fold-out bed. One was about Ferdinand Magellan; one was *Sailing Around the World Alone* by Joshua Slocum; and the third was *Around the World Submerged* by Edward L. Beach.

"I don't know, I guess Dad was trying to tell me something, but I've got nothing in common with those guys. They each had setbacks during their circumnavigations, but their biggest problem was they traveled too early, way before technology made everything easy." She smiled. "And they didn't have a billionaire for a dad."

. . .

"Welcome to Vitiaz," Neb said, while the humming-cam hovered above them.

"It's a relief to be here," Zalika said with a smile. They sat in one of the quiet and splendid restaurant modules of Nova Canton seastead within the Republic of Vitiaz. Far beneath them, Zalika knew, robotic mining machinery extracted valuable minerals from an oceanic trench, making Vitiaz a rival to Quebrada in wealth among aquastates.

"You're most of the way across the Pacific now," Neb said. "Please tell our audience what happened back there in Penrhyn."

"A misunderstanding, that's all." Zalika sipped her drink. In this subdued light, she thought, Neb didn't look half bad. "I docked at Motusia."

"Let me break in again for a moment. The landers in our audience may not know that, unlike cities on land, some seasteads, like Motusia, can move about. I'm sorry—please go on."

"I needed to recharge my fuel cell. Motusia was the only 'stead in Penrhyn with an underwater dock. They told me they weren't scheduled to move for a few days." She shook her head. "Anyway, I woke up forty nautical miles farther west. They'd moved during the night to avoid a hurricane. I couldn't let that invalidate my trip, so when I left, I steered the sub back east to where Motusia had been, and continued the trip from there. The data logging system will show that."

"I see. And then you entered Manihiki on April 24th, is that right?"

"Flotz! Those stupid people!" Zalika burned inside with the painful memory. "Those sea-slugs with legs! Those shrimp-brained—"

"Can you describe what happened?" Neb appeared to be making an effort to stifle a smile.

That made Zalika madder, but she couldn't help finding his smile alluring. "All right. Well, you know how Penrhyn and Manihiki overlap."

"That's right. To remind our audience, part of the border between these aquastates is at the 150-meter depth, with Penrhyn being above that level and Manihiki below."

"So, I'd undocked from Motusia and backtracked the forty nauts. I'd loaded a lot of food in Motusia and it took a while to adjust weight and trim of the sub. I was in the overlap zone and I might have dipped below that 150-meter border a little, I don't know.

"Anyway, suddenly I was boxed in by three Manihiki border patrol subs and they ordered me to follow them."

"What did you do?" Neb's face held that neutral reporter expression once more.

Zalika sighed to collect herself. *I can do this without crying.* "I explained who I was, of course, but they kept babbling on about their trespassing law. Worse, I couldn't just hover back up to Penrhyn; they'd positioned their subs above and in front, trapping me in Manihiki! So, I followed them to one of their deep seasteads, Research Station Number Six, I guess they call it."

Zalika shut her eyes a moment to steel herself, but found the shame and rage bubbling up. "It all happened so fast. They brought me in front of some judge. He wouldn't let me call my dad. He didn't care that it was just an accident. 'We are concerned with facts here, young lady, not irrelevancies,'" she imitated the judge's deep voice.

"Then," her lower lip trembled and tears began flowing. "Then they threw me in jail! Me! Me!" She slammed a fist on the table and bent her head down to sob. Zalika could sense a deeper hush flowing through the restaurant and supposed others might be watching her, but she didn't care. *Let the fools stare.*

"I'm sorry," Neb's voice sounded low and soothing. "I've read that, in Manihiki, scientists lead the government. I heard their people value reason and the scientific approach."

"Yeah, reason, sure," Zalika raised her voice, then sniffled. "Were they reasonable to lock me up for an honest mistake? In Neptune's name, is that reasonable? Do you know how long I rotted in that cell? Do you? Four days! They wouldn't accept Dad's offers of bail money for my release. I guess there was some negotiating with diplomats or whatever. When Dad told them he'd sell no more subs in Manihiki, they got reasonable and let me go. As far as I'm concerned, that whole aquastate can go fu—"

"What was prison like?"

Oh, I get it. His audience would love to hear about the rich girl brought down to seabed level. Fine, whatever. "Horrible. Primitive and barbaric. Steel walls, a steel-barred door. A steel bed with a two-centimeter mattress. Worse, no access to social media or even basic cosmetics." She shook her head. "It was hell. I really don't think most people could take four days of that without going beached-whale crazy."

"But you made it through okay?"

"Yeah, I guess. I've got what most people don't have. Something that gets me through any rough spot in life."

"A deep faith? An inner peace?"

"No." Zalika dabbed at a final tear. "My dad."

She pauses halfway out of the open hatch, blinking in the sun and smiling for the crowd of photographers, journalists, and fans. This photo of her, she thinks, will surpass the iconic images of John Holland and Hyman Rickover posing in the hatches of their submarines. "She's done it!" someone shouts, "gone around the world, alone and submerged." People clap and cheer. She climbs out and her bodyguards join her to keep the throng back as she strides through. For some reason, her bodyguards begin blowing whistles, loud and shrill whistles, with a pulsing rhythm, whistles going on and on...

Zalika awoke in her berth aboard the sub with a loud alarm going off. Though fatigued from the many false alarms of the voyage so far, Zalika arose to check out every one of them. Without AI capability to do the thinking, the sonar could only sound an alarm for close or medium range contacts, not classify them or turn the sub to avoid them. So long as she didn't intervene, the autopilot just maintained a steady course, speed, and depth.

"What the flotz is going on?" Suddenly wide awake, Zalika stared in disbelief at the sonar screen. The display showed dozens of loud noise sources, all of human origin. Some were fixed, some moved left to right across her bow, and some moved the other way. Zalika supposed the fixed ones to be surface ship active sonars pinging away. The fast-moving sources scared her.

"Torps," she said aloud to nobody, after making sure that all those sound traces were heading elsewhere. "It's a damned war!"

A deafening noise blanked the screen and a loud *whump* resounded from the speakers. Several other implosions followed, signaling the destruction of a combatant submarine. Zalika squeezed her eyes shut and bit her lip in sadness, knowing that dozens of submarine sailors had just met their end.

Just two weeks earlier, when she had docked at the ReefView seastead off the Australian coast on the 8th of May, the authorities had warned her of a border dispute between India and the aquastate of Kumari Kandam. With a seafloor rich in oil and minerals, the contested zone would bring vast riches to the victor.

Some border dispute! Get out of this battlefield now, girl. She steered the Zalicaprice to the south.

A high decibel sonic blast marked where a torpedo had exploded against a surface ship. Zalika flinched with the noise.

The high-pitched whine of another torp motor sounded loud and close. *Where'd that come from? Probably some combat sub waiting in silence.* She turned her craft in a direction most likely to escape the torp's detection cone and cut power to coast without sound.

The torp turned toward her for a few seconds, taking an acoustic sniff. Zalika sat in open-mouthed, heart-hammering fear, convinced her final moment had arrived.

Something made the torp turn away. It whipped past her, leaving a thick streak of light across her screen. *Whew! Zalicaprice must not have matched its target parameters.*

Less than half a minute later, a massive series of implosion shocks slammed into her sub like jackhammer impacts.

· · ·

One month later, Zalika paused the computer's voice-to-text translation to let it catch up. She took a deep breath, then wrinkled her nose at the odor of oil, ozone, and food. *Zalicaprice has sure lost that new-sub smell.* She resumed her diary narration. "Looking back, that was the worst moment of this jaunt so far. When all those damaged system lights came on, I thought I was done for. I vowed to quit the whole trip if I made it out of there alive.

"I had one main thruster down, a broken radio buoy, no backup air monitoring system, a degraded sonar, and four minor hull leaks. Thank Neptune the fuel cell had enough juice for me to limp into Lemuria. I ended up staying there two weeks while Harrison Undersea techs repaired my sub.

"I know, I know—two weeks in the pleasure domes of Chagos, Lemuria is hardly reason for complaint. But I've been there five times before, and you only have a first time once.

"I actually had fun talking with Neb. The interviews flowed well. When we were off-cam he told me his reports about me were the most-viewed and most-read in *This Minute's* history. He's getting… tolerable." *Maybe more than tolerable.*

She paused to double-check her diary settings. *Yup, full privacy, security-linked to my retina scan.*

"It's frustrating," she resumed, "that Neb can ask any questions he wants about me, but he never answers any of mine about him. He's staying strictly professional—flotz it all!—so if he feels any interest in me, he's not letting it show. Maybe I intimidate him, I don't know.

"It doesn't really matter. Between you and me, Diary, I've never had any problem getting a guy interested, if and when I chose.

"Did I mention how good-looking Neb is? I'm surprised I didn't notice it at first. He's no vid celeb, but there's ruggedness there, serious intensity, like there's some rock-solid core of certainty and determination inside. He'll ask me a question, and then look at me—those brown eyes imploring, daring, probing—I sometimes forget, for just a second, that I'm Zalika and he's just another reporter."

She paused and stared out the viewdome as her sub passed through a school of fish that separated before it. "Anyway, it feels good to get that out. So, I left Lemuria and started the most uncomfortable part of my trip—the part nearest land. It was bad, back when I passed so close to Australia and Indonesia, but not this bad. I had to squeeze through the Gulf of Aden and the Red Sea. It felt so cramped. And don't get me started on Suez. If it weren't for all the favorable publicity my trip brought them, I don't think the Egyptians would have let me through their canal submerged at all.

"The Mediterranean feels so restricted, so congested. There's an oppressive sensation, being so close to land. I can't explain it. Land is just—I don't know—dry and old. No, not just old—ancient and static. So much better to be in the oceans where the flow is, where the action, is. That's where dynamic, fun people are—people who want to enjoy life, not cling to dusty relics.

"It's the 15th of June and I'm headed to New Phoenicia. I don't need to stop there for food, and the fuel cell has a full charge, but I just want to visit and enjoy the only aquastate in this whole sea that isn't part of a land country. Then in a few days (Neptune help me), I've got to squeeze through Gibraltar."

After passing through the strait, Zalika entered the aquastate of Gibralion. Then she stayed at Áquaforte in the Monarchy of Madeira. Few people, even in that aquastate, understood how their monarch was chosen, but the country had long been prosperous and well-led. During her short stay there, Zalika found the people friendly and content. They'd fawned over her. With cameras rolling, she boarded a tourist sub and visited the wreck of an old sunken submarine, the *Scorpion*. The Madeirans kept the wreck as an honored tomb and shrine under a special agreement with the United States.

Now nearing the western border of Madeira, Zalika intended to detour south into Ridgia to avoid the Ungoverned Region. People actually lived in the UGR, but under a state of violent anarchy. *Stay clear of that place. Don't invite trouble.*

The hours dragged while she sat at the control console, looking at instruments, occasionally glancing out of the acrylic viewdome. Not much to see. The sonar showed two tractor submersibles working the Ridgian seaweed farms far above.

Loneliness—yeah, I way underestimated that. She came from a world of friends, fans, and crowds.

And it's my birthday, July 3rd. She picked up an imaginary wine glass and downed it. "Happy twenty-third birthday to me! Woo-hoo! What a beautiful cake." She mimed blowing out candles. For some reason, she thought about Neb, and wished he could be with her to celebrate the day.

A dolphin swam alongside the sub and seemed to smile as it stared into the dome at her. "Hi, friend. Want some cake?" She giggled and held out an imaginary plate to the dolphin. As if offended, the mammal broke off and headed away, returning the forward view to its uninterrupted field of dark blue. She craned her neck to follow the dolphin. "Hey, don't go. Plenty of wine left."

Zalika didn't know if she could ever get used to such loneliness and boredom. Nor could anyone else, she suspected. *Well, Joshua Slocum did it, sailing around the world alone.* She idly thumbed through his book. *Okay for him, an old man without a fan base. Plus, he had a horizon to look at, and the sun, moon, clouds, and weather to keep him company.* Zalika had a blank vista, dark blue by day, black by night.

Thought it'd be easier. Didn't think I'd have problems, especially not boredom. I could quit this now, take a flight to Quebrada and be partying tonight. Stupid jaunt hasn't been that important to me, after all. Just a silly stunt, really. Let somebody else be first.

She touched the controls, about to blow ballast tanks, surface the sub, and end her submerged journey. Her eyes fell on the logo of Harrison Undersea Enterprises, and she paused. *Yeah, I know what you'd say about this, Dad.*

Zalika shook her head, thinking back to when she and her father performed the final inspection of the sub in drydock, just prior to her trip.

"You know, Dad," she'd said, tracing the four-bladed design painted on the hull, "you should change the logo to match what your sub's propellers really look like."

He'd cocked his head and squinted. "Propeller? All these years you thought our logo was a propeller? It's the four oar-blades of the *tabono*, the ancient Ashanti symbol of perseverance."

"Perseverance," she now said to the empty sub, taking her hands off the ballast controls. All her father's lectures about enduring hardships, about finishing what she started, came back to her now. She'd never internalized the concept, and hadn't needed to. For all her father's talk about persistence, he'd always saved her when she'd quit midway through things.

"Ah, Dad," she said. "Too bad you didn't give me the life hack for boredom."

A rustling, swishing sound startled her. "What in Neptune's name?" Zalika looked up, since the noise seemed to come from there. A long frond of seaweed draped over her forward viewdome, then slid off. She saw other lengths of sargassum drifting down around her.

Harvest time at the farm. Let's get out from under this, Zalicaprice. These would be the aged, over-ripe plants that lacked air chambers to stay afloat, the waste from the harvesting process. She goosed the throttle to twenty-five knots, well over efficient cruising speed. A few more plant fronds pelted her as she sped up.

The sub pitched downward and descended at high speed. The depth gage flashed in yellow as the number of meters mounted—410, 420, 430...

"What the—?" Zalika blinked, unable at first to believe the indications, but well aware her sub's rated crush depth was five hundred meters. The bow planes showed *full dive* and wouldn't respond in any mode. By instinct, she reversed the throttles to slacken speed. But emergency actions for stuck bow planes also stated to blow ballast and surface. She hesitated over the controls, knowing that would invalidate her trip.

Only if I broach the surface, she realized, and blew ballast tanks.

Her descent slowed, but not fast enough. The numbers flashed in red. 470, 480…490…500.

Zalika held her breath and winced, knowing the pressure would soon crush her sub like an egg. 510.

Somewhere, a portion of the hull groaned. 520.

At 530 meters, the depth gage reversed and began showing lower numbers. When back above 500 meters, Zalika let out her held breath in a whoosh. *I'm gonna kiss all the Harrison Undersea structural engineers on the lips. That was too close.*

When speed slowed to zero, she set the throttles to all stop. After she'd risen to 25 meters, she vented ballast tanks and set depth controls to hover. Now Zalicaprice would stay at that depth, just drifting with the current.

"Who wants a million Quebradan pesos to fix a jammed bow plane?" Zalika asked her empty craft. "Nobody? Guess I'll have to do it myself."

She unbuckled from her seat and got her dry-suit from a locker. In minutes she had suited up for the cold North Atlantic water, and donned her DIGMA gear. Less than a decade earlier, scientists from Manganor had developed the Diving Gill Membrane Apparatus, which separated entrained air from water and freed divers from compressed air tanks, thus replacing scuba gear.

Zalika encountered no problems operating the submarine's small diving chamber, and soon swam toward her craft's bow, aided by swim fins on her feet.

As I figured, fouled by seaweed. The bow planes jutted out like miniature wings on both sides. A long frond had wrapped around the rotating mounting post, jamming the starboard plane in the full dive position. Mechanically linked to it, the port bow plane also slanted downward.

Unsheathing her dive knife, Zalika hacked at the plant tendril that had nearly caused her sub to collapse. The fibers had wound tightly around the post, wedging into the hull seal, making the work tedious. Only after five minutes of sawing and cutting could she free the bow planes enough for them to rotate. Though she wore a heated dry-suit, her extremities had begun to freeze and stiffen where the heating elements couldn't keep up.

No sooner had she turned to make her way back to the upper hatch, when she spied movement close by.

Zalika had never seen a shark this close, and it terrified her to the core. Twice as long as she was tall, it moved with graceful smoothness, flicking its tail back and forth, always nearing her at an angle, always keeping one eye on her. Though the shark's actions seemed unhurried and nonthreatening, its apparent indifference only heightened Zalika's fear.

Though paralyzed with horror, Zalika soon regained a glimmer of rational thought. *Can't buy my way out of this. What do I know about sharks? Make slow movements; don't flail. They're attracted to shiny objects. The dive knife, Stupid!* She hid the blade behind her.

She heard her own shallow, ragged breaths in her DIGMA regulator. *Breath slowly; they can sense fear. Well, if they sense my fear, I'm already a goner.*

The shark drew closer, and she knew it could attack at any moment. *It's got tender spots—snout, eyes, gills.*

The tail lashed and the shark lunged. But it turned, sliding its body along her torso with great force. Its sandpaper-rough skin scraped her dry-suit.

She struck with the knife, but missed its eye with her clumsy thrust.

With another flap of its tail, the shark glided away. Zalika hesitated, watching to see if it would circle back, then made her way up to the hatch.

Once back inside the diving chamber with the hatch closed, she gulped for air, not realizing she'd been holding her breath. She bent down and sat on the deck in a ball. Arms around her knees, she cried with suppressed sorrow and relief. Shaking with sobs, she let out a scream of anguish, thinking how close she'd come to death.

It was testing me. I wasn't its usual prey, so it was checking to see how I'd react. I didn't try to speed away, and even fought back, so must not have been worth the trouble.

Wiping her eyes and blowing her nose, she stood, and set controls to equalize pressure across the inner hatch. She needed to decompress slowly, in stages, to avoid the bends, so she programmed the whole sub to serve as her decompression chamber.

Zalika changed into dry clothes and sat back down at the controls. She tested the bow planes and felt pleased when they worked.

"Okay," she announced to the empty sub in the empty ocean. "Ready for boredom now. Anxious for it. Bring it on."

Following one minute of welcome boredom, four strong signals showed on her sonar, all from submerged sources, all increasing in strength. The sonar system resolved the signals as likely UGR pirate vessels, closing on her position.

"UGR pirates?" Zalika checked her inertial navigation system and noted with dismay that it located her in the southeast corner of the Ungoverned Region. *Neptune's armpit! Current must've swept me here while I was fixing the flukin' bow plane.*

This area had once been the site of a legitimate aquastate, New Chiapas, but it had collapsed when drug cartels overturned the government. Now, independent warlords and gangs operated in a region devoid of law.

The four mini-subs neared hers, assuming a formation like a four-sided equilateral pyramid, a shrinking pyramid with a pirate sub at each corner and hers in the center. *No way out.*

Zalika had come to a hovering stop and watched one of the subs through her viewdome. If they'd once been Harrison subs, it was hard to tell. No logos or other identifying marking showed on the outside. Different colored hull sections and appendages suggested these vehicles had been assembled or repaired from pieces of other subs. Rusty hull plating, and some dents and scrapes indicated poor maintenance and rough operation. Each sub possessed only small viewports, not a large acrylic dome, so Zalika could not see the pilots or crew of these subs.

Speaking in Spanish, a voice came over the acoustic underwater telephone. "You will follow us to our base now. Comply and we will not harm you. We'll take your submarine, but you will be released."

Released? That's a lie. According to rumors, very few women occupied the UGR. She shuddered. *Not hard to guess what they'd do to me.*

Zalika picked up her microphone. "I'm Zalika Harrison. You must have heard of my round-the-world trip. I'm here by accident. I just want to leave the UGR peacefully. Please let me do that."

"Who you are and how you got here are irrelevant." A different voice spoke this time, also male. "Either follow us now and live, or refuse to comply and die."

"I have money," she said. "Lots of it. I'll put up my radio buoy and signal my father to transfer funds to your account."

"We want your submarine, not your promises," a third pirate said. "Follow us or we'll torpedo your sub."

Zalika thought fast, but came up with no options. Surrounded by equally-spaced, fully-armed subs, she lacked weapons of any kind. *My fortune for a torpedo.* Harrison family subs didn't have them, and several aquastates would never have permitted entry if she'd been armed. Some of them had inspected her sub at the border to verify that.

Odd that a different one of them speaks each time. Can I use that?

"You're not making sense," she said. "If you shoot a torpedo, you'll destroy my sub, and that's what you claim you want." Without waiting for a response, she went on. "I've got a better idea. But I'm only going to deal with one of you. Which one's the leader?"

After a hesitation, four voices spoke at once, but one voice rang louder. "We ain't got no leader. This is an equal partnership. Now follow us."

"I'm not going anywhere." Zalika tried to sound firm. "One of you—and only one—can have the sub," she gulped, hoping this would work, "and me. But you'll have to mate your sub on my upper hatch and come aboard. Now which one of you men will it be?"

All four pirate subs sped toward her vessel's upper hatch. They collided and used thrusters to shove each other out of the way.

Zalika applied random thruster movements and hovering adjustments to shift position, complicating matters for the competing pirates.

"Stop moving, woman!" one said. "Hold still."

"Sorry," Zalika said. "I'm not as good at piloting a sub as I am at other things." She heard the clanking and scraping above her and saw the four subs jockeying for the best position over her hatch. *What happened to that equal partnership, boys?*

When they were all together over her position, Zalika blew ballast tanks and vented at the same time, sending a froth of huge air bubbles upward. She played her active sonar on maximum, sending a loud blast of noise intended to further disorient the pirates. Then she set throttles to flank speed and raced away.

Eventually, a volley of torpedoes sped toward her, but she'd gotten a substantial head start and the anti-torpedo countermeasures she launched fooled the incoming weapons. Though her high speed drained her fuel cell dangerously low, she didn't slow until she entered the aquastate of Aquarius and met up with their border patrolling sub.

"Cam off," Neb said. The little robotic humming-cam's red light went out and the robot fluttered to rest on the fold-out table in Zalika's sub. "Wow! Diving past crush depth, fixing a stuck bow plane, then single-handedly holding off a pirate attack!" He shook his head, chuckling. "This is pure gold. You thought you were famous *before*!" He started packing up the humming-cam. "It's a shame you're almost done."

Zalika wasn't thinking of pirates or fuel cells or the end of her journey, but of Neb. They had just concluded an amazing interview, and his first thought had been of the increase in her fame, not his own, or that of his zine. Just one of the wonderful things about him.

"Neb." She reached across the table and touched his arm. "It's time I interviewed you for a change."

"What?" He looked puzzled and wary.

"Yeah. You've had seven interviews with me and you asked all the questions. I want to learn about you."

"Me? I'm no celebrity. I'm not going on a record-breaking trip around the world."

She poked his chest. "Ah, but you're the star reporter for a major news zine. That's something. Come on, let me interview you. It'll be fun."

His eyes narrowed. "Okay. What do you want to know?"

Zalika had no humming-cam, no datapad, not even a pen or paper. She didn't need them. "First question. With all your travelling around to keep up with me, how is your girlfriend dealing with your absence?"

The sequence of shock, regret, then understanding that played on Neb's face told Zalika what she wanted to know. "Boy, you go straight for the personal stuff," he said, coughing.

"Oh, we're just getting started. Second question. I know how lonely it's been for me aboard this sub. On a scale of one to ten, how lonely has it been for you, hopping from 'stead to 'stead, trying to cover my trip?"

He averted his eyes for a second, then got dismissive. "I haven't felt lone—"

"All right then. Third question." Zalika pushed a button and the table folded away. She moved over and sat next to him on his seat. "What would your girlfriends say if I asked them how good a kisser you are?"

His lips parted in surprise and Zalika gave him no time to answer. She leaned in, wrapped her arms around his neck, and kissed him. He resisted at first, then gave in to it, running his hands through her hair.

With the glorious moment over, she backed away and opened her eyes. "Wow. Forget that question. Who cares what they think?" That kiss had made her feel tingly and warm; it had helped her reach a decision. "Last question. Will you come with me? Let's take this sub and go somewhere together."

He jerked back as if struck. "What? Oh," he let out a little laugh and relaxed. "You're joking."

"No, Neb." Zalika looked steadily into his eyes. "I'm very serious. Let's go far away, just you and me."

He recoiled again. "But you can't do that. If I go with you, it would invalidate your whole voyage. You wouldn't set the record."

Silly Neb, you just don't get it yet. "I'm quitting all that," Zalika shrugged. "I never cared that much about it. It was just something to do. I'm tired of rotting in prison and fighting pirates. I want something else now. Some*one* else."

Neb glanced around as if checking for exit paths, then gazed at her in disbelief. "You're almost done, Zalika! The Caribbean, the Panama Canal, and you're home. You can't give up when you're so close."

"Sure, I can." She flicked her hand as if to banish all doubt.

"But I don't understand," his brow furrowed in puzzlement. "What...what are you suggesting?"

"A simple marriage contract. Let's say three years, with an option for two more. We can get hitched right here in Aquarius."

His eyes widened in shock. "Zalika, I..."

"All you have to do is say *yes*," she smiled at him. "It's what I want."

His eyes seemed to search hers for any sign she wasn't serious. Then he looked away as if someone has written answers to his dilemma on the bulkhead of her sub. He shut his eyes, signed, and rubbed his temples.

What's the matter with him? Six billion guys on the planet—did I propose to the only one who'd hesitate before saying yes to me?

"I'm flattered, Zalika." Neb opened his eyes but didn't meet her gaze. "But I can't marry you, or go away with you."

"Why not?" She tried to hide her surprise with a little smile. He looked away, then back at her. "Marriage is something you commit to, with heart and soul. Not something you decide on a whim, a caprice."

The reference to her sub's name stung, but Zalika felt relieved he'd left an open possibility. "Oh, you need more time to decide. Well, think about it. You can get back to me tomorrow."

"No," Neb shook his head. "I don't need more time. There's just no nice way to put this."

She frowned and her voice turned harsh. "Just tell me straight."

"Zalika, if you can't finish a four-month journey when you're in sight of the finish line, how do I know you can stay married for three years?"

From a place deep inside her, rage bubbled up to the surface. *How dare you!* She stood up and pointed to the hatch. "Get out. Get out of my submarine right now! I never want to see you again."

Neb stood up and hastened to the hatch without a word.

"Get out!" Zalika cried, tears streaming down. "You're acting like my father! You hear me? Get out!"

Five hours later, Zalika undocked from the Calypso seastead in the aquastate of Aquarius. Still shaking with anger, her eyes blurry from tears, she let the Zalicaprice drift with the current with no set course while she thought about where to go next.

No seastead in Aquarius appealed to her. She liked the ecological basis of that aquastate, but somehow the reality didn't live up to the promise. Ever since its first seastead, GreenSea, had perished in a hurricane, Aquarius had struggled economically. Not a place for a good party.

That's what she needed now—a good time, with friends, or even just fans. She needed to forget.

Flotz! Why did Neb refuse me? It doesn't make any sense.

This Minute had once called her a spoiled rich girl. She hated that. Is that what her dad was trying to say too, only more nicely? That she was spoiled?

Did Neb also think she was spoiled? *But I love him.* She did, more than anything. But he didn't love her, the spoiled rich kid, that was sure.

She blew her nose and wiped her eyes. *Money won't buy the solution to this problem. I can't buy Neb's love.*

Zalika stared out into the blue ocean for several minutes and it seemed to stare back. *I've given up on stuff my whole life, as soon as I see the next glittery object. Nothing to show for it. Got a million fans and a hundred friends, but no one who really, really loves me, except Dad. And the man I love won't have me because I can't stay the course.*

With one finger, she traced the four oar-blades of the *tabono* logo on her console. *Perseverance. Oh, Dad, you were right. I am spoiled. But I can change. I can finish things that I start. That's really the only way to get the things you want most.*

After two decades of taking the easy path, of acting on whims, of preferring instant gratification, it took all the will she had for Zalika to set the autopilot for a southwest course toward Panama.

"Diary," she said, "I get it now. Things worth having are worth striving for. Some things you can't give up on. I'm going to finish this journey around the world, underwater and alone. I will do it, I promise you. After I'm done, I'm going to do something much harder. I swear to you, no matter what I have to do, or how long it takes, I'm going to earn the love of Neb Douglas."

Taught to Kill

Excited from their dive, the man and woman swam back to the diving chamber, sat and watched as the water level lowered, removed their breathers, smiled at each other, and went to sleep forever.

Ten days later, Major Seán Kelmaryn walked along the steel-walled corridors of the underwater seastead Ascenseon with his subordinate. He liked to grant his people some latitude as they ran their investigations. They learned more that way. But this was ridiculous. "You think some half-brained adolescent can crack a murder case?" he asked.

Lieutenant Yasmin Almareo winced and her dark brown eyes flared for a moment when she faced him. "You don't know her. The kid's good. She's done this stuff before."

Seán liked the young lieutenant. She'd picked up her police skills fast and seemed poised for a successful career. Seán couldn't understand her reliance on that odd teenage girl, though. "We're wasting time—time we don't have. I'm getting pressure from the 'stead director's office to solve this thing fast. I gave you this case 'cause I thought you could handle it."

"With *her* help, I can," Yasmin said.

"I hope so. Solve this case and our market share will go up. We'll be the top police firm on the whole 'stead. If you *can't*, the government will give the biz to a rival. If that happens, I'll have to let some good cops go." *Meaning you*, he didn't have to say.

"That won't happen," she said as they rounded a corner. "This kid's uncanny. Major, you *know* her rep."

Seán nodded. Everyone in Ascenseon knew. Fluke it, the whole aquastate of Ridgia knew. A year ago, Hanna Webmarix had been an average fourteen-year-old, out on a recreational submersible ride with her father. Her old man had been one of the finest cops in the 'stead.

A malfunction in the sub caused it to hit a rocky seabed at full speed. The impact killed her father and left her barely this side of dead.

The kid's skull got crushed, but sixty percent of her brain had still worked. Doctors tried something risky; they connected her brain to an experimental computer in a medical operation that had never worked before. It worked with Hanna. Somehow her brain and the computer began operating as one, who the flotz knew why. Now the *average* girl was setting new standards in IQ testing.

Seán suspected the press of exaggerating her exploits. The kid simply couldn't be *that* good. Still, it was a shame about her prognosis. Due to deterioration of her other internal injuries, doctors only gave her two more years to live.

"Here we are," Yasmin said. They'd stopped before a door partway along a corridor. She raised her hand to push the doorbell.

"Wait," Seán stopped her. "How long do you figure she'll need to solve the case after she's heard the evidence?"

"I've never seen her take more than five minutes."

"Ten irids says she can't solve it in that time."

"Make it twenty and you're on," she shook his hand, then pressed the button.

Mrs. Webmarix, a smiling woman with sad, blue eyes, greeted them and let them in. A needlepoint logo of her late husband's police company adorned one wall. Framed news articles of his achievements, along with photos of his various promotions through the ranks decorated others.

Following Mrs. Webmarix into the living room, Seán got his first in-person glimpse of young Hanna. His stomach lurched as he looked at the wheelchair-bound girl. The lower half of her face seemed normal enough—a soft, well curved chin and jawline with youthful, pretty lips that formed a heart-melting smile. Her left eye lit up the room with the most penetrating bluish hue.

From there, things went askew. The right side of her skull sloped down at a wrong angle, as if it had been sliced off. A plastic membrane covered that area and seemed to blend with her skin at the edges. From that membrane projected a small, flat electronic box. Her right eye drooped at a slant and appeared almost pinched shut except for the glint of a black iris.

On the floor nearby rested a one-meter black cube. The computer, Seán surmised, linked in a wireless manner with her brain. Both deep within and on the surface of the cube, he could see flashing pinpoints of light, ever-shifting three-dimensional galaxies of them, arrays of luminous patterns that formed, moved, and died out in unpredictable ways. The display could have mesmerized him for hours.

He recalled hearing that Hanna's enhanced brain combined instant Internet access with photographic memory and magnified attention to detail. She'd dabbled in mathematics and physics, and now had theorems named after her.

"Yasmin, it's great to see you," Hanna had just said to Lieutenant Almareo while Seán had been distracted. "Major Seán Kelmaryn, I'm glad to meet you."

Seán fought against revulsion, moved closer, and shook the girl's outstretched hand. "My pleasure, Miss Webmarix," he lied.

"Just Hanna," the girl giggled. "If it makes you more comfortable, Seán, you can face away from me; I don't mind. I make a terrible first impression, and every impression after that."

"No, I—" Seán thought he'd hidden his reaction. "My apologies, er, Hanna. I'll be fine." He remembered hearing how much Hanna enjoyed police work. Once investigators had found her father's sub had been sabotaged, every police firm on the 'stead joined the hunt for the murderer. Security companies might be tough competitors on everything else, but when a cop killer was loose, they teamed up. Scores of detectives were stymied by the case of the sabotaged sub. Hanna begged them to show her the evidence. Finally, one company relented and she'd named the only possible killer in four minutes flat, from deduction alone.

"Why don't you both sit down?" Mrs. Webmarix pulled up chairs facing Hanna across a low table. "Would you care for something to drink?"

Yasmin took a kelpee with sugar, no cream, and Seán asked for instant coffee, black. Hanna pulled out a pack of gum.

"You have doubts about me, don't you, Seán?" Hanna asked. From her pack she withdrew one stick, unwrapped it, and popped it in her mouth. "I hope I can earn your trust. Now, Yasmin, I assume this is about the death of those two diplomats?"

"Right," Yasmin said. "I suggest a standard verbal detective services contract, version six point five. Same terms and payment rate as our last contract. Acceptable?"

"Agreed," Hanna said.

Yasmin held up her datapad and rattled off legal terms with accustomed ease. Seán expected Hanna to hold up a datapad to sync with Yasmin's, so the contract would be digitally signed by both, but she didn't. Then he realized Hanna, in essence, *was* a datapad. After a minute, Yasmin and Hanna had executed the agreement.

Mrs. Webmarix brought in a tray with their drinks, then excused herself.

"Well, I hope this case is interesting," Hanna said after blowing and deflating a red bubble. "Lately they've been pretty easy."

Hanna's gum-chewing did nothing to raise her reputation in Seán's mind. From the packaging, he recognized it as Rainbow Gum, the current fad for the kindergarten set. The stuff changed color when chewed, taking on each hue of the spectrum in turn, then repeating until it stopped cycling.

"The two victims were found alone in a sealed chamber," Yasmin said, "without a mark on them and without anyone else in the vicinity."

"I knew that much from the news," Hanna said. "The press is quoting your company as saying it was an accident, some sort of computer malfunction." She smirked. "Of course, it wasn't."

"We haven't ruled out a malfunction," Seán said. He sipped his coffee.

"Though some think that's almost impossible," Lieutenant Almareo said in a flat, professional tone.

Hanna looked from Seán to his subordinate. "So, you told the press something they'd believe, hoping the government would ease off on the scrutiny you're getting and allow you to solve the case without the hot spotlight treatment."

Seán almost coughed up a slug of coffee. *Flotz, how'd she figure that out?*

"Sounds like a good strategy to me," Hanna went on. "Tell me about the victims. Not the stuff I already know from the news. I want to know who might have had a motive."

"Who *didn't* have a motive to kill those two?" Yasmin asked. "Sofia Rossmarell and John Willmarium were Ridgia's top diplomats. They were the driving force behind every recent treaty our aquastate signed. They took on the toughest conflicts and always struck a favorable deal. Most recently they'd negotiated a border dispute, settled a case involving rights to a sunken wreck, and stopped a civil war before it started. The problem with swinging delicate deals," Yasmin said, "is someone always feels like they lost—and they harbor a grudge."

"When each of their families came here from a land country, they converted to a surname with 'mare' as a middle syllable, like most Ridgians. A beautiful woman, Rossmarel was of Italian stock. Willmarium had been American, older but with a distinguished appearance and a poker face that revealed nothing. The two had been inseparable and unbeatable. Rumors swirled about a sexual relationship, never proven."

"How did they die?" Hanna asked.

"Every Saturday morning the two of them went DIGMA diving together," Yasmin began.

Seán enjoyed doing that too. DIGMA, the Diving Gill Membrane Apparatus, had freed divers from bulky scuba tanks.

"They generally used DiveFac Five, nearest one to their quarters," Lieutenant Almareo said, checking her datapad, "and that's the one they used that day. They weren't the first to use the facility that morning, and it had operated flawlessly up until then."

"Is Number Five arranged and operated like Number Two?" Hanna asked. "That's the only one I've been to."

"Yes, an unmanned, automated facility. It's a standard layout," Yasmin called up a view on her datapad. "Entrance foyer, changing rooms, the diving chamber itself, computer room, and equipment room. Run like a franchise with separate operator-owners for each one."

"Got it," Hanna said, nodding as she chewed her gum, "so back to that Saturday morning."

"The fac's computer called all medical and police companies at—" Yasmin checked her datapad, "nine forty-six AM. Ours was the first police firm on the scene and we cut a contract with the franchise owner, Luca Bermara, before any others arrived. The victims were in the diving chamber, slumped on the bench. No marks. No signs of struggle. Nothing apparently out of place. The med company reps pronounced them dead on the scene at ten fourteen."

"Hypoxia," Hanna said, then blew an orange bubble.

Seán had to admit he was starting to be more impressed with the teenager's questions, and with how much she knew, though he still considered her gum juvenile. He took another swig of coffee.

"Right. According to the autopsy report," Yasmin clicked to a different screen, "it was hypoxia combined with ebullism. Basically, they were trying to breath vacuum."

"And if the pressure drop was fast enough, they never knew what happened," Hanna said, shaking her misshapen head. "They just fell asleep and never woke up." She sighed. "What safety features did the DivFac have?"

"All switches and valves are controlled by a computer with a perfect safety record. Two independent vacuum breaker valves open automatically to vent the chamber when they detect a vacuum."

"Wait—you said all valves were controlled by the computer, right?"

"Yes."

"Not truly independent, then," Hanna said, pursing her lips. "I assume you checked the valves?"

"Hanna, we hired a separate diving facility company to check every component in the system. Every mechanical component— valves, pumps, compressors—operated flawlessly."

"Okay, tell me about this computer with the perfect safety record."

Now we're getting to the real problem, Seán thought. He'd let Lieutenant Almareo run her investigation, so she knew more of the details, but he'd learned enough to convince him the computer had failed somehow.

"It's a NeuronTech ANN Model X2301. The NeuronTech rep named it Pluto."

"Was this tech an astronomer?" Seán asked.

"Nah." Yasmin snorted and shook her head. "A cartoon fan. His other computers were Mickey, Minnie, and Goofy, names like that."

"X2301," Hanna said, nodding. "I know that model. It came out five years ago. "Mine," she patted the black cube with the roaming light patterns, "is a Model X4601."

"This computer, Pluto, never had a problem leading up to that Saturday morning," Yasmin went on. "We hired an independent expert to check Pluto out. First, they disconnected it from the DiveFac and fed it simulations. Then they hooked it back up and put test dummies in the chamber. Pluto never made any mistakes when we used a series of diver certification numbers taken at random from the list of qualified divers. But when we used the diver cert numbers of Sofia Rossmarel or John Willmarium—either one—Pluto partly flooded the chamber, shut the vent, shut both vacuum breakers, and opened the water drain."

Hanna let out a whistle. "Water drains out and air can't replace it. Sudden vacuum."

"But the computer only did it for those two people?" Seán asked. "Somebody must've programmed it to do that."

Hanna and Yasmin shared a glance, and Seán wondered if he'd said something wrong.

"You don't exactly *program* an ANN," Yasmin said. "Hanna, you can explain it better."

"The old digital computers were *programmed*," the young girl said, "with a strict set of instructions written in some computer language. Artificial Neural Networks, or ANNs, are different. You don't program them; you *train* them. No coded computer language at all. Give them various inputs and compare their output to what you want it to be. Reward good outputs and punish bad ones; repeat until the ANN is trained and gives the desired output every time.

"Think of an ANN as a huge number of very simple computers, or nodes, each one connected to several others. Although each node is really stupid, when they're all connected and trained, the result can behave very well. ANNs are most useful for complex, changing situations where inputs are incomplete or unclear."

"Like in a DivFac," Yasmin nodded, "where there are lots of switches and valves to control, and a sensor could go bad at any time."

"Exactly," Hanna said. "ANNs mimic the behavior of animal brains, dealing well with uncertainty. Unlike animals, though, they have no instincts; they just behave according to their training. They're not as smart as people yet. More like dolphins or dogs." She blew a fist sized bubble, yellow this time.

"So, somebody *trained* this computer to kill Rossmarel and Willmarium?" Seán frowned. "Who could have done that?"

"Our suspect list is short," Yasmin tapped her datapad. "Pluto was trained at NeuronTech four years ago, but we can disregard those original trainers because Pluto operated correctly for all that time, including for many dives by the two victims, according to the logs. Rossmarel and Willmarium went rec diving most Saturday mornings, including the week before their deaths."

"Who had access to Pluto during that week?" Hanna asked.

"Just three people," Yasmin told her, "and according to the log, all three accessed it for about forty-five minutes each."

"That's all?" Seán was surprised and looked at Hanna. "Not enough time for training, is it? You said there'd be a lot of inputs and outputs involved."

"More than enough time, Seán," Hanna said. "With software automating the training process, you can do many thousands of training runs in forty-five minutes." Hanna turned to Yasmin. "Let me guess—the log is no help in figuring out who did the training, right?"

"Right," the lieutenant said. "It doesn't show that any training took place all week, just standard maintenance and verification checks."

"How is the log kept?" Hanna asked.

"Pluto records the log of its own activities and all interactions with it."

Hanna gave a grim smile. "So, the murderer also trained Pluto to go back and alter its log entries to cover up evidence of a training session."

"Wouldn't that be stupid? Seán asked. "If the killer was smart enough to train the computer to erase its own log entries of training sessions, why not have it erase *all* evidence of *any* access by the murder himself?"

Yasmin shook her head. "That would have disrupted a pattern and led us right to him. See, these same three people access Pluto every three months, as part of their job. If one of them had no log entries recording normal access, *that* would have attracted our attention."

That made sense to Seán. "So, we're dealing with a smart killer. You said all three accessed the computer in the week before the murder. If each one accesses only once a quarter, isn't it odd that they each did it the same week?"

"No," said Yasmin. "That's their normal pattern, quarter after quarter. See, one's from a safety monitoring firm. She has to recertify Pluto to operate every three months. The NeuronTech rep always does his checks right before her cert to make sure Pluto will pass her tests. And the DiveFac Manager does a check before *that* to satisfy himself that Pluto won't flunk the other two people's tests."

"Did they access the computer in that order? Seán asked. "I mean— first the DiveFac manager, then the computer rep, and then the safety inspector?"

"Yes," Yasmin nodded.

"It's the last one, then," Seán said. "If it was the first or second, he'd be taking a risk that the inspector after him would detect his tampering."

"Only a tiny chance," Hanna had just sucked in a green bubble. "Remember, Pluto got trained to kill only two specific people. To detect that through testing, the later inspector would have to randomly pick one of those two names from the hundreds of qualified divers in Ascenseon. Not very likely." Hanna then turned to Yasmin. "Tell me about these three people. You interrogated them, right?"

Lieutenant Almareo opened some new screens on her datapad. "Yes, and I've got the videos." She tilted her datapad so both Hanna and Seán could see the screen.

It showed a pudgy, middle-aged man. Some remaining blond hair formed wispy curls around a bald spot. His reddish skin made Seán wonder if that resulted from anger or embarrassment, or if it was his normal skin tone. The man's eyes bulged, and his face glinted with sweat. Gass addict, Seán thought. The drug gass, an extract of sargassum seaweed, had been legal in their 'stead since its founding, but few people used the stuff in doses high enough to be habit-forming or to have the visible symptoms.

"Luca Bermara," Yasmin said. "Forty-three-year-old divorced male of French descent. Franchise owner of DiveFac Five for the past eight months. He's a prediction market gambler. When he wins, he buys gass; when he loses, he gets high."

Probably addicted to both the gambling and the drug, Seán thought. This guy took risks, lived on the edge.

Yasmin clicked play. Bermara kept mopping his sweaty face with a handkerchief. Underarm stains showed through his gray jumpsuit material. The interrogation must have taken place in a computer room; in the background behind Bermara, patterns of pulsating lights danced and shifted in a display much like Hanna's computer cube. Bermara seemed nervous, his bug-eyes shifting around. Might well be the man's habitual demeanor, Seán realized, or an effect of the drug, or both.

"...no, I didn't know 'em," Bermara said on the video in response to a question from Lieutenant Almareo, sitting off-screen. "It's just horrible. Never really trusted those swishin' ANNs myself. One of 'em was bound to go squido one day—just bad luck it had to be in *my* DiveFac."

"We understand you gamble on the event prediction markets, Mr. Bermara. Is that so?" Lieutenant Almareo's voice asked.

"Yeah," Bermara said, squinting.

"Did you bet on the Demerare dispute?"

"Flotz, that's goin' back aways. Yeah, I think so."

"Lose a lot?"

"I don't really...yeah, some I guess."

Seán recalled the border dispute between Ridgia and the neighboring aquastate of Demerare to the west. At first Demerare had held the stronger claim and most thought that country would gain kilonauts of area. Then Rossmarel and Willmarium turned the tide somehow and angled a better deal for Ridgia than anybody had thought possible.

"Were you angry about the outcome?" Yasmin asked Bermara. "Mad at the negotiators?"

"You blubbin' me, officer? I was just down a few thousand irids, is all. That's not worth someone's life!"

"You accessed Pluto a few days before the deaths, Mr. Bermara. Is that right?"

"You bet I accessed Pluto. But just to check it out. I can't afford to have the flotzin' thing fail a quarterly cert. That'd put me outa biz for *weeks*."

"Do you know how to train a neural net computer?"

"Yeah, I guess I could train an ANN; I was a repair tech myself for two years. But like I said, I'd *never* teach the swishin' thing to *kill* someone!"

Lieutenant Almareo played the whole video, but none of the rest added any useful information for Seán.

"Why didn't you interrogate him at the station?" Hanna asked. She puffed out a blue bubble with her rainbow gum.

"Our interro room's being renovated, so I did all three in the computer room at the DiveFac."

Almareo clicked to the next video. "Ebo Shahari," she said, "but his Oceanist name is Wade."

An Oceanist all right, Seán thought. The man's green-dyed skin, webbed fingers, and a black starfish tattoo on his forehead, all revealed him as a devout adherent to the new religion spreading throughout world's seasteads. A slim, bald guy, he appeared younger than Bermara and wore a brooding expression. "Wait. Shahari, you said? Without the 'mare' syllable in his name?"

"Right. A rebel."

Not long before, a group of Oceanists had launched a movement to overthrow the government of Ridgia. In defiance, they'd changed their 'mare' names back to their original surnames.

"Twenty-five-year-old male of Senegalese descent," Yasmin went on. "Single. Shahari *lives* online. Operates a website dedicated to renewing the civil war. Has a dozen known internet personas, probably more we don't know about. Active VR gamer. He started working with NeuronTech just two weeks after the rebellion collapsed."

Glancing at Hanna for her reaction, Seán saw she looked intent, thoughtful.

Yasmin started the video.

As it played, Seán thought about Oceanists in general. He had nothing in particular against them. The way they'd permadye their skin and surgically web their fingers and toes—that used to creep him out, but no more. From what he knew, Oceanism hyped itself as a religion of peace, so it had seemed strange when a group of them within Ridgia had begun agitating for rebellion against the government. This guy, Shahari, seemed like another of the angry foot soldiers in the rebellion's failed cause.

"I can't understand what went wrong with Pluto," Ebo Shahari said on the video at one point. "You got to believe me. I did nothing!"

Seán noticed Shahari seemed upset, his eyes wide, his head shaking in denial. On the screen behind him, lights blinked on and off. The man's hands fidgeted on the table, and at times his webbed fingers drummed out a rhythm.

"You accessed Pluto during the week before Rossmarel's and Willmarium's deaths."

"Yes, but just to run quarterly checks, I swear! That's all I did, all I ever did. You can check the log if you don't believe me. Pluto keeps a log."

"Do you know how to train an ANN, Mr. Shahari?"

"Wouldn't be much of a tech if I didn't, would I?"

"You were a rebel, Mr. Shahari, were you not?" Yasmin's voice asked in an even tone.

"I keep telling you—call me *Wade*. That's my name, Wade. Yes, I was a reb. So what? Ancient history."

"Were you angry with Rossmarel and Willmarium when they negotiated an end to the civil uprising?"

"Why would I be mad at those two? They only did their job. It was our movement's own leaders who sold out. They gave up without a... Wait. You think *I* did this? I thought you wanted to know how Pluto broke down." His hands were thrashing about the table now. Shahari's voice was raised, agitated. "You're flukin' crazy if you think—you know what?" He folded his arms. "I changed my mind. I *do* want a lawyer."

The video ended at that moment.

Lieutenant Almareo smiled at Hanna. "We followed up and interviewed him with his attorney present. I've transmitted that vid to you, but—"

"—but there's nothing useful on it," Hanna finished.

"Right. Let me show you our final suspect." She got to the opening frame of the next video, showing a middle-aged woman. "This is Júlia Lomarez. Fifty-seven-year-old female of Spanish descent. Never married. Worked for CompuCert Labs since their founding fifteen years ago."

Seán shook his head. "Fifteen years? Kind of unlikely that our killer would happen to be in the right job when—"

"Her working territory got shifted four months ago to include Ascenseon DiveFacs, just one month after our victims negotiated that sunken wreck ownership deal. I talked to her supervisor and he said the shift was by mutual consent, not her request." Yasmin went back to her datapad notes. "Hobbies are knitting and reading science fiction. From friends and co-workers, and her own testimony, I learned she's terrified of the coming Singularity."

Hanna smirked but Seán just nodded. *A reasonable fear, in his view.* Beyond the theorized event known as the Singularity, the point where computers would become more intelligent than people, no one knew *what* would happen.

"She's claimed that's why she likes her job as the final certification authority for ANNs," Yasmin said. "She helps keep them in their place."

Despite his own misgivings about a potential Singularity, Seán felt a mental chill at hearing those words. *Down the ages people have used similar phrases to justify some of history's worst atrocities. Could this pleasant-looking lady really be a killer?*

Lieutenant Almareo ran the video of Júlia Lomarez answering questions. She was plump, Seán noticed, with a double chin and a body that strained against her mauve jumpsuit. Her brown hair bore streaks of gray throughout. The screen in the background showed several flashing points of light. Lomarez's voice, scratchy and high-pitched, reminded Seán of his lovable grandmother. Her facial wrinkles heightened the effect of her smiles, but also turned her frowns into stony disapproval.

"...simply horrible what happened to him, and to the woman too, of course," Lomarez was saying. "Just tragic." She shook her head.

"You renewed the certification of the computer, Pluto, just a few days before the deaths, is that correct?" Yasmin asked from off-screen.

"Yes, I did, and believe me, Pluto passed every test. There must have been some serious mechanical problem. Something wrong with the pumps or valves. I'm afraid I don't know much about those things."

"Ms. Lomarez, we checked out all the mechanical systems and found nothing wrong. Pluto's log shows that it directed the valve sequence leading to a vacuum being drawn in the chamber. You were the last person to access Pluto before the deaths of Mr. Willmarium and Ms. Rossmarel."

This brought on Ms. Lomarez's stony frown, though Seán thought he saw the twitch of a sneer at the mention of Rossmarel's name.

"Well, I simply don't know what could have happened then," she said. "Pluto checked out perfectly during my tests."

"You came to Ascenseon from Spain, is that true?"

Lomarez brightened at the change of topic. "Yes, I did, but that was many years ago. I came here during the 'stead's first year."

"Were you upset when Willmarium and his partner negotiated the rights to the Hija de Cádiz?"

Seán watched the screen for Lomarez's reaction. Hija de Cádiz had been a Spanish galleon of the 1540s, lost during a transatlantic voyage. The discovery of the wreck and its cargo of New World gold within the aquatorial border of Ridgia had set off a major dispute with Spain regarding ownership. While warships of both countries faced each other in the waters above the sunken galleon, Rossmarel and Willmarium had pulled off another diplomatic feat. The resulting treaty gave Spain title to the wreck and all its contents, but required

Madrid to pay Ridgia a finder's fee for locating the sailing ship. The fee nearly equaled the value of the gold.

"Why would I be upset?" Lomarez asked. "I'm a Ridgian now, not a Spaniard."

"One more question, Ms. Lomarez." There was a pause. "Were you once in love with John Willmarium?"

Lomarez's lips formed a flat line; her jaw set and her stare went ice-hard. Then she relaxed and her features softened. "Officer, you're a young, pretty woman. I hope you never find out what it's like to love with all your heart and get nothing in return." She turned away and gazed into a distance only she could see. "It's a hurt you can't simply forget. Or get over."

Lomarez turned back to face the lieutenant, and gave a slight smile as she wiped her eyes with a tissue. "But you really want to know if I *hated* John. Enough to kill him." She paused, then shook her head. "No. My love was too deep for that. I could never harm him."

She paused, then gave short chuckle. "And no, I'm not a jealous person. I could not harm Ms. Rossmarel either."

There it was again, Seán thought, a tightening of the mouth and a slight squint of the iron gray eyes as she said Rossmarel's name. Or did he imagine it?

The video concluded moments later. Lieutenant Almareo looked up from her datapad. "Well, that's it, Hanna. I've synched my datapad with your system so you have the test reports on the DiveFac, the autopsy reports, Pluto's complete logs going back to its factory training, and all the interrogation interviews. That's all the evidence. What do you think?"

In a nonchalant motion meant to look like he was scratching an itch on his arm, Seán started his watch timer. If Hanna saw the movement, she didn't comment on it.

Hanna stared for a moment at the wall behind Seán and Yasmin. On the floor, the black cube swirled with a fantastic light show, an electronic aurora borealis. Hanna blew a violet bubble with her gum, then collapsed it and resumed chewing.

Her odd face bore no discernible expression other than intense thought. Seán felt sorry for her, a victim of a terrible crime and a horrible trauma. Now the youth who had solved so many perplexing problems must have finally met her match. Seán could think of factors for and against each suspect. They seemed perfectly balanced to him. Any of the three could be guilty.

"Let me see your datapad a moment, Yasmin," Hanna said. Taking the pad, she positioned its screen so all three could see it. She played the beginning of the Bermara video.

"Please state your full name," Almareo's voice asked.

"Luca Pierre Bermara."

Hanna scrolled back over those seconds of the video three times, then clicked on the next one.

"...your full name."

"Wade Ebo Shahari."

Hanna replayed that, then the opening seconds of the Lomarez video.

Seán had no idea why the suspect's names were important to Hanna. He only knew he was well on his way to winning his twenty irid bet. Unfortunately, it meant they'd be no closer to solving the case.

Hanna set down the datapad and smiled. "So, Yasmin, the evidence is clear. Why haven't you arrested the murderer yet?"

"What? You mean you solved it already?" Seán couldn't believe it. Only two minutes and forty seconds had passed according to his timer.

Hanna's smile lessened to a Mona Lisa half-smile. "Not really. See, all three suspects have motive, means, and opportunity. None of them has an alibi. After I reviewed the evidence, I couldn't decide between them."

Seán looked at Lieutenant Almareo. "I told you we were wasting our time. We've got to get back to—"

"Seán, please," Hanna said. "Let me finish. "I said *I* couldn't decide between them." Both her good eye and the deformed one stared at him. "But Pluto could."

"Pluto? What do you mean?" Seán frowned, unable to figure out her logic.

"You'll have to thank the workers renovating your interrogation room at the station," Hanna said, her full smile returning. "That forced you to make these videos elsewhere, and you chose to do them at the DiveFac, in full view of Pluto. So each video amounted to two interrogations—of the suspect and also of the ANN."

Seán thought back to the light patterns in the background of each video.

"You're saying Pluto reacted differently to—" Lieutenant Almareo began.

"I'm suggesting you ought to think like a computer," Hanna, the half-computer, said. "More accurately, think like a computer with the intellect of a dolphin, or a dog. You can't speak, but you know humans make sounds, each one with different tonal variations. Moreover, it's been four years since you were last trained at the factory. Four years since someone gave you the equivalent of fish, or dog biscuits. More rewards for each trick you performed correctly."

She looked at each investigator. "Then one week someone comes in and gives you another training session, lasting forty-five minutes. You're a computer; you don't have human morality. You don't know you're being trained to kill. Only trained to do a more subtle trick. You have to operate the DiveFac normally for almost everyone, but in a slightly different way for two specific humans. You don't know why, but you're getting rewards if you do it right.

"The very next Saturday comes and you do your job. A few days later, you hear the voice of your new trainer, or master, the one who gave you all those rewards. You get excited—intense neural activity— as you wonder if he'll give you more rewards today. That's what Pluto was thinking. Look at the videos and see for yourselves."

With a few display manipulations, Hanna put all three videos on the screen and ran the first few seconds simultaneously. The difference couldn't have been more obvious.

"Bermara," said Seán and Lieutenant Almareo at the same time. "The DiveFac franchise guy," Seán added. While only a few lights sparked behind Shahari and Lomarez, the background of Bermara's video danced with a myriad of luminescent points, flowing in and out of various shapes, some like spiral curves and others like starbursts.

"Like a dog wagging its tail," Seán mused. He began thinking ahead to how they'd present this to the prosecutor. "Wait a minute." He'd spotted a logical flaw. "Will this hold up as solid evidence in court? The computer isn't smart enough to communicate in words; it can't testify or be cross-examined. It's just giving a different reaction to one guy—there could be a lot of ways to explain that."

Hanna paused, but only a moment. "Point, Seán. But I think the evidence will hold up if you get a good prosecutor. As a backup plan, I suggest you call NeuronTech and find out the technician who originally trained Pluto. Arrange to get a video of that tech with Pluto's status screen in the background, just as you did with Bermara and the others. Trust me; Pluto hasn't forgotten that tech, even after four years. It will light up like it did with Bermara, proving that only the trainer would cause that reaction. An open-and-shut case, Seán." She gave Lieutenant Almareo a playful glance. "You *are* going to bring me a *difficult* case someday, aren't you, Yasmin?"

Seán stared in awe at the teenage girl, now inflating a red bubble from her gum, who'd just solved a case that had bedeviled half his department for a week. After seeing the evidence, she'd cracked it in less than three minutes. *She may have just saved Ridgia Protective Services, Inc. as well.*

Far beyond uncanny, he thought, *this kid's a national treasure. What I could do with a handful like her at the firm, each making crime solving his or her career. I'd give them all the rainbow gum they wanted. Instead, there's just this one kid, with two years left to live. There's the crime.*

Hanna fixed him with a deep stare. "I get that look a lot, Seán. You're pitying me. Please don't. Dad always told me life isn't fair; bad things happen to good people. I'm grateful for the time I've had and glad to help the police when I can. I don't need your pity, Seán, but I do need you to arrest that bad guy. Please do that for me, and for my dad."

"I will, Hanna," Seán felt a little choked up as he rose and shook her hand. "It was nice meeting you."

"Same here," she smiled. After he and Lieutenant Almareo turned to go, Hanna added, "Oh, just one more thing, Seán. I know you were skeptical of me, and I'm guessing you aren't above making an occasional friendly low-stakes wager." She winked at him. "Perhaps next time you'll bet *on* me, not against me."

Across Oceans Wide

*A*t the age of four, Brenna couldn't fathom her sister, Halcyone. She would stare at people and things in a way that made Brenna wonder if Halcyone were seeing things differently, not as they are, but as they could be. She gazed at her toys and at the adults in her family as if studying them, figuring out how they could be useful.

Most of the time, Brenna enjoyed playing with Halcyone, also a four-year-old. They loved singing the popular children's seasteading song:

> "I wish, I wish, upon a fish,
> To grab a whale right by its tail,
> And ride the tide 'cross ocean's wide,
> Dance in the deep before I sleep."

She and Halcyone sang it over and over.

The children of *landers*, who lived in the dirt countries, wished upon stars, Brenna knew. But for those seastead children who lived undersea, it made more sense to wish upon a fish, since that's what they saw when they opened their drapes. Brenna had also heard that lander children sometimes had whole rooms with lots of floor space to spread out their toys. But life in a seastead meant accepting very restricted volumes, and most children played on their beds, the only space available unless their family was wealthy.

One day, they sat on Halcyone's bed since she was recovering from surgery to remove two branchial cysts.

"I hate my scars," Halcyone said. "See?" She swept her hair back and pulled her shirt collar down enough to show two red, vertical lines, one on each side of her neck. "J-Mom said the scars will always be there. Now I'll never be pretty like you." They called one of the women in their family *J-Mom* since her name was Jallulah. Each of the family's other women worked, but J-Mom stayed in their compartment to look after the children.

Brenna looked at the scars. "They might get better after a while."

"J-Mom said my hair will hide them, but I still think they're ugly. And I hate having to stay in bed. I feel fine."

Brenna and Halcyone belonged to the same family, surname Tillerman, the result of a contract marriage of five women, seven men, and four children at that time. The adults changed every few years. The girls called themselves sisters, though they had separate bio-moms and bio-dads. Being almost the same age made it fun to play together. One brother was already a teenager and the other a four-month-old infant, and they weren't interested in the same things.

After a knock on their bedroom door, J-Mom's voice asked, "Girls? Adrian's come over to play with you."

Brenna saw Halcyone sigh. She leaned closer and whispered to Brenna. "He never plays nice." Five-year-old Adrian belonged to a family in a neighboring compartment. Brenna knew they shouldn't refuse his visit. J-Mom had her hands full with the baby and Adrian's caregiver must have errands to run again. Maybe he'd only be here a short time.

The door opened and J-Mom looked in at them. "Go on in, Adrian."

Brenna noticed Halcyone shift her dark brown hair to cover her scars. Adrian shuffled in, frowning, and Brenna guessed he hadn't asked to be sent over to play with two girls. He looked up and brightened when he saw one of the toys on Halcyone's bed.

"You've got a Dolly Dolphin!" he said. "Does it talk?"

"It's Brenna's," Halcyone said.

Adrian snatched the plastic toy from Brenna's lap, shook it, and looked at it head on. "What can it say?"

After some dolphin-like chittering, the toy said, "Hi! I'm Dolly Dolphin. What's your name?"

"I'm Krafty Kraken," Adrian told the toy, naming a character from a popular cartoon video, the bad guy who always opposed the brave hero, Bradley Breakwater.

"Hi, Krafty Kraken," the toy dolphin said. "What do you like to do?"

"That's long enough," Halcyone said, giving Adrian that intense, serious glare that made her look grown up already. "Give it back to Brenna now."

Brenna was about to say it was okay for Adrian to play a while longer, but Adrian spoke to the toy. "I like to spit in toy dolphin's mouths." He spat.

"I know a fun counting game," the dolphin said. "Let's play that instead."

"I warned you, Adrian," Halcyone sprang out of her bed. Before Brenna knew what was happening, Halcyone had pinned Adrian to the deck and was punching him in the face. Though a year younger than he was, Halcyone was a little bigger.

Adrian cried out, and Brenna saw his lip bleeding. Halcyone backed off of him when the door opened and J-Mom rushed in.

Halcyone stood up, handed Brenna back her toy, and said, "this is the Family Tillerman compartment, Adrian. You don't come here anymore."

The thirteen-year-old sisters giggled. Brenna and Halcyone stood naked, side by side in their room, gazing at their reflections in the bulkhead which they'd voice-commanded to become a mirror surface.

"This is going to take some getting used to," Brenna said.

Halcyone flicked her hair back. "Wonderful. Just when my scars were starting to fade, this treatment *accents* them."

"They don't show. Really." Brenna swept Halcyone's hair back in place. "See?"

Earlier that day, they'd undergone the Immersion treatment. Required for full acceptance into the Oceanism religion, Immersion mandated more than recitation of doctrine, correct responses to questions about the faith, and solemn affirmations of belief. Immersion also meant a full-body skin color change to blue, green, aquamarine, turquoise or some other water tone; the application of a tattoo with an approved Oceanism symbol; and the permanent surgical addition of stretchable skin-like webbing between fingers and toes.

Brenna had chosen a single-hue pastel green for her skin coloring, a tone she saw as calming and peaceful. Her blue starfish tattoo glowed on her forehead when she triggered it, like the controllable bioluminescence in deep-sea creatures. As with most seasteaders, even non-Oceanists, she'd also had a controllable white-light tattoo applied to both palms; these served as crude flashlights during power failures.

"The boys will really notice you now," Halcyone told her. "Especially *Hudson*." She drew the name out.

Brenna blushed, and saw in the mirror how her slight reddening still showed despite the skin treatment. "I don't think he's interested in me, or any girl right now. He just talks about being a submariner when he grows up." She sighed. "Maybe I'll contract with a submariner someday."

"*Contract* with one?" Halcyone scoffed and spread her fingers, examining her webbing. "I'm going to *be* one."

To Brenna's way of thinking, Halcyone had selected very odd Immersion options. Her skin showed waves of bold green and blue, alternating in curving patterns. Strangest of all, she'd gotten a glowing hammerhead shark tattoo on her right forearm, far more typical of the symbol and placement chosen by boys, though hers changed color with her mood. Brenna started to put her clothes back on, wondering if she'd ever understand her sister at all. "Kinda dangerous, don't you think?"

Shrugging, Halcyone reached for her own shorts to don them. "Compared to what? I just want to do something important with my life." She frowned. "The way things are going, I might not get the chance anyway."

She referred to the decline of the Manihiki aquastate, Brenna knew. After the initial rush to colonize the seas, some aquastates had prospered while others decayed and ceded area until they got absorbed. On occasion, mobile seasteads crossed borders and petitioned to join neighboring aquastates. A vocal minority of adults in Brenna's and Halcyone's steastead, Tongarva, had already proposed departing Manihiki.

"Oh, I think you'll shake up the world someday," Brenna said, both to reassure her and because she admired and envied Halcyone's drive and intensity.

"Hmm," Halcyone grimaced and sat on the bed. "If that's true, I'll have to overcome a lot of biological baggage. What do you think of T-Dad's announcement at dinner last night?"

Brenna lifted her shoulders and sat next to her. "It's bad news, but not the end of the world." Among the adults in Family Tillerman, Troy earned the highest income. His employer had announced cutbacks and Troy would be forced to suffer a cut in salary. T-Dad had told the family he'd checked their financial status, and they would have to move to a smaller compartment within the seastead.

"Oh, it's bad news," Halcyone touched Brenna's arm, "but I don't think you know *how* bad." Her voice lowered to a passionate whisper. "T-Dad's my bio-dad, and he always tells me how he's descended from the Hopi Tribe. That tribe was always getting uprooted, forced from its home, and they always just accepted it and moved on. Now here we go again. Why won't he stand and *fight*, for once?

"I swear," Halcyone went on, her eyes flaring in anger and her shark tattoo glowing, "I will fight back whenever someone tries to take what's mine."

. . .

"So, Halcyone, tell us all about the exciting things you've been up to." Brenna's question wasn't just polite chatter at her new family's dinner table. Nor was it only a technique learned from her double major in journalism and communication at college. Brenna hadn't really been able to keep up with her sister while Halcyone was at sea, but knew she hadn't yet joined a family.

Upon graduation at age twenty-two, Brenna had been pleased to land a job as a junior staff writer at the vid-zine *This Minute*, and she'd also contracted to join Family Plimsoll, bringing that group up to three women, four men, and six children. With Halcyone having been granted a few days of leave by the Manihikian Navy, Brenna had invited her to dine with her family. Halcyone had appeared attentive while listening to the other adults talk about their occupations.

Caught with a mouthful of broiled bonito, Halcyone couldn't answer right away. With the gap in conversation, the family's six-year-old asked, "What are those marks on your neck?"

"Christopher!" one of the mom's scolded. "That's not polite."

Halcyone had gotten her brown hair cut short in a raised, spiked style, apparently having lost her self-conscious worry about her scars. In general, her time in the military had seemed to harden her features and given her a tougher appearance.

"They're gills," Halcyone said, smiling and tilting up her chin to display them.

"Really?" Christopher asked in a voice full of wonder.

While the older kids elbowed each other and giggled, Brenna noticed Halcyone flaunting the scars she'd once detested.

"To answer your question, Brenna," Halcyone said, "they're trying to drum me out of the force."

"Great Neptune!" Brenna said. "What happened?"

"I was aboard the *Cachalot*, patrolling along the eastern edge of the Disputed Zone with Penrhyn. *Four* subs patrolled the Penrhyn side while we could only afford one. I stood watch in the control room while all the other officers ate in the wardroom. Suddenly the toxic gas casualty alarm sounded." She made a high-pitched "bweep, bweep" sound that

Christopner tried to mimic. Halcyone continued, "It turned out we had two problems—a mishap with the fuel cells that released chlorine gas and a faulty ventilation lineup that sent the gas to the wardroom.

"Our sonar showed all four Penrhynian subs had entered the DZ. A voice from one of the sub's commanders came over the laser telephone saying they'd heard our alarm and wanted to offer assistance. With all our other officers incapacitated, and me only a junior ensign, I was the senior ranking officer on our sub. All the enlisted personnel in the control room looked at me, waiting for my orders." Halcyone looked around the table. "I'm sorry. Am I boring you?"

"No!" said the family's nine-year-old boy, who leaned forward, his eyes wide open.

"Well," Halcyone set down her glass of kelp beer, "I told the techs to give new instructions to six sharks—do any of you kids know what sharks are?

"They're robotic underwater vehicles, right?" asked the fourteen-year-old girl.

"I was going to say it," said the six-year-old boy.

"That's right. They're much smarter than the torpedoes they used to use," Halcyone said. "I told the techs to instruct each shark to swim back toward base, then to spread out and come back in a wide pattern lining up with me. As they came back, I wanted them to mimic the sonar behavior of a large, manned sub. It's like inflating them to the size of whales. Sort of like a pufferfish does."

The younger children puffed out their cheeks or drew their hands apart to imitate the expansion effect.

A few minutes later," Halcyone continued, "it looked to the Penrhynian subs like we had seven subs against their four. Needless to say, the four Penrhynian subs turned fluke and retreated back to their side of the DZ."

Halcyone sat back and spread sweetened roe jelly on a seaweed cracker.

"Wait," Brenna frowned. "I missed the part where they're trying to force you out of the Navy."

"Oh, yeah." Halcyone showed a confident little smile. "Once he came to, my commanding officer was shark-frenzy mad at me. By the time reports went from the Navy to both Pod houses and the administration, I was being accused of inciting an international incident, aggravating an already tense border situation."

"That's just wrong," Brenna said. "They can't get away with that." She brightened as a crazy idea occurred. "I'm going to write a feature story about that. I'll bet I can get it into *This Minute*."

Halcyone made a dismissive hand motion.

"I can see your captain's point," said the diplomat, a man named Douglas in his late thirties. He examined his wine glass. "Our politicians are working to maintain a delicate balance—"

"Anyone want some whale's milk ice cream?" Brenna interrupted, all too aware of Halcyone's explosive nature when she got riled. "Douglas, won't you help me get it?"

Halcyone fixed her laser stare on Douglas, and the shark tattoo on her arm began glowing red. *Too late*, Brenna thought. *This will get ugly.*

"Weak people with passive attitudes," Halcyone's voice lanced out like a narwhal's horn, "are the ones who'll send our country to its doom."

Brenna ushered the children from the room, and within five minutes Douglas left the compartment red-faced and on the verge of tears. *Diplomats aren't used to being screamed at, especially the way Halcyone does it.*

Nine years later, Brenna sat in a hotel room with Halcyone, watching the wall screen.

"With eighty nine percent of the votes reported," the announcer looked exhausted, "*This Minute* can at last project the winner..."

Brenna clinked glasses with her sister just as the digital time hologram changed to 0124. "Congratulations."

"Thanks." Halcyone smiled and sipped. While watching, she'd been humming something Brenna recognized but couldn't name.

"...a remarkable upset of an incumbent who served six terms in the Lower Pod," the announcer said. "'Hammerhead Halcyone,' as her supporters call her, came out of nowhere, it seems, and captured voters' attentions with her message of Manihiki pride, naval strength, and toughness in international relations. Obviously, in the end, that message seems to have resonated with—"

What is it she's humming? Oh, yeah. It's that silly kid's song—I wish, I wish upon a fish. How odd. "Room screen off," Brenna said, ignoring the buzz of her netphone. She shook her head, still amazed at her sister's achievement. "They're probably at a fever pitch down in the ballroom. Better get down there and give your victory speech."

Halcyone stopped humming and frowned. "Did I ever tell you I hate giving speeches?"

Laughing, Brenna said, "All the time. But you're good at it."

"Helps to have someone giving me the right words to say." Halcyone stretched her arms out and yawned. "Thanks for joining my campaign; I know you hated to quit your other job. Now as a Lower Podmember, I'll need an advisor. Are you up for that?"

"No." Brenna shook her head. "I wouldn't mind staying on as your speechwriter and spokesperson, though."

"You're hired, Sis," Halcyone clapped her shoulder. "And tomorrow, you can start planning my campaign for the Upper Pod."

"What?" Brenna looked at her in surprise and set her drink down. She knew Halcyone held ambitions as large as the Pacific, but to be thinking about the Upper Pod at age thirty-one? It seemed so sudden. "Are you serious?"

Halcyone's ultramarine eyes glowed. "Oh, this is just the beginning. I'm going to take Manihiki to greatness. But there's only so much I can do from the lower house."

Brenna looked at her, trying to grasp the brash presumption of Halcyone's ambition. The youngest member of the Upper Pod was twice her age.

Admittedly, Halcyone was an easily promotable package. Young and fierce, with that spiked hair, focused gaze, and sharp-angled face, she'd win no beauty contest, but she projected a charisma few could match. Combine that with her reputation as the only naval hero in the war recently fought, and lost, against Penrhyn, and it was inevitable she'd unseat the incumbent.

My article had started this whole tidal surge, Brenna realized. After it had appeared on *This Minute*, recruits for the submarine service had flooded in, and the Navy couldn't very well let Halcyone go. The brass tried to push her into a corner, assigning the upstart ensign to research new weapons and tactics. Instead, from what Brenna could glean from outside the closed doors of security classifications, Halcyone sparked ideas that might well revolutionize submarine warfare.

But the technologies came too late for their nation's war against the Penrhynese. Naval leaders had taken a chance and made Halcyone the first officer of the fleet's oldest sub.

Tears welled in Brenna's eyes whenever she thought about what happened next. In the heat of battle, apparently Halcyone declared her own captain weak and unfit to command, and relieved him. She then executed a one-sub rampage that left three enemy subs destroyed and two barely able to limp home. Her own vessel suffered extreme damage, killing half the crew, but rescue submersibles recovered the remainder from the bottom. This had proved Manihiki's one courageous moment in an otherwise humiliating war, and served only to limit the amount of area ceded to Penrhyn in the peace treaty.

What, Brenna wondered, *is she aiming for*? As always, Halcyone raised more questions than she answered.

"Why don't you throttle back a bit? Enjoy your success?" Brenna asked. "You could settle down, find a man, and contract with a family."

"I might do that," Halcyone met her gaze, "when I find a man who's my match."

Brenna considered this. Who would be a match for Halcyone? What man *wouldn't* feel a bit intimidated by her? Likely her sister had already rebuffed some advances. She sighed. It was a matchmaking task for another day. But for now...

She slid a data pad across the table. "Your victory speech. And yes, you have to give it. Go get 'em, Hammerhead."

* * *

Below their tower, a crowd had begun gathering in the arena. Forty-year-old Brenna marveled at the preparations President Halcyone Tillerman had made for the high priest's visit.

Halcyone had ordered the seastead's helipad converted to an amphitheater, complete with small stage, live orchestra in a pit, and hundreds of chairs. Behind the guest seats, holographic images began appearing, of people in other seats, those from Manihiki's other seasteads, watching the event remotely. It gave the illusion of a vast—almost infinite—crowd. 'Steaders weren't accustomed to such open spaces, and Brenna saw many gazing about in wonder.

"Here's your speech." Brenna handed Halcyone a datapad. "It's loaded in the teleprompter. I suggest you read it over first." Fairly standard 'welcome to our aquastate' stuff, Brenna knew, but geared toward High Priest Ford Broadwater, who had founded Oceanism and become its highest official.

Halcyone handed back the datapad. "He's not here just for a visit. I've got something else planned."

Brenna stared at her. Only a year earlier, President Nekton had chosen Halcyone as his running mate. Soon after the election, he'd been impeached over a bribery scandal. No one seemed to know how the press had uncovered his misdeed, and journalists weren't saying. Untainted by the scandal, Vice President Halcyone had ascended to the higher office and immediately strengthened the undersea Navy and engaged in a more aggressive foreign policy. The public and the military adored her, the president-submariner who'd fought battles alongside her warriors rather than staying behind in a plush seastead office.

"Why didn't you tell me?" Brenna narrowed her eyes. "You're keeping me out of a lot of your plans these days."

A flash of sheepishness came over Halcyone's face before she assumed command of herself once more. "Sorry. Things just fell into place for this today. I'm sure you prepared a fine speech."

An hour later, Brenna sat in the amphitheater, watching the arrival of the high priest. He walked out on stage while the orchestra played the serene Debussy tune *En Bateau*. He looked older than he did on his televised sermons, with his dark blue skin and flowing, sky-blue beard. He sat down near two people already on stage, one of his five pentapriests and Halcyone's vice president, an elderly and well-respected politician who'd been lured out of retirement to balance Halcyone's youth and perceived rashness. *More important,* Brenna thought, *he has no political ambitions of his own.*

With a hiss of hydraulics, the entire stage began ascending and stopped four meters above the pit orchestra. A glass panel allowed viewers to see beneath the stage. A car-sized, rectangular hole opened on the stage floor in front of the seated dignitaries.

Brenna saw movement. A vehicle emerged from behind a wall to the right, moving slowly beneath the stage. A minisub, gold in color, motored toward mid-stage. Only then did Brenna realize the stage sat above a transparent box of water and its clear front allowed spectators to see the sub. Through its acrylic bubble nose, Brenna saw Halcyone at the controls.

The audience, both live and holographic, burst into applause and shouted, drowning out the orchestra's playing of Handel's *Water Music.* Brenna shook her head at the spectacle. *Really? A golden submarine?*

Once it reached the stage's midpoint, the sub surfaced vertically through the hole. An upper hatch opened, and Halcyone climbed out, assisted by the vice president. She wore nothing special for this occasion, just her blue military-style jumpsuit with the presidential seal on the left side of her chest.

Halcyone strode to the high priest, shook his hand, and welcomed him to Tongareva seastead. She bowed to him, and he placed a gold, laurel-leaf crown on her head, saying, "By the power of Oceanus, I crown you Empress Halcyone of Manihiki."

Brenna's jaw dropped, even as the crowd resumed cheering. If any citizens disapproved, they kept their silence, for Brenna heard no cries of dissent. *Empress? You planned this long ago; it didn't just fall into place.* She sighed, and clapped along with the others. *At least you didn't go full Napoleon and crown yourself.*

The Vice President draped a purple robe over Halcyone's shoulders. Brenna would never have chosen purple to go with a blue jumpsuit, green-and-blue skin, and blond hair, but somehow the hues didn't clash when Halcyone wore them. Her vice president—*or whatever new title he has now*, Brenna thought—handed Halcyone a golden scepter.

The empress held up a hand and the audience fell silent.

"For too long," she said, speaking louder as she went on, "Manihiki suffered under leaders who were cautious, indecisive, and weak. Starting today, that changes. I hereby dissolve both the Upper and Lower Pods. No more endless wrangling and debating. Now nothing stands between me and the people of Manihiki. Starting today, together we will make this aquastate the greatest nation the world has ever seen!"

An eruption of applause and shouting filled the amphitheater with sound.

Great Neptune, Brenna thought. *What have you done, sister?*

Aboard the Chimaera, a manned submarine in combat, almost everyone viewed Brenna's role of spokesperson and biographer as surplus. For that reason, she sat wedged in a corner on a board placed atop the radar unit, between the bulkhead and a large sonar cabinet. She would never have been allowed aboard at all, let alone in the control room, were it not for Empress Halcyone.

"As you can see, Excellency, the situation is foggy now," Admiral Bollard, a tall and distinguished man, pointed to the three-dimensional holographic display. It showed precise blue dots for all Empire subs and robotic vehicles—all given the names of sea creatures—but red uncertainty spheres and ovoids for enemy forces. The red blobs overlapped, creating a nebulous, confusing cloud. "Once we launch a few more minnows and sharks out there, things will clear up and we can—"

"No, Admiral," Halcyone pressed buttons and rotated the display. "Their command sub is right here." She pointed near the edge of one of the red spheres. "Have one of our sharks transmit, in the clear, on acoustic, that we expect them to surrender their forces, and their seastead, in ten minutes or we will destroy one of their manned subs."

Showing a look combining bewilderment and awe, Admiral Bollard said, "Yes, Excellency." He turned and conveyed the orders to lower ranking personnel.

"Now position your forces in a semicircle around that location," Halcyone told the admiral, "and prepare the Hull Hammer."

Brenna had heard of that weapon, but never seen it used. In the nine years since winning a seat in the Lower Pod, Halcyone had championed a number of advances that had altered undersea warfare. New tactics called for manned subs to linger on the fringes while a cloud of autonomous vehicles fought for position and advantage. These communicated with manned subs, dubbed 'whales,' with secure blue-green lasers.

Brenna took notes as the minutes of the ultimatum passed. Somehow, Halcyone had pierced the fog of war to pinpoint the enemy command sub's location, as if by some sixth sense beyond even the capabilities of the unmanned vehicle swarm.

"Admiral," Halcyone took her eyes off the chronometer to look at him. "We've given them ten minutes. They haven't withdrawn, haven't surrendered, and haven't recovered their critters. They didn't even acknowledge or ask for more time. Send this location," she pointed her finger again, within a red sphere, "to our forces and fire the Hull Hammer."

The admiral passed this order on. Half a minute later, a low-pitched noise blasted from somewhere forward in the sub. It sounded as if someone had compressed a foghorn to a short, electronic pulse of noise. Brenna felt it shake her bones.

As a scientist had explained to her, the Hull Hammer was a coordinated set of these pulses. Each sub in Halcyone's force emitted a similar tone, all precision-timed to arrive together at a specific point—the spot Halcyone had directed—with magnified power. To anyone else in this sector of ocean, it would seem like several loud, short, foghorns. But to anyone unlucky enough to be at the designated point...

Muffled booms came over a nearby speaker, and it seemed redundant for the sonarman to report, "Implosion. I'm hearing breaking-up noises on that bearing."

Minutes later, the Republic of Vitiaz surrendered.

So it had been for months now, Brenna reflected as she took notes documenting the occasion. Halcyone's underwater armada defeated seastead after seastead, conquering a new aquastate every few months. Each time she did, the newly subjugated state became part of her empire, paying taxes and earning her protection. The remnants of each defeated fleet joined hers.

The first few of these conquests had gone off with little trouble, Kernaria and Spectruma simply agreed to merge with Manahiki. Gallego and Quebrada had fallen next after brief resistance. The last several aquastates put up a real fight, but each had succumbed in their turn. Word had gotten around about Halcyone's treatment of defeated countries; she allowed them to keep a number of their own leaders and most of their laws. So far, this had helped minimize internal friction in the Empire.

"I'll accept their formal surrender tomorrow," Halcyone told the admiral. "Please make the arrangements. For now, I'll be in my cabin."

The admiral smiled and acknowledged the order.

When Halcyone turned, Brenna spoke. "May I have a word, Excellency? In your stateroom?"

"Of course, Brenna. Come." The empress beckoned her. Halcyone's step seemed close to a strut, Brenna thought as she followed her sister down the passageway. The exertions of battle might leave most people exhausted but Halcyone drew energy from it.

"All right, sister," Halcyone said once both of them had entered her stateroom. The empress sat on her bed and indicated by hand for

Brenna to sit in a chair. Large for a submarine cabin, the compartment still seemed cramped and very spartan in style. A single brass plaque had been affixed to one bulkhead, a plaque with the children's rhyme, 'I wish, I wish upon a fish' etched on it. "Make it quick." Halcyone said. "You're holding up my post-battle entertainment."

"I'm sorry." Brenna knew how Halcyone used sex to reward whichever submarine captain in her fleet showed the most fighting spirit during the day's battle.

"I imagine," Brenna said, "some of your captains think they'll father the one foretold by prophesy." Oceanists had long predicted that one day a demi-god would be born with functional gills for breathing seawater. Halcyone had encouraged Brenna to spread the rumor that her neck marks were, in fact, half-formed gills. She'd even gotten a doctor to testify to it. This further enhanced her mystique, drew people to her, and caused many to believe the spreading of Oceanism to be the main reason for the Manihiki expansion.

Halcyone threw back her head as she laughed at this comment, revealing the faded scars. "I'm glad that myth still works. You're one of the few who knows these aren't gills. What you don't know is that I got my tubes tied years ago; I'll never have children, let alone the prophesied one."

Before Brenna could react, Halcyone sobered. "But you didn't want to talk to me about that. What's on your mind?"

Even though Brenna had prepared her thoughts, she still found it difficult to say the words aloud. "It's all happened so fast, all this." She swept her hand toward the chart on the bulkhead showing the ever-widening expanse of the Manihiki Empire in the central Pacific. "In the rush of things, I've drifted from where I wanted to be. I'm not a journalist anymore, not even your biographer, really. I'm nothing but a propaganda minister now, putting out more outrageous lies every week." She'd admired Halcyone, and been blinded by that admiration. Brenna saw that now. But the empress had a dark side and she'd done ugly things along the way. Brenna didn't want to be dragged farther into that abyss.

"You want out," Halcyone tapped her lips while considering this. "You realize, of course, there are many who covet what you have—close and frequent access to me. I grant you that access because you're my sister; we've shared everything, grown up together." She turned away. "But it would be troublesome to have a journalist of your knowledge and skill out loose, separate from my inner circle. Have you ever noticed how few such people there are? Ever wondered why?"

Brenna wondered if Halcyone had been silencing dissent somehow, perhaps by ordering troublemakers jailed, or killed. Brenna had begun to regret writing the hero-worshipping article that started it all. "Are you threatening me, Halcyone? Because there was a time, back when I was a beginning journalist and you a low-ranking submariner, when—"

"Don't go any further with that, sister." Halcyone's dark blue eyes narrowed a fraction and the shark tattoo on her arm glowed crimson. "If you think you created me with that frothy article of yours, you're wrong. You helped, yes, but I would have gotten here without you. Let's be clear about that. As to threatening you, well, you can take it how you like. I'm only saying it would be better for you and your family if you stayed on my staff."

And there it was. Taken aback, Brenna understood in that moment she had not been an observer, admiring the passing of a mighty blue whale. Instead, she'd been swept along, grabbed a whale right by the tail, as the nursery rhyme went. There could be no letting go.

Brenna's netphone buzzed, and the screen showed it to be an emergency call. She excused herself from J-Mom's bedside and went to the sea-hospital's waiting room to answer the call.

Halcyone's face appeared on the screen, looking haggard. "Brenna, I don't have long to talk."

In Halcyone's background, someone said, "Passing two thousand meters." The empress looked off screen and snapped, "Belay those depth reports."

"What happened?" Brenna asked, beginning to worry.

"The Alliance hit us," Halcyone said. "Hard. Some kind of new weapon we haven't seen before." She frowned. "It looks like this is it."

Brenna understood then. Halcyone's sub was sinking, unable to regain control. Her forces must have been defeated. Brenna herself would have been aboard, except that J-Mom had become very ill, so they'd substituted a different biographer for this campaign to allow her to be by Jallulah's side.

"What statement do you want me to put out?" Brenna asked.

Halcyone gave a slight smirk. "I don't really care."

"But what's to become of the empire now?"

"Why, it collapses, of course." Halcyone shrugged. "My remaining admirals are all too weak to rule in my place."

Brenna stared in shock, unable to respond. At age forty-nine, Halcyone led the largest empire the world had ever known, stretching across the Pacific, spanning South America, and extending into vast sections of the South Atlantic. In recent years, the battles had been increasingly hard-fought, and the rest of the world's countries—both lander nations and aquastates—had banded together into an alliance to oppose her.

Behind Halcyone, a tech said, "Passing design crush depth, Empress."

"It collapses," Brenna repeated Halcyone's words as she felt her eyes fill with tears. "I don't understand. What's it all been about? What was the point?" At various times, her own propaganda had declared the empress to be promoting the Oceanism religion, to be spreading Manihikan culture, to be uniting the aquastates against the landers, and to be establishing great seasteads.

"Shut up and listen, sis," Halcyone leaned closer to her screen. "I don't have much time. Remember the song we used to sing as little girls? I want you to sing it with me now. I wish, I wish upon a—"

"Halcyone, I don't...it's just a silly song for kids." Brenna was crying now.

"Sing it!" The empress gave her that commanding glare. "And really listen to the words."

Brenna joined in the song, though some parts came out as sobs.

> "I wish, I wish, upon a fish,
> To grab a whale right by its tail,
> And ride the tide 'cross ocean's wide,
> Dance in the deep before I sleep."

"Thanks, sis," Halcyone smiled. "Did you ever know anyone who followed that wish better than me? I guess I'm gonna learn to dance in the deep next."

Her flowing tears blurred Halcyone's image on the screen. Brenna covered her mouth and shook her head. "No, sis," she spoke softly through her sobs. "Nobody ever followed that song better than you."

The screen switched to a text display: Connection Lost.

Some Time Together

***R**ule One of combat, Lieutenant Zolin Merlo thought—*
never send a copilot on a mission with a pilot he hates. *I guess
I don't* hate *her, exactly, but she registers pretty high on my dislike meter.*

He banked their craft left to join the squadron as it formed up,
and to clear the path for the two remaining fighters to launch. After
that, the temporary runway would submerge again, hiding Seastead
Pelagia under the sea.

Zolin's aversion to Lieutenant Delfia Guerrero sprang partly
from a personality conflict and partly from her oddball religion.
Why the command saw fit to assign such opposites together in one
vehicle, he'd never know. How she'd ever managed to graduate from
the Academy at all made an even bigger mystery.

With the squadron fully formed, the leader changed course
to the West and Zolin followed in turn. At the pre-mission brief, the
squadron commander had imposed strict radio silence except in
emergency, and early maneuvers were known to everyone.

He stole a glance at Delfia in the seat to his left and winced
inside at what he saw. Light blue skin and matching hair, webbed
fingers on both hands, and the squadron insignia standing out as a
black tattoo on her right forearm. As a religion, Oceanism seemed silly
to Zolin, but those adherents who dyed their skin and webbed their

digits truly repulsed him. Kind of a shame, really, since she might even be attractive but for all that sky-blue cultish nonsense.

Long range radar started picking up a massive cloud of dots to the west, stretching like a straight, impenetrable wall. Zolin sensed Delfia stiffen and look at him, so he met her glance without a word. The enemy. A huge, opposing force.

Zolin gritted his teeth, thinking of one other thing that bothered him about her. That tensing, and the little fidgeting she did, weren't signs of fear. He'd learned she loved the fight, craved battle, and lived for war. She'd taken reckless chances in the simulator time after time. Sure, she'd scored well, but one day her lack of reasonable caution and flouting of established doctrine would kill her and her copilot. He hoped today would not be that day.

The radar cloud resolved into triangular blips, hundreds of them. *Ay Dios!* They must have sent the whole Manihikan Air Force against them. Zolin's and Delfia's aquastate, Gallego, could only muster five squadrons of twenty-five fighters each. No wonder the Manihiki aquastate had succeeded in spreading, expanding through the ocean, gobbling up seastead after seastead with numbers that overwhelmed all defenses. Led by their maniacal dictator, Halcyone Tillerman, they advanced like a tidal wave.

Rule Two of combat, Zolin consoled himself—victory doesn't always go to the side with greater numbers. Other factors such as intelligent tactics and iron discipline could prevail. Manihiki must fall sometime, and perhaps in this battle, they would at last.

A glance at the virtual, holographic readout confirmed weapon status showed green across the board. Railgun, lasers, missiles, and short-range guns all checked out okay. Zolin gazed at the fighters arrayed to either side and wished once again he could fly one of those, rather than the experimental craft he and Delfia flew. They'd been picked for Bolador One, the first combat flying submarine. A stupid concept, Zolin thought, marrying two opposite types of craft together. With all the engineering and design compromises, it meant the stupid thing couldn't perform either function well. Though he and Delfia had cross-trained for both air and undersea combat, he preferred the sky and she the ocean.

More fidgeting from the seat beside him. Delfia was actually grinning as they neared weapon range to the enemy. She *loved* being assigned to this unproven kludge of a craft. Sure, it probably enhanced *her* career, such as that was. The assignment came as an unwelcome interruption to his, though. He should be commanding one of the sleek, fast, agile fighters, a true master of the air, rather than this stubby, inappropriate melding of sea and sky. Even the stupid name, Bolador, was Filipino for flying fish, Zolin recalled, a name unlikely to provoke fear in any enemy's soul.

The railgun's range indicator flicked from amber to green and Zolin fired at a target he'd picked earlier. Bolador One shuddered as the electromagnets sent a projectile at Mach 8. A moment later, the fighter to their right disintegrated as an enemy's railgun slug slammed through it.

Zolin jinked right to fill the gap and sensed an unheard whoosh as a railgun projectile meant for them screamed past.

"Flotz!" Delfia said, but kept any further thoughts to herself.

A moment after that, she said, "Laser on us."

"Got it," Zolin answered, keeping irritation in check. She should have known he'd seen the warning lights. If the enemy laser stayed locked for five seconds, it might melt through. He released a missile programmed to follow the Manihikan fighter's laser toward its source and swerved left.

He scanned the battlespace. Formation integrity had broken up as both lines met and the melee began, each fighter on its own to kill the enemy and avoid collisions or firing at friendlies.

Zolin focused on his zone of control, banking and swooping to seek and engage enemy fighters, loosing missiles, firing the machine gun, plunging and climbing to elude incoming fire. On occasion, Delfia aided him by pointing at something on the display he'd missed, but the air was his realm, not hers.

Around them, the skies darkened from the smoke of explosions, crisscrossed by beams of laser light and lit by the flaring blasts of missile strikes. Downward spirals and arcs of smoke marked the final trails of dying aircraft.

With missiles nearly out, Zolin switched to the laser, supplemented by the guns. He searched for damaged enemy aircraft, hoping the laser could down them with only brief exposure.

By instinct, he knew the moment to break off to evade return fire. Missiles zinged past, but some enemy gunfire got through. Damage warnings lit up the virtual display.

"All Gallego squadrons break off, break off immediately," a voice on the radio spoke. "Head back to base if able. Bolador One, you are ordered below. Subron Nine requires assistance. All other craft—"

The message broke off and Zolin hoped it had not been due to the explosion to his left. Following orders, he descended, lowered the landing skis and slowed to lessen their impact with the water.

When they hit at the optimum entry angle, the tough little craft took the jolt and Zolin felt all his air rush from his lungs, but the bags deployed to restrain him.

When the impact bags deflated, he heard the hiss of the magneto-turbines giving up their heat to the ocean and saw the waves lapping over their plastonium viewing bubble.

He turned to Delfia. "Your show, Lieutenant."

"Couldn't let you have all the fun," Delfia Guerrero looked at her copilot. "You did all right up there."

She saw him shrug and relax in his seat. His flight suit collar had darkened with sweat. With his curly black hair and penetrating brown eyes, he might have been handsome, except for being such a stiff, rule-bound pain in the ass. Still, he'd put in a good fight and downed five enemy fighters. He'd become an ace now. But still a jerk.

She turned to the virtual instruments, displayed as see-through hologram images, and darkened all other lighting in their bubble. The message had said Submarine Squadron Nine needed help, and by Oceanus, she was going to give it.

The bladeless, magneto-hydrodynamic turbines had cooled for subsea use, so she fired them up again. Number two showed only eighty nine percent efficiency; it must have taken a hit. Torps five and thirteen, two of her twenty mini-torpedoes, indicated as nonfunctional. All others showed green, though, and the hull wasn't leaking, so she had more than enough to join the fight.

She grabbed the stick and angled them downward. Other than muffled explosions and the impact splashes of downed aircraft, silence ruled. Darkness settled over them and she dimmed the display lighting to minimum.

They'd entered her world now.

Delfia felt a familiar twinge of electric connection, more imagined than real, as she merged with her vessel. The sonar became her eyes, the fuel cells her heart, the turbine propulsors her legs, and the torps her hands. One with the machine.

And Zolin in the seat to her right? He seemed an irritant, that out-of-place, irregular grain of sand which nags at the smooth, fleshy surfaces of the oyster.

Why the command had assigned Zolin as her copilot, Oceanus only knew. She'd been the top mini-sub pilot of her squadron, or any squadron, and had learned all the aerial stuff well enough to take Bolador One out solo. She really didn't need a copilot at all.

True, he'd been a top fighter pilot, and had done well today. *But I might have done even better.*

Bearing lines to torps and other subs appeared on the screen. She altered course to let the ranges resolve. All distant, so she goosed the throttles to hasten toward the action.

Delfia didn't mind his standoffish nature, or the way he looked down at her. He was smart, and it was in the nature of smart people to act condescending.

No, what got to her was his lack of warrior spirit. He seemed to treat this as a job, something to do to keep money flowing to his account. He showed no hatred for the enemy, no zeal for combat. His unemotional demeanor might point to a lack of commitment to the fight if push came to total knock-down. Fluke it, she just didn't know if she could count on him.

There was that foghorn pulse again, the one she'd heard just before the last implosion. Other tones of different frequencies joined in, and the sea thrummed with the clash of slightly offset tones.

A series of sickening booms marked the implosions and breaking-up noises of another Gallegan sub.

Flotz! This was the rumored Hull Hammer of the Manihikan sub forces. They coordinated sonic pulses in timing and pitch so the noise would concentrate into an enormous pressure spike at one precise location, that of an enemy sub. It was akin to the shockwave lithotripsy procedure doctors used to disintegrate kidney stones.

Against it, the Gallegan forces had no defense. Worse, they'd been unable to duplicate the weapon themselves.

One thing Delfia knew as she loosed two torps at the nearest enemy sub, now in range, the Manihikans couldn't wield the Hull Hammer if they didn't have enough subs located at optimum points. Maybe she could break up that network.

She set course toward the next enemy sub, zig-zagging at random times and directions so they'd be unable to target her. When well within range, she fired torps again.

Bolador One was smaller than every other sub in the battle, though faster and more maneuverable. However, each sub had released numerous unmanned vehicles, all smaller than Delfia's vessel, all roaming about looking for manned subs to attack. She had to avoid these robotic vehicles while attacking only the manned enemy subs.

Among the compromises forced on Bolador One's designers was the lack of room or weight capacity to carry any of her own unmanned vehicles, beyond simple torps and anti-torps. Moreover, hers were merely mini-torpedoes, and it would take a large salvo of them to destroy a full-size sub.

Delfia set her anti-torps to fully automatic so they'd respond by launching themselves at any detected threat without her direction.

The undersea battle differed greatly from the earlier air skirmish. Everything moved like molasses. This underwater struggle raged in utter blackness, and could only be heard, not seen. Kills were marked by implosions, not explosions, with the gruesome sound of hulls and interior tanks collapsing.

Delfia weaved Bolador One between and among the Manihikan subs, slinging torps in every direction, trusting anti-torps to protect her from incoming weapons and robots.

At one point she caused their vessel to ride upward at the bottom of the huge bubble resulting from the implosion of an enemy sub beneath. This confused several enemy torps enough that they turned away to search elsewhere.

Minutes later she ducked in just behind an enemy, right behind its propulsors where she couldn't be heard and where no enemy dared shoot. When the sub ahead brought her to a prime tactical position to rejoin the fray, she launched two weapons and peeled away, out of the wake.

"Out of antis," Zolin said without emotion.

Delfia grunted that she'd heard him, but it irked her that he'd felt the need to tell her.

She shot her last two torps at the nearest enemy sub, then frowned as the display showed two inbound torpedoes on her tail.

"See those?" Zolin pointed to the sonar screen.

"Yup." She watched the dots closing in and heard the whine of their propellers.

"You gonna—"

"Yeah. Hang on." Closer…closer… She saw Zolin tense in his seat, gripping the armrests. With seconds to go, Delfia burped their reserve air, causing a large bubble to rise from their location, and cut engines.

She saw the torps angle toward the bubble, strike it, and explode. Bolador One got buffeted, but sustained no damage. *Thank Oceanus.*

Zolin wiped his brow and blew out a breath. "Lucky."

She grinned at him while scanning the sonar display. "It's called skill." Few friendlies appeared on the screen.

"Let's vamoose before they target us with the Hull Hammer," Zolin said.

"They can't target us if I keep changing directions." The sonar showed enemy subs and unmanned vehicles all around them. *A target-rich environment. Sweet.* "All right, who wants to be next?"

"What the flotz? Have you gone squido?" Beside her, Zolin sounded incredulous. "We're out of weps, Lieutenant. Time to pack it in."

Sometimes you can be such a jelly. "We still have your air weps. Will the railgun work underwater?"

He shook his head. "Doubt it. It's not designed—"

"You didn't say no." She jabbed a button and a thunderous roar deafened her for a moment. Her sonar screen went white. When it cleared, she noted the enemy sub ahead had imploded.

"You melted our railgun," Zolin pointed at the cluster of red panel lights. "It'll never fire again."

"Neither will that sub. Worth it."

No more subs from Gallego's Squadron Nine remained in action, and some of the enemy had left the battlefield to press the attack against the seastead itself.

"Oh, no you don't," she said, and gunned the turbines to follow.

"Torps, incoming." Zolin pointed at the holo display.

Three of them had come from nowhere. She swerved, circled, spiraled, and reversed, but couldn't shake the weapons.

One torpedo crossed her bow and she activated the remaining air missile, thanking Zolin in her mind for leaving her one last shot.

"Missiles won't work under—" Zolin began.

"Watch and learn, minnow," she said.

The missile dropped from Bolador One's stubby, swept-back wings and lit off. Much slower underwater, it nevertheless sped toward the torp and smashed into it, imploding it at a distance.

The two other torps still came on from behind, too close to avoid.

"Flotz!" she yelled as she blew ballast to lift her vessel at the last second.

The exploding torpedoes felt like a titanic sledge-hammer striking them from beneath. Delfia blacked out.

"Lieutenant?" He patted her blue-dyed cheek, but her eyelids remained shut. "You hear me? Wake up." Delfia had been breathing but unconscious when he'd woken up.

He slapped her harder and both her eyes opened. He noticed for the first time how closely her eye color matched that of her skin. *Knowing her, she'll probably demand a situation report first thing.*

"Ow. Flotz it. I'm awake," she said, then coughed. "Sitrep, Lieutenant."

Knew it. "We're bottomed and half-flooded at a depth of 983 meters. Propulsion's out. Atmosphere control is gone. Emergency batt is at ninety percent. We've got sonar, and all contacts have left the area."

She shook her head. "Turned tail and ran, did they?" She moved her hands, and looked down at the water that filled their cockpit to their waists. "Is the emergency buoy up and working?"

"Haven't tried it yet. Figured I'd wake you up first."

She nodded. "Pop the buoy."

He reached a wet hand out of the water, which had stopped rising, and touched the virtual display. Nothing happened.

She looked at him, reached above his head and banged on the overhead with her fist. He heard a faint clank, then the sound of unspooling cable.

"Must've gotten stuck," she said.

"Yeah." *The ops manual says nothing about banging on things.* Perhaps the buoy wasn't the only thing stuck and in need of jarring loose. "Look, about that battle. I need to tell you—"

"Forget it. Happens to the best."

"Huh?"

"You know," she said, "thinking things are hopeless when they're not. Giving up. You don't have to apologize for it."

"I wasn't going to apologize. I was...never mind." He'd wanted to offer some praise for how she fought the battle, her unconventional tactics and perseverance. If not for her launching that final missile underwater, they'd probably be dead.

"What?" She pressed.

"Buoy's topside," he changed subjects. "What do you want to send?"

"Tell 'em our location and situation and request rescue ASAP. Coded burst transmission only."

Zolin did so, then called up a couple of equations on the virtual display and entered some numbers.

"What's all that?" Delfia asked.

"Well—" he began, then the voice reply to their radio message came in.

"Pelagia now under attack. Can't send (garbled) to you. Relayed your request to Seastead Gofaria. Earliest (garbled) rescue UUV to your location is five hours. Good luck. Out."

"That squirts ink, doesn't it?" she asked.

Zolin looked at the result of the final equation. "Flotz. This isn't good either."

"What?"

"Remember when I said atmosphere control is out?"

Fear shown in her eyes. "You're saying we'll run out of oxygen?"

"No, no. We have plenty of O_2. Remember the training on emergency situations?" He couldn't help feeling a little superior.

"Must have slept through it."

"It's the carbon dioxide. We're CO_2 factories, you and I. It's toxic in high concentrations. If CO_2 gets to ten percent in here, we die. According to this equation, it'll get there in three hours."

"But the rescue UUV doesn't get here for five hours."

"Right. At the earliest." He could tell she was working through the implications.

"What if we both went to sleep? We'd make less CO_2, right?"

164

"A bit less, yeah. That would take us out to about four hours."

"Not long enough." Her blue eyes seemed to search his, looking for a spark of hope, a solution.

"Nope. Not enough, unless you're one of those *aquans* I've heard about." There had long been rumors that scientists could enable certain rare people to breathe water as well as air. Sea stories, myths, with no proof.

"No such luck." Delfia flicked her hair away from her neck. "No gills. You're saying one of us has to stop making CO_2 so the other can survive."

"That's right." He watched to see if her hands moved, if she'd make some effort to unsheathe a knife. She didn't.

"Oh, come on. There's got to be some other way, for Oceanus' sake."

"There isn't. And appealing to some deity won't help."

"Oceanus isn't..." She trailed off, looked at him with narrowed eyes, then signed. "Look, you and I have never gotten along. I don't know all the reasons and right now, I don't care. But I'm not the flotzing enemy, okay? I'm on your side. We're a team." She looked around and splashed one hand in the water. "A broken-down, dysfunctional, distrustful team, I'll grant you. But a team. We've gotten out of some tough scrapes today, you and I. We can figure our way out of this one."

"You don't understand." He shook his head. "Math equations aren't rules you can flout. No happy team talk will help us 'figure our way out of this.'" *Rule Three of Combat—people die in war.* "Worse, all this arguing only increases our breathing and makes even more CO_2."

"You're a defeatist," she sneered. "You're just giving up. Again."

"I'm a realist. You've always just gotten by, with your rule bending and your cock-sure attitude. Well, you've met your match this time. You can't ignore these cold facts." He jabbed at the holographic equations. They flickered, blurred, then snapped back into focus.

"We'll see about that." She hit a virtual button to record a message to base. She explained the situation, listing broken equipment. "Please advise on possible options allowing both of us to survive." She hit the buttons to send focused, burst transmissions to both Pelagia and Gofaria.

"Now," she turned to him. "Let's go over this in more detail. First, how long can we both sit here yakking before one of us has to die?"

"Another hour, but then one of us has to…stop making CO_2."

"And we're too deep to ascend using the escape gear."

"Right. It's only rated for fifty meters."

"And there's no way to pump or blow out all this water?"

"Right again. The emergency batt doesn't have enough power to start pumps, and we used the last of our ballast air during the battle."

Delfia frowned at him.

"I'm not blaming, just saying."

"Can we remove the CO_2 somehow?"

"Normally yes, but the CO_2 scrubber is beyond repair, and under water. Even if we could fix it, we'd need more than the emergency battery to run it. They should have given us lithium hydroxide canisters as a backup, but to save weight they didn't."

"In your equation, it looks like you calculate the time left using the volume of air, the percent CO_2 we can stand, the number of people, and our breathing rate."

"Yeah." He sighed, having thought through every factor already. "If we could increase the volume, or the level of CO_2 we can stand, or decrease our breathing rate enough, we might make it."

Biting her lip, Delfia looked down. "The only other factor, the only one we can control, is the number of us. One survives, two don't."

The silence that followed felt deep and lonely to Zolin, disturbed only by their breathing and a soft dripping from somewhere.

The radio sounded like a raucous din when the voice crackled to life. "This is Seastead Gofaria. Pelagia has fallen. We've managed to hold off the Manihikan forces for the time being and we now serve as the capital of Gallego. We've been apprised of your situation, and our rescue UUV should reach your location in four and a half hours. We've been considering your problem and have no solution that permits both of you to live. We'll keep working on the problem, but a more favorable answer is doubtful. Sorry for the bad news. Good luck, Bolador One. Gofaria out."

Zolin looked at Delfia, and it seemed as if all her bravado had drained out. Her eyebrows curved in worry, and she looked scared for the first time since he'd known her. Strangely pretty, but scared. He clicked the transmit button twice to acknowledge without speaking.

He let the deep stillness lengthen, then said, "Pelagia fell. It's under Manihikan control now."

Her eyes narrowed and she looked at him with suspicion. "You know, if you kill me, you'll be court-martialed. Did you know that?"

That had not even occurred to him. "I'm just saying we can't go back to Pelagia again, not with Empress Halcyone Tillerman in charge. The rumor is that she doesn't kill military people who give up, so maybe our friends are safe."

She spoke softly. "You *want* to kill me, don't you?"

Zolin thought a moment. "No, I don't. I admit things would be better for me with you dead, and better for you with me dead. But I don't want you to die by my hand. It's not a court martial I'm afraid of, but my own conscience."

She sighed, perhaps with some relief, and looked out into the black depths. "I feel the same way. That means one of us must commit suicide to save the other."

"Looks that way." Zolin tried to think of the fairest way to make that awful decision.

"That means," she stretched one of her blue hands toward a small pouch mounted near her side of the seal where the plastonium bubble met the rest of the hull, "it's me who has to die."

"What? No, it doesn't mean that at all." Zolin grasped her arm. He knew the two pouches, one on each side, contained emergency items such as lights, and food, but also a small knife and a pistol. "Why would you think that?"

She shrugged. "It's in the regs."

He snorted. "There's no regulation like that."

"The captain is supposed to be the last to leave a ship," she said. "I'm the pilot, the closest thing we have to a captain."

"That's not a reg. It's an old custom."

"Okay, how about this?" She gave him a stern frown. "As the officer in command of Bolador One, I order you to allow me to commit suicide."

"No," he said. "We can't decide it that way. This is too important. We have to come up with a fair way, one with equal chances, one we both agree to."

Delfia looked at him for a long time. Was there, he wondered, a glimmer of relief there? "What do you have in mind?"

"A coin flip."

She half-smiled, a facial expression that looked good in blue. "Bring a coin?"

"I never fly without my lucky squadron coin." Zolin pulled the oversized coin from his pocket, really a memento bearing the squadron emblem on one side and the Gallegan Navy emblem on the other. "Where's yours?"

"Lost in a bar bet," she shook her head.

Zolin couldn't imagine betting his coin on some trivial matter but could well see her doing so. No doubt her reckless and risk-taking nature extended beyond the battle arena. Too bad her luck hadn't.

"By the way, why does Lieutenant Rational have a *lucky* coin?" Her eyes twinkled as she grinned.

"In the sim, I found I did better with the coin and worse without it." He shrugged, "It stopped being superstitious and started being rational."

"Is it a fair coin?"

"Let's find out." He flipped it ten times, being careful not to let it plop in the water. Ten times he tossed it, arcing up from his right thumb, over and down to his left palm. The heads of the squadron side appeared six times, and the tails of the Gallegan Navy four.

"Fair enough," she said.

"If we do this," he held up the coin to her, "we do it based on one flip alone. No 'best-two-out-of-three' and no switching to drawing straws or some other thing. One flip and that's it. Agreed?"

He caught the flash of irritation in her eyes. *Doesn't like me setting the terms.* But the sharpness eased as she saw the logic. She nodded. "One flip. And if you flip it, then I call it in the air. If it lands the way I call it, I live. If not, I die. Fair?"

Zolin gulped. Something so easy to talk about became tough to really absorb, to appreciate in his gut. Their lives hinged on the spinning of a small metal disk. Either way it landed, one of them must die. "Yeah, that's fair. Ready?" He got the coin in position atop his right thumb.

"Wait." She put her blue, webbed hand over the coin. "How much longer do we have together? I mean, before one of us has to..."

"Half an hour. But the CO_2 symptoms will be affecting us more by then. We'll be getting headaches, dizziness, and twitching. Later we'll be nauseous and have trouble breathing."

"I don't care. Don't flip the coin until then. There's no need for us to know right now which one of us has to die."

"Okay. What do you want to do?" He almost added, *play a hand or two of poker?* but refrained.

"I thought," she looked down at the control stick in front of her, "we could tell each other messages to pass on to family and other loved ones." At the last two words her eyes looked up and into his, but only for an instant before looking down again.

"Final messages," Zolin said.

"That's right. You first."

"Me? Well, okay." He stared out into the black abyss and imagined his family. "I don't know. Just tell my family I loved them."

"Who's in your family?"

"There's Mamá and Papá, and my older brother, Acalan."

"Acalan and Zolin. From *A* to *Z*, eh? What does Acalan do?" She looked at him with genuine interest.

"He works for Military R&D. He develops new technologies to win the war for Gallego. Or he did until today, until Pelagia fell."

"I've heard of him, I think. Dr. Merlo is your brother?"

"Yes." Once again, resentment stirred inside Zolin. Everyone knew his brother, it seemed.

"Wow. How much older is he?"

"Six years."

"And a scientist. I've heard he's very smart."

"I suppose so. He thought up the idea for our bladeless turbine-propulsors." He pointed down and outboard to where the huge cylinders lay, probably half-buried in ooze.

"The technology that made this flying sub possible." She leaned away from him and looked at him with an appraising eye. "That explains..."

"What?"

"Nothing." Delfia blinked and looked away, then put a webbed hand to her temple. "I think the high CO_2 is getting to me. I've got a headache and I'm not thinking straight. But don't worry. If you're the one who loses the coin flip, I'll tell your family you love them."

"You might have to go to Ilhuicaltepetl to do that. I'd expect them to move back if they're allowed to."

"Your family is Aztec?"

Zolin shrugged. "We're a mix. Papá thought he had more Aztec blood than Hispanic, so he moved to Ilhuicaltepetl where he met Mamá. The family moved to Gallego later." He didn't need to add why. The resurrection of an Aztec country at the aquastate of Ilhuicaltapetl had proven an economic failure, and the Manihikans had already overrun it.

Delfia nodded.

He glanced at the clock portion of the holo display. When it flickered, he rapped on the hologram projector and the image steadied. "Not much time left. Tell me the messages you want me to give."

She sat a little straighter in her seat. "Tell the rest of the squadron, whoever remains, that I did my best to honor them and all of Gallego."

When she fell silent, he asked, "That's it? What about your family?"

"I have no message for them." Her mouth formed a straight line and her jaw was firm.

"Really?" Then he had a thought. "Are they..."

"My parents are still alive, but they didn't want me converting to Oceanism, so we don't talk. I had a twin sister—Sofia—but the Manihikans killed her five months ago."

Zolin looked but saw no sadness in her expression, no tears forming in her eyes. Her air of determination was scary in its ferocity. *"Qué horror,"* he said softly. He understood now why she was so tough, why she had to be. He also realized some of the depth of her loathing for the Manihikan aquastate. "I'll...I'll pass your message to the squadron."

"Time's running out." She nodded at the holographic time counter, then shivered. "And it's getting cold. I'm glad I got a chance to know you better. I only wish I'd taken the time to do that before today."

"Me too." He smiled at her. "Are you ready for this?"

"Flip it," she said. "It's not going to get any easier."

His hands shook as he positioned the coin, but he knew it wasn't all due to the cold water. His head pounded with a painful headache and breathing had become more difficult; he needed to take a few breaths before tossing the coin in the air.

It arced up, tumbling as it went, both its faces reflecting the display lights as it turned over and over.

"Tails," Delfia called, and Zolin had just time to recall that tails had come up only four times in their ten-flip trial. To the end, she'd wanted to give him the edge.

The coin dropped into his left palm.

Tails.

"Tails, I lose," he said, and reached for his emergency pouch, where the dive knife was located.

"Zolin, no. Let's—"

"We agreed," he told her. "One flip only." He opened the pouch and found the knife. It had a sharp, pointed tip, and a serrated cutting edge. One stab to his heart should do it. "Please deliver my message."

He looked and saw she was crying. Lieutenant Delfia Guerrero, the toughest warfighter in the squadron, sat bawling her eyes out. She held her blue, webbed hands to her face, but that couldn't hide her tears. He wished he could stay alive then, for she seemed beautiful somehow, and it would have been so good to see if she could find a way to like him as much as he liked—no, *loved*—her.

He held the knife before him, its tip aimed at the left side of his chest. This would be the most difficult thing he'd ever done, and he wondered for a moment whether it was worse for Delfia. She'd be left behind to remember this moment forever.

The instrument holograms flickered again, and then went out. Emergency lights remained on but seemed dimmer. As he'd learned from Delfia, Zolin wacked the holo projector, but nothing happened.

Mounted next to the holo projector sat his escape gear, in its storage bag. "Escape," he read in the faint light. *Something about that gear.* His thoughts formed slowly, and he frowned with the effort.

"What?" she asked, following his glance. "You said the escape gear wouldn't work at this depth."

He shook his head, then palmed his forehead, worsening his headache. "So stupid. Our escape gear is DIGMA." The DIving Gear Membrane Apparatus had replaced scuba technology years earlier. It used a nano-engineered membrane to filter entrained air from water. "Yeah, we can't use it to escape, but that's not our immediate problem. We just need to quit breathing air with so much CO_2 in it. Do you remember," he asked, "what DIGMA does with CO_2?"

"No." She shook her head. "You're the smart one."

"Water on one side of the membrane, right?" He tried to recall. "The air that's normally absorbed in water passes through so we can breathe it in. But the CO_2—"

"The CO_2 we exhale passes back through the membrane," Delfia parroted the words from a training lecture, "and—"

"—and gets absorbed in the water," Zolin finished. "We've got plenty of water here." He splashed it with one hand. "Enough to absorb the CO_2 from both of us, until that rescue UUV from Gofaria gets here. All we have to do is breathe through our regulators under the water until then." He patted the hull. "Like our Bolador, when we're underwater, we must be like a fish."

"You're a fluking genius, you know that?" She leaned over and kissed him. When the kiss went on and on, he felt her webbed hands running through his hair.

Then it was over. She backed away from him. "Hang on. How in Oceanus' name did you happen to think of the DIGMA thing? It's not covered by your equation at all."

"Maybe your happy team talk inspired me."

She resumed kissing him. *Rule Four of Combat—sometimes the pressures of war can bring out the best in people.*

Five humming-cams from the major Gallegan news services, and seven more from others around the world, hovered just outside the window of the decompression chamber. Delfia watched them jostling for position as they tried to get pics of both her and Zolin while they rested and recovered in the chamber.

"Do you realize each of you is now a combat Ace?"

"Is it true you exceeded the time two people can breathe in a confined space? How did you do that?"

"How long will your decompression take?"

The questions seemed numerous and never-ending.

The unmanned underwater vehicle had rescued them and taken them to the Gofaria seastead, but since they'd been under pressure, they needed to recover in the treatment chamber to prevent decompression sickness. Compared to the cockpit of the Bolador One, this chamber was spacious, with chairs, a table, computer connectivity, and bunk beds.

From their military debrief, they'd learned how their battle, and the subsequent one at Pelagia, had depleted the Manihikan forces such that they'd abandoned Gallego for the time being. The Gallegan aquastate had reached out to other countries on land and at sea to form an alliance against Halcyone Tillerman's growing empire.

In answering the questions from the press, Delfia did most of the talking, because it was in her nature, and she couldn't very well let them find out he was the smart one. *He's not the sand grain in the oyster, he's the pearl.*

"It's been great talking to all of you," she said at last. "But I hope you understand, after what we've been through, Zolin and I need some time alone together." She winked for the cameras, muted the chamber's microphone, and pulled down the window's shade.

The Source

*T*o find his missing father, Adrian Penshell knew he must rent a submarine. *Why can't Mom understand that? Doesn't she care about Dad?*

"Last week they said it wasn't a rescue anymore," Adrian told his mother. "They've stopped searching altogether. They're convinced he's dead. *Somebody* has to look for him, and if I don't, nobody will."

She stood at the kitchen counter, preparing a seaweed and swordfish salad. "The UUVs will keep looking," she said. "They'll find him." Her glance flicked to the living room wall with its scrolling images and videos marking Adrian Senior's significant moments—lecturing at a scientific conference, posing with Oceanism's founder, pointing to key layers of a core sample, and giving guidance to the helmsman of a research submarine. Adrian Junior had never noticed it before, but the images all showed his father pointing, finger outstretched, directing or commanding, showing the way.

"The UUVs," he snorted and stood, thinking of the unmanned underwater vehicles the authorities deployed to continue the hunt. "They're just doing programmed search patterns." Too full of a twenty-year-old's energy to sit, he paced around the adjoined kitchen and living room, pausing to glance out the window of their Templemere seastead apartment module. The sea looked restless, agitated, swept one way by currents and the other way by wind. "It'll be months before they stumble on him. They don't know his methods of exploring vents like I do."

"Why don't you tell the police where to send the UUVs, then?" his mom asked. "There's no need for you to risk your life." An Oceanist, she'd undergone the Immersion procedure; she'd had her skin dyed sapphire blue to match her eyes, and she bore a seahorse tattoo on her forehead.

"Mom, this isn't something you do remotely. We've been waiting for others to find him, but they haven't. I have to take charge and go myself. It's what Dad would do if you or I were lost." Five years earlier, Adrian had chosen to have his skin dyed jade green and get an octopus tattoo to match his father's.

She shut her eyes and bowed her head. When she looked up, tears ran from both blue eyes. "I couldn't bear it if I lost you both. I couldn't."

Adrian stopped pacing and understood. For the first time he considered she might be right. Perhaps he shouldn't go. Soon, his determination returned and he racked his brain to think of one, final convincing argument. Against hers, though, there wasn't one.

He held both of her webbed hands and faced her. "You won't lose me, Mom. Dad's missing. Both of us need to know what happened to him. I have to do this."

"I don't like it." His mother looked up at him through her tears. "But I can't stop you. Please be careful, Adrian."

"If you can't help me," Adrian said to the bartender, "then may I speak to your manager, please?" Having come this far, he wasn't about to take no for an answer.

"Sure. I'll get him." The young woman leaned closer. "I want to help you, but we have a privacy policy." She went through a back door.

Adrian had travelled to six seasteads in four aquastates in the past two weeks. He'd questioned submersible repair technicians, supply store clerks, hotel receptionists, and seastead dockmasters. The trail had led him to the Blubbering Whale, a dingy bar in the aquastate of Quebrada.

The bartender came back and introduced the manager, but Adrian was too intimidated by the hulking guy's size to catch the name. This giant could have served as a bouncer, too, and probably did. He had blue skin with a forehead tattoo of a shark. An Oceanist.

He growled and leaned close to Adrian, "didn't my tap angel tell you—"

The bartender tugged his sleeve. "His dad is Adrian Penshell."

"Penshell?" he asked, rubbing his chin. "Hold your halyards. Isn't that the guy who—?"

Adrian nodded. Everyone had heard of his dad—a famous marine biologist and chief proponent of Oceanism's creation theory. Oceanism, the largest religion in most aquastates, maintained that the god Oceanus had created life at a single undersea hydrothermal vent, the Alpha Vent. The fourth prophesy of Oceanism predicted it would be found. Three months ago, Adrian Senior had gone missing while searching for it.

"And you're his spawn, huh?" The manager had pity in his eyes. He turned to the bartender. "He's a special case. If you know something, you can tell him."

She gave a nod. "Your father came in here with his crew about three months ago. I remember him 'cause of his picture in the news and 'cause he tipped well."

"What else do you remember?"

She shook her head. "Nothing. They were just typical customers."

Adrian sighed. "Did you hear them say anything in particular? Even something zany or odd?"

She shook her head, then stared into space and a smile formed. "There was something." A smile formed. "It's going to sound batfish crazy."

"Go on."

"They were sitting at that table right there, close to the bar, and at one point I kept hearing them say 'SpongeBob SquarePants,' only they seemed to be serious, not laughing, you know?"

"SpongeBob SquarePants? Are you sure?"

"Well, yeah. That topic doesn't come up often in this place, so it kinda stood out."

Adrian smiled and laid enough Quebradan pesos on the bar to cover the beer five times over. "Thank you. Believe it or not, you've been very helpful."

After leaving the Blubbering Whale, Adrian searched the online hydrothermal vent database for a feature called SpongeBob SquarePants. He'd known deep-ocean explorers often bestowed quirky names on their discoveries, names such as Scooby, Godzilla, and Salty Dawg. The United Nations Geographic Information Working Group discouraged such silliness, but dutifully registered the names if provided evidential documentation. In the database, Adrian found the SpongeBob SquarePants vent—the type known as a white smoker—and attempted to file a Float Plan with the dock-master in Quebrada.

"Your float plan's no good, not unless you sign this waiver." The dockmaster pushed an e-pad across the desk toward Adrian. "That location is in the middle of a declared war zone in Nazcator. Manihiki and the Alliance both have warsubs in that area. You can file your plan, but your insurance won't pay for death, injury, or damages. I'm required to notify your rental company, and you must sign this *no rescue* waiver."

Without hesitation, Adrian signed.

Five kilometers from the SpongeBob Vent, Adrian pushed his sub faster than the rental company's recommended cruising speed. Beyond the acrylic bubble viewport, a school of fish scattered from the glare of his external lights. His excitement increased as his chances of finding his father rose. Odds ran against his father and the small crew still being alive in their small submersible with limited food, drinkable water, and oxygen generating capability. But Adrian's father was intelligent and resourceful, so Adrian held out hope. So far, though, his sonar showed no returns indicating a downed submersible.

A blip did show moments later, but not that of his father's exploration vessel. This one moved fast, on an intercept course with Adrian. A military sub, most likely. He hoped they'd recognize his commercial active sonar as that of a rental sub and leave him alone.

The sub neared, slowing as it did. The sonar image indicated a craft not much larger than his own.

From the comms panel came a feminine voice, distorted by the blue-green laser transmission through water. "Unknown vessel off my port bow, this is Submarine November Seven Two Niner. Identify yourself."

Adrian had learned Spanish in school and understood her well enough, despite her clipped dialect. He picked up his underwater telephone microphone. "This is Adrian Penshell Junior, aboard an unarmed rental submarine on a peaceful exploratory mission." He took care in pronouncing his famous name and the words *unarmed* and *peaceful.*

"You're in a war zone," the woman said, without giving any sign she knew of his father. "Come to a stationary hover immediately or I will fire on you. Prepare for lock-on, boarding, and inspection."

Didn't she hear me? He keyed the mic. "I'm not your enemy. I just want to—"

"Tubes flooded, outer doors open, torps ready to fire," she said in a flat, firm tone.

Flotz. Adrian killed the thrusters and set his ballast control to hover. "You win. I'm ready for lock-on."

Her sub approached and Adrian saw it through his upper viewport. A sleek, silver, elongated teardrop, it glided under expert control. Half again as large as his one-person rent-a-sub, this vessel sported many shapes—circles, ovals, and rectangles—outlined in black on its hull, evidently openings or appendages its captain could close or retract to render them flush against its smooth surface. While he watched, circular weapon ports shut like eyelids. By comparison, his Harrison compact rental sub looked clunky and low-grade.

A cylindrical trunk exuded from the military sub's hull and formed a seal around his own upper hatch. Struts extended out and clamped his sub to hers with a series of clangs.

"How many people do you have aboard?"

"Just me," Adrian said.

"Open your upper hatch, then stand forward of it with your hands empty and extended so I can see them."

A minute later, an olive-skinned and athletically fit young woman wearing body armor stood before him. It looked like some drunk hairdresser had wreaked havoc on her black hair using blunt scissors. She wore no Oceanist body modifications.

She aimed her barb-pistol at his chest. "Where are you from, Mr. Penshell?"

If she'd heard of his dad, she would have known he hailed from the aquastate where Oceanism started. "Kernaria."

"Put your hands against the bulkhead and don't move."

While he did so, she conducted a search of his submersible, glancing at her hand-held scanner from time to time.

When she finished, she holstered her weapon and told him to relax. "You've strayed into a war, Mr. Penshell."

"I'm sorry. I'm just searching for—"

"I don't care. I'm taking you in so my people can arrange safe transit for you back to your home."

He shook his head in frustration. *Not now, when I'm so close.* "I'm no threat to you, or to anyone. I just want to—"

"No. You're coming with me. Am I going to have to handcuff you?" Her hand moved toward her pistol.

He glared. "You can't take me prisoner. I have rights."

"Rights?" She snorted. "Might makes right in a war zone. You're lucky I didn't implode you first. And I'm not taking you prisoner. Kernaria joined the Alliance two weeks ago, so you're not even a neutral; you're a friendly. That's why I'm being so gentle." She pointed up the ladder to her sub. "You're riding in my sub where I can watch you. Get going."

Gentle, she calls it. He climbed the ladder.

• • •

Spartan, functional, and clean, her sub's interior felt uninviting, cramped, and uncomfortable, all bare metal and right angles.

"Sit there. Strap in." She pointed to a seat with no controls or screens of its own, centered behind the two piloting chairs.

He did so. Behind him, she slipped off her body armor and stowed it in a locker. Her zippered red-and-white jumpsuit displayed the Nazcator emblem—the Nazca line drawing of a whale—above the left breast pocket but showed no military rank insignia anywhere. She squeezed past him and sat in the left pilot seat. Turning to glance at him, she said, "I'm Weps-Spec Mayu Villca, by the way." A corner of her mouth twitched upward. "Sorry for the shark-eye treatment, but I had to assume you were Manihiki until I could confirm otherwise."

"I understand, Mayu, but once you confirmed that, you could've just let me search for my father."

With his sub still attached to hers, she turned her vessel back in the direction she'd come from and increased speed. "I've heard of your father, but you picked the worst possible spot to go looking for him. I did you a favor. If the Manihikans had found you, well…they ask questions later."

"Did me a favor?" He glared at the back of her head and its poorly hacked hair. "I was doing just fine."

She spoke without looking at him. "This humanitarian rescue took me away from searching for the enemy. I don't expect gratitude, but right now I need you to tamp down your froth while we're in enemy waters."

Adrian fumed silently for a few minutes, then calmed. From what he'd heard of the Manihiki, she might have been right about how they would have treated him. At the moment, there seemed little point in antagonizing her. He could deal with her superiors later.

Visible through the viewport ahead, a vast school of jack mackerel parted all around them as their attached subs passed through it. It always fascinated him to see such swarming behavior, thousands of creatures flowing together as if a single, graceful entity danced and shifted shapes before him.

Mayu didn't seem inclined toward conversation as she monitored her instruments and steered her sub. Fifteen minutes passed in silence while Adrian wondered when he'd be able to resume his search. If only she hadn't spotted him, he'd probably have gotten to the vent by now, and perhaps even begun rescuing his father and his crewmembers from their trapped sub. He couldn't permit himself to believe his father was dead. Surely Adrian Senior had found some way to endure.

Adrian's thoughts turned to his mother. He hadn't contacted her in days. "I hate to interrupt you, but can I get a message to my mom?"

"Yeah. When we get to the c-sub."

"C-sub?"

"Colony submarine." She pointed ahead. "Look."

A huge shape loomed in their forward viewport.

"Mother of Neptune!" He leaned forward to get a better view. By far the largest submarine Adrian had ever seen, it seemed at first a colossal version of Mayu's mini-sub, gray-silver in color and teardrop shaped. As they drew closer, Adrian perceived it as an assembly, a collection of smaller units. Dozens—no, hundreds—of craft linked together to form this giant. The pieces ranged from tiny, unmanned vessels to subs twice the size of Mayu's. While he watched, transfixed, one submersible detached from the collective and two others docked in available niches.

"Wha-what's its name?" Adrian managed to ask.

"Naming it would be useless." Mayu maneuvered closer and engaged thrusters to nudge her sub sideways to nestle against the giant vessel. "At any time, it might split into fragments. Many of the unit subs you see may leave to join other c-subs. It depends on the needs of the Nazcator Fleet."

Shaking his head in amazement, Adrian puzzled over the idea of a gigantic submarine solely made up of smaller submarines. It seemed bizarre. Mayu had said she was a weapons specialist, and dozens of torpedo tube doors dotted her sub's outer hull. Perhaps all subs in the Nazcator Navy were similarly specialized, some for sonar, others for propulsion.

With a metallic thud, Mayu's sub latched to the c-sub. She powered down her electronics and unstrapped from her seat. "Come on. Let's get you to our admin group for processing. Then you'll be on your way, and I'll be back in the hunt."

As he undid his own seat restraints, Adrian reflected with disapproval on her eagerness to do battle. He harbored no desire to fight in a war and detested the whole notion of combat. War wasted lives, but religion and science saved and uplifted them. His dad had become a leader in both, and Adrian aspired to sail in his father's wake as best he could.

They exited through a side hatch and into another small submarine. People didn't look up at or speak as Mayu and Adrian passed through; the c-sub crewmembers stuck to their various tasks. He and Mayu entered another sub, and then another. Each featured a different layout and different equipment, but nobody greeted or even acknowledged Adrian and Mayu.

"There's no need to take me to your admin group," Adrian said to Mayu while she led him into another submarine. "Just show me the way to your commander. I can take it from there."

"Don't have one." She walked a short way and turned right toward yet another watertight door.

"Your supervisor or leader, then." Adrian tired from stepping through all the hatches and doors. "The one who gives you orders."

"No one gives us orders."

"You *are* in the military, right? Someone has to give the orders. How else would you know what to do?" At a hundred dinnertime discussions, Adrian's father had spoken of the importance of strong leadership. That, he'd said, was the most vital aspect of getting any large project done. Adrian yearned to be the type of leader his father had always been.

"Shh." She quieted him while they crossed through a sub devoted to crew quarters, a darkened space with curtained-off bunk beds. In the next one, the aroma of food greeted him, and he saw white-clad crewmen preparing meals.

"It's not like that with us," she said in answer to his question. "We don't do what others tell us. We each do what needs to be done."

To Adrian, that seemed a recipe for utter chaos, yet everyone he'd seen had been working at some task, or sleeping, or eating. No arguments, no shirking. He was about to ask how a c-sub could function without a captain, but Mayu suddenly stopped and he almost collided with her.

She held up her hand and stared into space. She frowned, then nodded and faced Adrian. "Change of plans. The Manihikans are attacking and the c-sub's dispersing. Come with me." She led him back in the direction they'd come from.

"What?" Adrian had heard no alarms, seen no flashing lights. "How do you know?"

Ahead of him, Mayu tapped her poorly shorn hair. "Implants. All Nazcatorans are linked, at least over a short range."

Now Adrian understood why he'd heard nobody talking aboard the c-sub except him and Mayu. "A hive mind."

Mayu laughed. "Nothing that creepy. We're still individuals. Watch your step over those cables."

The change became obvious to Adrian then. People now moved with a solemn purpose, each to their own mini-subs. The flow of personnel followed some logic invisible to him, no doubt agreed to within their mental network. He and Mayu never passed others going the opposite way. As they moved to the outer sectors of the c-sub, Adrian began to hear the muffled metallic sound of latches disengaging. "Why do I have to go with *you*? Can't I stay with one of the subs that's not fighting?"

She shook her head. "We all fight. Hurry up."

He hastened after her, struggling to grasp her answer. Thinking back to the galley sub and the sleeping quarters sub, he wondered how those could be expected to wage battle. Perhaps each sub, though marginally specialized for one thing, was still able to do all things to a limited extent. The c-sub, for all its unwieldy and labyrinthine hatches and doors, had traded efficiency for ultimate flexibility. On a moment's notice, this huge sub could become its own fleet.

Finally, they returned to Mayu's sub and she sealed the door behind them.

"Um…you know my rental sub is still attached below yours, right?" Adrian knew which seat to take, and buckled in.

"Yeah." Mayu moved with an astounding economy of effort, seeming to flow into her seat, strap in, and energize her panels and displays in one combined motion. "It'll slow us down a bit, but it's not blocking any weapons ports, and there's no time to jettison it now."

Through the forward viewport, Adrian marveled as the immense c-sub broke apart. By the dozens, individual subs detached, broke free, drifted a short distance, and then sped off.

Up until now, there'd been no time to think. He'd been swept along by events, and by Mayu. Now, a feeling of depression and dread rose within Adrian like an inexorable tide. He was in a war, headed straight for a powerful enemy. At least his father, if dead, had died pursuing something noble, the search for ultimate truth, the source of all life. Senior's son now would die in a senseless battle, just one more casualty added to the wastes of war. As his mother had feared, she'd lose both husband and son.

"Look, I'm sorry about all this," Mayu said, seeming to care about his feelings for the first time. "But at least you're in a weapons sub. We stand a pretty good chance, unless they target us for a Hull Hammer."

That term meant nothing to Adrian. He'd heard the Manihikans possessed some kind of super-weapon and had forced other aquastates into immediate surrender, but he'd paid no attention to details he wouldn't understand anyway. Everyone knew Manihiki, with its fierce Empress Halcyone Tillerman, had conquered vast stretches of ocean area and several land nations. By some estimates, she'd soon control half the world. Aquastates bordering her expanding empire had banded together in a loose and disjointed Alliance, but so far that coalition had offered not the least hindrance to the burgeoning juggernaut of the Manihikan military.

Adrian began hearing muffled booms. The forward viewport turned opaque and, in its place, appeared a kind of tactical display, with luminous dots and arrows and accompanying text, none of which he understood. At first, he thought Mayu had called up the display for his benefit, so he could follow the battle's progress. But he realized she'd done it for her own convenience, since the viewport was larger than her screens, and there'd be nothing to see through a port at these ranges.

On the display, a huge number of blue dots moved as one, like a spotted amoeba. It split up, rejoined, advanced and retreated in complex contoured shapes that shifted in response to the red dots. *Like a school of fish.*

Some lighter dots fanned out from the red ones, moving so fast they appeared as orange lines. When these met other dots, both winked out of existence, and that correlated with the distant explosions he heard. Vessels were being destroyed, some of them manned, their pressure hulls imploding and death coming in an instant to the occupants. A complete waste of precious life, Adrian thought, the life that had found its start over four billion years ago, perhaps in these very waters. How much longer did he have to live, before he become merely a dot vanishing from some other sub's display?

"Things aren't going too well for us," Mayu mused. "If only..." She turned, wearing one of her half-smiles. "Do you still have the e-key for your rental?"

He blinked at the unexpected question. "Uh, yeah. Is something wrong with *this* sub?"

"No. Gimme your key."

Adrian hesitated.

Mayu glared back, full evil eye. "Nazcator will pay for any damages. Don't make me force it from you."

He handed her his e-key. She set some controls, unbelted, and returned a minute later. "This should get interesting," she said while strapping herself in. She worked her console like a musician, and Adrian felt the hull shudder seven separate times.

Without turning to facing him, Mayu said, "I just fired hypersonic torps at every Manihiki contact I've identified. I'm trying to draw their fire so our damaged Alliance subs can limp away."

"Draw their fire?" Adrian felt a cold shiver. "Doesn't that mean—?"

"Yeah. Look." Mayu pointed to the display, where six streaks of orange lines drew nearer to a single blue point. "That's us. Watch."

She pushed a button and Adrian heard the hydraulic clamping struts release his rent-a-sub. Next came a motor's loud whirr just outside Mayu's hull.

"Such a shame how some people drive rentals," Mayu said. "Yours is angling upward at forty knots."

"It won't do forty."

"It will now, but not for long. As for us, we're going to quiet mode." She lowered her voice. "Nothing above a whisper."

Sound from her sub's propulsion motors ceased, as did the ventilation fans and the power module. Through the hull, Adrian heard only the receding scream of his rental sub's engine.

Fear mounted within him and he started hyperventilating. The six orange lines grew ever closer to the blue dot, which had separated from a new, green one. He couldn't take his eyes from the display. His life would end when those lines converged.

Mayu seemed not to notice. Every time one of her outbound torps found its target, she nodded and whispered something Adrian couldn't hear.

Adrian bowed his head and prayed to Oceanus, vowing to worship at the temple every week if the god of Oceanism would only spare his life.

When it came, the boom caused him to scream involuntarily and jolted him out of his seat against the restraint straps. He blinked, then realized he *could* still blink. *That must mean—*

"We're still in the fight," Mayu whispered to him, a big smile brightening her face. "Got some minor leakage, but the pumps will handle that when I turn 'em back on. For now, we'll just sit here until the tactical picture clears." She looked back at her instruments, then turned to add, "Sorry about your rental. Here's your e-key back."

"Thanks." Adrian took it. "Harrison Rental will be so thrilled when I return it." To his surprise, the small joke helped calm his shaking and quench his fear.

Mayu's sub drifted downward in utter silence and touched bottom a short time later. "My little ploy cleared out the battle zone," Mayu whispered. "I've been watching the Manihikans re-form up to seek out the fleeing Alliance subs. See how they all took up positions to protect that one there? Big mistake to identify their leader that way." She glanced back at him and winked. "Or to have a leader at all. It looks like that sub might pass almost directly over us. I'm going to try my new weapon on it."

Adrian cocked his head. "New weapon? Why didn't you use it before now?"

"It sucks most of the juice from my power module. I only get one shot. It's a saser."

"A what?"

"A saser." She grinned. "Like a laser, but sound, not light. A narrow, coherent beam."

"Uh-huh." Adrian wondered how anyone could get so excited about a new way of killing people.

"Come on, baby…" Mayu whispered to the approaching image on her display. "That's it…closer…closer…*there*."

A low hum came from the power module restarting. Then Mayu pressed a button and held onto a joystick. Adrian heard an irritating whine like a dentist drill.

"Just a few more seconds…"

From what Adrian could see, Mayu was working to hold crosshairs steady on a spot at the forward underside of a moving submarine's hull. In the image, the surface puckered, indented, and then gave way.

She turned off power and her sub fell silent again. He barely heard her whisper, "Smaller hole than I'd hoped, but at this depth… Anyway, I'm going silent. We may get incoming torps."

The fear-filled silence stretched for Adrian, but no orange lines appeared on the tactical display. No one fired torpedoes. The sub Mayu had targeted drifted lower and lower.

Hissing broke the silence. "They're blowing ballast," Mayu said.

Still the sub descended, though not as fast. A loud bang started Adrian, then more followed, the sounds of a submarine imploding.

Mayu murmured again, then kept watching displays. "That's odd."

"What?"

"Look at the other subs. Just holding position. Not searching for us."

"Isn't that…good?"

"Maybe. It's just weird. Oh, they're moving now."

Above and around them, the enemy subs fanned out and turned to a course back to Manihiki. In fifteen minutes, they'd vanished beyond the limits of Mayu's display.

"We're pretty low on power," Mayu said. "I'll wait a few more minutes to ensure they're gone, then—" She cocked her head at a sudden sound from her panel. "Some idiot's out there broadcasting on open, unscrambled acoustics." She turned a volume dial.

Despite the warbling distortion of the water, the excited tones of the man's voice came through. "…fire. I repeat: All Alliance forces cease fire. Manihiki has surrendered and called for a peace conference to discuss terms. The war is over." The voice paused, then resumed. "Mayu Villca, if you're still out there, please acknowledge by acoustics."

Her brow furrowed. "Strange." She chewed her lip. "A Manihikan trick?" She shook her head and picked up the microphone. "Mayu here. I acknowledge message and understand cease fire."

The reply came moments later. "Mayu, your shot brought down the Manihikan flagship. Party at the c-sub in your honor tonight."

Adrian rolled his eyes and snorted. "A war hero, huh? They throw parties for killing people. Sounds like fun."

She glanced at him sidelong but said nothing.

A confusion of voices came from the speaker, all congratulatory messages for Mayu. "Thanks, everyone," Mayu said. She lifted her sub off the bottom, turned off the tactical display, made the viewport transparent again, and steered a course back to where the c-sub would re-assemble.

Listening to the jubilant voices praising Mayu, Adrian began to regret his snide comment. How many more would have died, he wondered, if not for her actions?

About to apologize to her, he saw something in the viewport and gaped, wide-eyed. "Holy Oceanus! Stop, stop, stop."

"What?" Mayu slowed the sub. "What's the matter?"

"There." He pointed. "It's...it's SpongeBob SquarePants."

He couldn't mistake the formation. It matched the pictures in the hydrothermal vent database. Narrow, pointed spires jutted from the bottom, forming a spindly gray castle of irregular and complex contours. "Sweet Neptune, there's his sub."

Bristling with external tanks, thrusters, collection baskets, and mechanical arms, the research vessel lay on the bottom. One arm reached at an awkward angle and grasped a part of the white smoker's structure that arched between two eternal cylinder tanks.

"He's trapped!" Adrian said. "We've got to rescue him."

Mayu frowned. "I'm almost out of power. I'll call for another—"

"No time for that," Adrian pleaded. "We've got to get him—I mean *them*—out now."

She shook her head. "I can't risk it."

He gripped her shoulder. "You risked it for me, and there was a war on, then. A humanitarian rescue, you said. Come on. They may be down to their final minutes in there."

Her narrow-eyed glance didn't look pleasant, but she sighed. "All right, we'll try. But I'm calling for help, too. We might need a tow to get back."

In a few minutes Mayu had transmitted her request and maneuvered so she could extrude a trunk onto the forward upper hatch of the stricken submersible and latch on. She pointed at one of her screens. "It's not flooded, but nobody could be breathing that air. Oxygen's low and CO_2 is way high. We'll wear respirators."

Adriain unstrapped from his seat. "Let's go." He felt buoyant. He'd soon see his father, after all his searching. Maybe Adrian Senior had found a way to survive on his own respirator, somehow. Maybe even now he was nearing the end of his air supply.

The trunk connecting the two subs served as an airlock, so bad air wouldn't enter Mayu's craft. Adrian breathed fast and deep in his respirator, unable to quell his anticipation.

Mayu opened the research submersible's hatch and entered first. Descending the short ladder, Adrian found the interior chilly and misty. A body still sat at the controls, unmoving. It had been a young research technician, not his father. Farther aft, Adrian saw a man lying face up on the deck in the bunking area, and he rushed to it.

His father stared upward, a bearded and older version of Adrian Junior, with the Penshell green eyes and other facial features unmistakable. No mistaking the chest wounds, either, with dried blood marring the light blue jumpsuit.

"Dad, can you hear me?" Adrian knelt by his father and dared to hope, but the cold body gave no response. He touched the octopus tattoo on his father's forehead, stroked the jade green skin of his cheek.

Tears ran from Adrian's eyes, tears he couldn't wipe away with his regulator face mask on. For months, he'd nurtured the hope his father had remained alive somehow, and now the contrary truth hit him in the gut. The man who'd shaped his life, whose unwavering strength of character had defined Adrian's personality and very existence, that man would guide him no more. "Oh, Dad," Adrian wailed. "I can't believe you're gone. What happened?" He shut his eyes, his frame quaking with sobs.

"I can tell you what happened." Mayu's voice came from the forward part of the submersible, "but you won't like it."

Adrian looked up and saw her through a haze of stinging tears. He blinked hard to clear his vision, but that only helped a little. "What do you mean?"

She summoned him with a tilt of her chin. "It's all here." She glanced at a console, then turned back to him. "If you really want to know."

Adrian stood and walked toward her. "I've got to know the truth, no matter what."

Tight lipped, she looked at him for a moment. "Okay. Humidity ruined the computer system, but I managed to recover some files. I've been reading text entries, but we'll get a better understanding from a couple of video logs." She reached over one researcher's dead body and tapped a button.

The face of Adrian's father appeared on the screen, full of life, facing the camera. In the upper right, a time stamp read 23 May1607Z. "So far, all samples obtained here at SpongeBob SquarePants," he said, "date to 3.92 billion years ago, matching that of the earliest life signs obtained at numerous other sites. Either our current dating techniques are insufficiently precise to distinguish which one is the true Alpha Vent," he shook his head, "or life originated in several places simultaneously, a hypothesis I'm unwilling to accept. I believe I can obtain better, earlier samples if I can nose our submersible closer to the base of the formation. Some on the team object to this plan—"

A young man's voice came from somewhere off screen. "Fluking right, I object. It's a stupid—"

"—and I have weighed these objections against the possible gain," Adrian Senior continued after staring with a frown to his left. "As the leader of this expedition, I've decided we must try it."

That video clip ended there. Mayu looked at him "Sure you want to go on?"

He nodded.

"Okay, last entry."

She pressed keys and another video came up, dated three weeks later than the other entry, but only two days ago, this one showing a young man's face, a visage of thick stubble, baggy and bloodshot eyes, and more lines than a youthful face should have. It was the young man whose body still sat at the controls.

"Not much air left." He spoke in gasps. "Probably beyond rescue now, if anybody's even looking. Kori and Strom are asleep. I'll try one more time to free us with the manipulator arm, then take a pill, too. Best way to go, but I had to say something in case someone listens to these recordings." He rubbed his forehead. "When we got stuck, the jolt knocked out our primary acoustic comms. We'd left port with our backup comms nonfunctional. Dr. Penshell didn't want to wait for repairs."

He shut his eyes, looked down, then back at the camera. "I hope people understand. It was simple math. One less person breathing—air lasts longer. He was the logical one—not only oldest, but that blowhole led us into this disaster. The three of us decided; the three of us did it. Can't say I regret it." His hand reached out as if to press a button, then he paused and gave a momentary smile. "Oh, yeah. We did take a sample at the base of SpongeBob and analyzed it. Still 3.92 billion, like the others. Guess this isn't the Alpha Vent." He shook his head. "Maybe there isn't one." The video log ended.

"They killed him," Adrian backed away from the screen and the young explorer's body, his mind swirling.

"I'm sorry," Mayu said, her eyes showing sympathy behind her respirator's lenses.

When Adrian thought of his father, he felt admiration, even idolization. Now, other memory scraps tainted that view—the times during childhood when he'd hated his father, the overheard fights with his mother, the muted criticisms from Adrian Senior's colleagues and the press. Adrian Junior had heard people call his father a glory-seeker and a reckless egotist. He'd dismissed those disparagements as mere jealous rantings, as had his father.

Now his father lay dead, murdered, and Adrian could imagine the event as if he'd been there. His father had pointed the way, rejecting opposition, intent on his goal, unmindful of the rising tide of his crew's anger. After the submersible had become trapped, its occupants unable to call for help, hot fury had merged with the cold logic of survival.

Adrian stood, staring at the remains of his father, while Mayu rested a hand on his shoulder. In a way, Senior's team hadn't killed him, Adrian realized. His own overconfident arrogance, domineering attitude, and dismal leadership had caught up with him at last.

"If you'd like," Mayu said softly, "my people will recover the sub, perform autopsies, and send your father's remains to you."

"Thank you, Mayu." Adrian turned his back on his father and headed toward the ladder to the hatch. As he raised his arm, he saw the panel lighting had given his green skin a blue tint. "That'll mean a lot to my mom."

The Lowly Shrimp

*F*ive-year-old Renata Novo could not understand why the stranger pulled her out of school. She'd been finger painting when a bald woman came in the classroom and whispered to the teacher. Senhora Mendonça had looked straight at Renata and called her name.

"You will go with this woman," Senhora Mendonça said.

Renata couldn't tell if her teacher was happy or sad to be sending her off, but Renata obeyed. The stranger was tall and looked a little mean. *She would look much prettier if she had hair on her head, or a wig*, Renata thought. The woman held her hand as they walked down the empty hall.

"Where are we going?" Renata asked.

"To the Bilge, a place more fitting for you." The stranger's voice had a growling sound.

Renata didn't know what the Bilge was, so she said, "I'm Renata. What's your name?"

"You will call me Guia. From now on, you will be called Camarão."

"But my name is—"

Guia's grip on her hand tightened until it hurt, then Guia relaxed it. "Camarão. That's your name now."

Renata didn't like that name. It meant shrimp. She didn't like Guia either. "I want my mamãe and papai."

"Hmmpf. We're going to the Bilge," Guia said.

Renata didn't want to go anywhere with this woman. She screamed, "I want my—"

Guia spun her around, picked her up and shook her. Glaring into Renata's eyes, she said, "You will be quiet, Camarão, or I will break every bone in your hand." She set Renata down and they walked out of the school in silence.

I'm being kidnapped. Renata had heard of children being kidnapped. This Guia couldn't possibly be a friend of her parents. But the teacher had let Guia take her out of school. She'd even pointed Renata out to Guia. Renata tried to squirm her way out of Guia's grip on her hand, but Guia held her even tighter.

Tears filled Renata's eyes and she whimpered softly as Guia led her out of the school sector of Áquaforte. The sole seastead in the aquastate of the Seamonarchy of Madeira, it was the only home Renata had ever known. Through the wide, brightly colored corridors, some people walked, others rode moving walkways, but none paid any attention to Renata. She dared not cry out, for she was sure Guia would break her hand, or worse.

Renata knew Áquaforte was big, and she hadn't seen much of it. When moving between its many levels, she'd always taken one of the elevators or escalators, but Guia guided her through a door to a stairway. It formed a square spiral going up and down a long way.

"Come on," Guia tugged Renata toward the downward steps.

Noises like Guia's voice and their shoes on the stairs echoed along the metal walls and metal stairs. They met no one else on their way down, though Renata sometimes heard the noises of people talking and walking either far below or far above them.

After a long time going down, Renata said, "I'm tired."

"I don't care. Keep going."

Eventually, after Renata slipped a few times, Guia lifted her and carried her farther down, always down, down a long way.

This far down, the stairs began looking worse. Renata noticed the steps were unpolished here. Then she saw dust on the floor and dents in the walls. Lower still, she saw brownish rust lining both the walls and hand railings. Where she'd seen fire extinguishers and comm panels beside each door above, down here some extinguishers were broken or missing and some comm panels damaged, with wires hanging out. On some levels, the lighting blinked and other levels had no lights at all.

They reached the lowest level and Guia stood in a puddle of gray water and set Renata down. Guia opened the door and led her out into a gigantic room, poorly lit and crammed tight with rusty pipes, chipped concrete columns, and oily machinery Renata didn't recognize. The place smelled a little like fish and a lot like a toilet. She saw one rat chase another around a corner.

Guia stared down at her. "This is the Bilge, the lowest part of Áquaforte, your new home, Camarão. You are so far behind your classmates, so unfit to be in the same school with them, and such an embarrassment to your family, that you will now receive special—and very rough—training. I will be your mamãe, your papai, your teacher, and everything to you."

Renata didn't understand all the words but knew this wasn't good. She put her hands on her hips. "Wait until my mamãe and papai find out you kidnapped me. They'll send the police and the police will put you in jail."

Guia shook her head. "I didn't kidnap you, Camarão. The police know all about me. So do your parents. They agreed I should take you away and train you."

Renata stared open-mouthed, feeling tears coming back. *My parents* know *about Guia? They actually agreed to let her take me?*

Ten hours later, Renata was so exhausted from everything Guia had put her through on her first day of training, it didn't take long to cry herself to sleep.

. . .

On her tenth birthday, Camarão ran away from Guia for the third time. She'd worked out Guia's schedule and knew the times her tormenter wouldn't be watching her. Where Guia went or what she did at those times, Camarão didn't know, but she felt grateful for these brief absences.

She squeezed between grimy pipes, squirmed through a crevice between a hot furnace and a bulkhead, and tight-roped along a narrow, elevated support strut, places she felt Guia would have difficulty in following her. Camarão then fell in with a group of miners riding up in an elevator at the end of their shift.

Camarão hoped to return to her home and her parents, if she could somehow remember where they lived or what they looked like. She barely remembered her own real name. *Renata*, she thought. *I think*.

Pressed against the back of the elevator, smelling the workers' sweat, she thought with a shudder about how her time with Guia had gone. She'd lived in the dreary Bilge among cockroaches and rats, and occasionally encountered other homeless people. These were the Bilge Folk.

Miners came down from the higher levels in shifts to don their deep-sea diving suits and extract minerals from the seafloor. Maintenance technicians also came down now and then to care for the geothermal pipes and the mighty furnaces and ventilation equipment. Camarão came to know many of these people of the higher levels, the Roof Folk, especially which ones would give her food if she begged.

Guia always kept her on the go. Her intense and arduous regimen covered mathematics, history, geography, writing, languages, music, and art. Where Guia obtained books, slate, chalk, and paper, Camarão never knew. She did know Guia's penalties for unsatisfactory performance. Most often, Camarão's efforts fell short of standards, so Guia forced her to do pushups, sit-ups, jumping jacks, and timed runs around the Bilge perimeter. Even when Camarão did something praiseworthy, Guia's highest compliment was "Hmmpf." Guia roused her too soon every morning and put her to bed in a pile of soft trash too late each night. She always felt tired. Moreover, Guia always stressed how far behind her peers Camarão was, no matter how hard she studied or how much she worked.

"You're hopeless at spherical trigonometry," Guia had said on the previous day. "You barely know just three languages; your handwriting is atrocious; you can't name all the Atlantic aquastates, and you can't identify the ten ministers in the Madeiran government. How do you expect to keep up with your former classmates? You'll just have to work harder before I can think of letting you re-join them."

"Am I the only one like me?" Camarão had asked.

"No, Guia shook her head. "This isn't the only Bilge sector either, and I'm not the only Guia."

Now, huddled in the back of the elevator, Camarão hoped to be free of her Guia forever. She didn't care how far behind she was. She wanted to live with her parents again, in their comfortable quarters.

The elevator stopped and the door opened on Level 147. The miners got out. *Is this the level where my parents live*? She didn't know. Unsure, she poked her head out of the elevator and looked around. As soon as she looked right, her heart sank.

There stood Guia, arms folded, one foot tapping.

"Flotz!" Camarão hung her head. "You find me every fluking time." *How did she know just where I'd be*?

"Come on," Guia said. "You'll double-time down the stairs, and you'll give me fifty pushups at the bottom. Also, no dinner tonight."

Camarão groaned. Her escape attempts always earned harsh punishments. "Last time I ran away, you only made me do thirty pushups."

"I added twenty for swearing."

Sighing, Camarão followed Guia to the stairs. They began jogging downward, with Camarão on the outside of the spiral. As fit as she was, Camarão knew the first several dozen levels would be easy, though she'd be gasping for breath at the bottom. Then she could begin her pushups. Another miserable day in a long string of them, with only more misery ahead.

· · ·

Five years later, Camarão hunched in her study corner, writing an essay on Queen Maria II of Portugal that highlighted her strengths and weaknesses as a leader. Camarão had a lot to do before Guia returned from her errand, whatever that was. Over time, she had carved out a bearable place for living and studying, a warm niche among the Bilge's ventilations pipes with flat, dry surfaces for her books and plenty of reflected light from scavenged mirrors.

Hearing a noise, she looked up, but it wasn't Guia. Barros was one of the Bilge Folk, a man about thirty years old, missing an upper front tooth, and always smelly.

Camarão had spoken with many of the Bilge Folk over the years, and found they only knew a single language, could barely do basic arithmetic, and lacked any understanding of their own aquastate's government. Yet none had Guias of their own, and they never studied or exercised. When Camarão had asked about that, Guia had said, "You'll end up among them if you don't work harder. If Madeira had better leaders in its government, there wouldn't be any Bilge Folk."

Barros' presence in Camarão's niche was unusual. The Bilge Folk generally stayed apart, away from each other's spaces.

"Hey, Barros," Camarão said. "What is it? You looking for food?"

He said nothing, just looked around Camarão's area. Then, with an unidentifiable expression, he moved quickly toward Camarão.

Startled, she scrambled to get out of his way, but he was on her. He grabbed her, pinning her arms and throwing her on her bed, a mat made from cardboard boxes and furnace insulation. From atop her, he unzipped the front of her jumpsuit from neck to crotch.

Camarão tried to push him away, but he was stronger. She cried out for help, but that earned her a jarring slap in the face from his meaty hand. He moved with a savage, vicious ferocity, panting heavily, his eyes wild. His foul breath made her nauseated, but that faded to insignificance as she fought for her life. She squirmed and writhed but couldn't escape from under him. With one of his massive hands clenching both her wrists together, he unzipped his pants with the other. She tried to recall the self-defense moves Guia had taught her, but in her confusion, nothing came to mind.

He focused on her breasts for some reason, cupped them with his hands and sucked on them. Camarão knew babies did that to their mothers, but didn't understand why Barros would suck on her dry breasts. Guia had explained many things as Camarão's body changed, but mostly talked about cleanliness. She had also mentioned that Camarão would one day choose a love partner.

Camarão had been left to imagine many things about "making love," but none included anything like this sweating, heaving, stinking monster on top of her. She felt him against her, hard, rubbing, like a giant misplaced finger probing, insistent. He reached down with one of his hands to position himself.

Then he was gone, his weight no longer pressing down. Through the mist of her tears, Camarão thought she saw two figures struggling, but they vanished around a corner. She lay on the bed, crying, confused, and afraid. Barros' odor hung in the air. Wiping her eyes with her sleeve, she looked around her empty niche. Between sobs, she saw the pictures of pink seahorses she'd drawn with a discarded crayon nib and stuck to the bulkhead, saw the misshapen doll she'd fashioned from gathered junk. They now seemed like items from someone else's room, belonging to a little girl she'd once known.

Guia came in and knelt by her bed. She looked different, with a dark bruise under her right eye and a bloody cut on her bald head. At least Guia had never shaved Camarão's head, and instead allowed her to keep her hair short. Now, Guia's eyes held an expression Camarão had never seen her show. "Are you in pain?"

She hadn't asked if Camarão was all right. She *wasn't* all right. Camarão felt her cheek where she'd been slapped. "No, I'm not in pain."

Guia glanced at Camarão's lower body. "Did he…?"

Dimly, Camarão understood what Guia meant, and shook her head. "No."

Guia blew out a sigh. Her face returned to its normal firmness, and Camarão already missed that fleeting, soft look of...concern? Caring? Camarão wondered what her punishment would be this time.

Instead, Guia said, "Let's get you cleaned up. Time you learned more advanced fighting skills."

The grueling schedule of studies and physical training worsened as weeks passed. As always, Camarão never measured up. Only in the self-defense exercises did she occasionally earn a "Hmmpf." Seven languages weren't enough. Integral and differential calculus weren't enough. Her reports on Homer, William Shakespeare, and Camilo Ferreira Botelho Castelo-Branco were woefully unsatisfactory, and her analyses of historical leaders was pathetic.

"You're not getting it at all," Guia said while watching Camarão do sit-ups. "All of humanity, and all of history, is a giant mass of ignorant followers steered by an unending chain of incompetent leaders. All leaders are either corrupt or on their way to becoming corrupt. On rare, glorious moments, some leaders show sparks of mediocrity. It's a tragic flaw of human nature that people must be led, and none of them is fit to lead."

Camarão suppressed the urge to ask if Guia was *her* leader. "What. About. Our. King?" she asked between sit-ups.

"He's like the rest—sub-par, uninspired. Humanity cries out for a true leader. That's why you study history. Remember, you owe me your report on the flaws of Winston Churchill tomorrow."

Two months after the attempted rape, Camarão settled into a depression deeper than any she'd felt before. It didn't matter how much effort she made, Guia would never let her rejoin her parents or classmates among the Roof Folk. After long suspecting it, Camarão became convinced Guia had some other reason for keeping her down here, that her teacher dangled a reward she'd never actually grant.

From her studies, Camarão had learned about one way out of the most hopeless situation. Life could present you with crushing burdens, depressing miseries, and desperate predicaments, but there was always a route of last resort, a final path leading toward relief of all troubles.

The Portuguese author Castelo-Branco had taken that path, and so had Shakespeare's Juliet.

Camarão owned no gun like the writer had used, but her rusty steak knife could stand in for the dagger used by the Capulet daughter.

One afternoon, Guia had left her alone to study. Guia's errands usually consumed ten to thirty minutes, which left Camarão time enough to stab herself in the chest, Juliet style.

There seemed no point in writing any final thoughts for Guia to read. The reason for her suicide would be no mystery. Camarão wondered where Guia would lay the blame—on the student for not measuring up, or on the teacher for pushing too hard? On the student, surely. Camarão had never detected a glimmer of self-assessment in Guia. The woman seemed indifferent to herself, incapable of the self-reflection that dominated Camarão's life. Guia seemed devoted to Camarão's misery and eventual destruction. No, Guia would feel no remorse, just a passing frustration over the chore of having to take on a new student.

As for herself, Camarão felt liberated already, knowing she'd soon have no more studying, no more calisthenics, no more looming projects, and no more painful laps around the Bilge. The knot she felt in her stomach whenever she thought about upcoming schoolwork or the next day of physical training—that tight knot of tension had vanished. The relaxation, the freedom, brought on a smile.

In exchange for that freedom, all she had to give up was her future life. And what was that? A life of suffering and pain. A life unworthy, as Guia said, of joining the rest of humanity. She was one of the Bilge Folk, and who really cared if there were one fewer of them? On balance, the loss of her life would be a net gain for society.

Sighing with finality, Camarão saw no reason to prolong the matter, and knew a real danger of being caught and stopped if she delayed further, so she held the knife perpendicular to the left side of her chest with her left hand. A vigorous blow to the hilt with the palm of her right hand should suffice. She extended that hand.

In a blur of frantic motion, a figure sped in, slapped Camarão's right hand away, and clenched her left wrist hard. The grip tightened and twisted until Camarão dropped the knife.

As always, it was Guia. She looked, not angry, but shocked and even afraid. She pulled up a chair opposite Camarão and faced her. Half a meter away, her eyes searched Camarão's.

"You were really going to do it, weren't you?" Guia's expression became neutral. She was in control once more, but something had changed between them and Guia must have known it.

A part of her felt like crying, but Camarão was well beyond that now. Her eyes full of fury, brimming with hatred, she glared at Guia. "Yes."

They sat looking at each other in silence. Finally, Guia said, "I see. Well, if you think there's no point in living, I'll give you a reason to live. We're moving."

At twenty, Camarão had aged five years since her suicide attempt. Sitting on one of the benches in the crew's mess of HMMS Machico, she studied and reflected. She'd come a long way since her time in the Bilge, but in another sense, hadn't come far at all.

Guia's notion of "a reason to live" had been a job, and she'd gotten one for Camarão in Áquaforte's nuclear power plant. Somehow, Guia had also arranged to get herself assigned as Camarão's supervisor. Although Camarão's duties had been rudimentary, Guia always kept her hustling, and forced her to study all aspects of reactor operation. In a year and a half there, Camarão figured she could have run the whole plant.

Then followed another job, this one at the Áquaforte sargasso farms. She piloted a harvester sub that saw-toothed through the seaweed crop, cutting and gathering ripe fronds for the food processing equipment. Once again, Guia became her boss and drove her hard. In both jobs, Guia ran her ragged during the day and continued schooling her at night. Camarão had no time for a personal life.

After Camarão worked three years at those two jobs, Guia had enlisted her in the Royal Madeiran Navy. Continuing her maddening habit, Guia was not only her chief instructor in boot camp, she became her division chief aboard her first submarine. As a newly reported enlisted sailor, Camarão had been assigned duty in the galley as a mess cook. Just now, the captain had just ordered the crew to Battle Stations, and Camarão's post was in the Damage Control party, which mustered in the crew's mess to await orders.

Shortly after getting underway, the sub had been directed to the Pacific to join the worldwide Alliance opposing the dreaded Manihikan Empire. Camarão sensed the tension all around her from crewmen who'd all heard rumors about a Manihikan super-weapon, one that imploded enemy submarine hulls without torpedoes, using sound alone. Everyone called it the Hull Hammer, but no one knew a workable defense against it. Around her, nervous crewmen drank their tea, trying without success to hide their fear. Having been near death before, Camarão quietly reviewed her submarine warfare tactics manual.

She glanced up at the clock to check the time, and saw the entire bulkhead dish in. It happened only for an instant; the vessel's outwardly curved hull dented inward, then sprang back to its normal cylindrical shape. Camarão blinked, not sure if she believed her own eyes.

From somewhere came the sound of rushing water, then the flooding alarm blared. The crewmen in the damage control party shouted questions in confusion, but Camarão fought against her mounting panic, knowing she only needed to await orders.

"Damage Control Party, lay to AMR One." She could barely hear the voice from the speakers over the sound of the ocean flooding in. "Secure the flooding and restore the drain pump." AMR One, the forward-most Auxiliary Machinery Room, was down one level, not far from the mess. Sitting at the end of a bench, Camarão slid off and was among the first to hasten down the ladder.

Three young men climbed down behind her, and then she heard a horrendous crash. Looking up, she saw a steel plate barring the way up. Something heavy had blocked the only entrance to AMR One. They'd get no more help for some time. Nor could they leave this room.

Glancing around the large space, with its mass of machinery, pipes, tanks, valves, and electrical cabinets, Camarão felt a flash of confusion. Water sprayed in from a dozen leaks, and sparks leapt from two circuit panels. The lights went out, blinding her, except for the flashes of arcing electricity. Red emergency lights flickered, then stayed on.

One man had already been in the space, probably his battle station post, she thought. He stood staring at a large pump, scratching his head. Behind her, the other three from the DC party stood as if puzzled about what to do. To Camarão's relief, one was a lieutenant, an officer with experience who would know what actions to take.

"What are your orders, sir?" She shouted to be heard.

His mouth opened and closed. He looked around the room, bewildered, and his eyes only grew wider. "It's…it's hopeless," he said.

"Sir, we've got to stop the flooding and fix the pump." She tugged his sleeve.

"It's flooding from *everywhere*," he said. "There aren't enough of us,"

She couldn't believe this officer didn't know what to do. "You," she pointed at a seaman. "Man the phones. Tell the Control Room that AMR One is on the line."

Camarão pointed at another crewman, a petty officer. "You. See those flood control valves up there? Shut 'em. All of 'em."

The man nodded and bolted up the ladder to comply. A set of handles at the entrance to all spaces allowed for shutting all valves leading to the sea. As soon as he pushed the last handle, water stopped gushing from every pipe in the space, and the electrical sparking died down and ceased.

"Tell Control we've secured flooding in AMR One," Camarão told her phone talker.

He nodded but cupped the headphone over one ear. "They say we took on too much water and the Hull Hammer knocked out propulsion. The ship's sinking, so we have to get the drain pump working."

She thought back to her training. "Can't they cross-connect the trim—?"

He held up a hand, listening. "The Hull Hammer wrecked the trim pump beyond repair. They want a status of repairing the drain pump."

She turned to the watch-stander who peered into the upper part of a pump motor. "What's the problem?"

He shook his head. "The motor controller. It can't handle the starting current." He pointed to an electrical cabinet, now charred and blackened.

Camarão pondered that. When starting, motors drew a large spike of current to start turning, then settled out at a lower value. "Could the controller keep the motor going at its normal speed?"

"Sure, but it can't start the pump from a dead stop."

"The ship's at 1400 meters," the phone talker said. "Control wants the status of pump repairs."

"Tell them it's impossible," the AMR watch-stander said.

"Belay that!" Camarão shouted. "Tell them we're working on it." She knew the submarine's normal depth limit was 1300 meters, and its design crush depth was 2000 meters. She looked around the room, wracking her brain for answers. "What's that?" She pointed to a large machine on a raised platform above.

"Air compressor number three," the watch-stander said.

"Does it work?"

"Yeah, but we don't need air, we need—"

Camarão saw some stiff, yellow fabric neatly coiled in a corner. "Could we rig those ratchet straps from the compressor to the pump motor shaft?"

The watch-stander's eyes grew wide, and he smiled. "Yeah, kooky, but it might just work."

Camarão pointed. "Lieutenant, bring one of those yellow straps here." Then she added, "Please, sir?"

"1600 meters," the phone-talker said. "They're demanding a status."

"Tell 'em to line up the drain pump suction to any bilge they want to de-water, and we'll tell 'em when it's running." She turned to the other men. "Let's get going."

The compressor's shaft protruded horizontally, and the drain pump's shaft stuck up vertically, but they tightened the ratchet strap as best they could around available flanges on both shafts.

The watch-stander shook his head. "Kookiest damn thing I've ever—"

"1800 meters!" The phone talker shouted, his eyes wide.

"Start the compressor at its slowest speed," Camarão signaled to the watch-stander. "Lieutenant, please stand by the drain pump motor controller and start the pump on my mark."

With a loud hum and a mechanical groan, the air compressor began rotating. The strap slipped at first, then caught and the drain pump shaft started turning. A hideous clatter sounded whenever the ratchet portion slipped around either shaft's flange. "Speed it up," Camarão twirled a finger.

That strap wouldn't last long. It had started to edge its way off the drain pump shaft. "Faster," she signaled. "Everybody, stand clear."

"1900 meters," the phone talker's voice cracked. His face was damp, but whether from sweat or tears, Camarão couldn't tell.

She pointed to the lieutenant. "Mark. Start the pump."

He pushed the pump controller button.

The strap lurched, then slipped off and sprang free of both shafts, flying away and slamming into the side of the oxygen generator. The drain pump motor stuttered twice, then spun steadily around.

Cheers erupted in the AMR.

The phone talker needed no direction. "The drain pump's working! It's working!" Then, he sobered. "2000 meters, still going down."

Camarão heard a loud metallic creak that trailed off. No doubt, the hull was straining to cope with a pressure of two hundred kilograms on each square centimeter of its surface, the maximum it was designed to take.

Everyone in AMR One looked at each other. They could do nothing more.

From her studies, Camarão knew submarine designers often added margins to their calculations, but only to account for real world uncertainties and imperfections, not to allow vessels to operate below crush depth. She and her shipmates had been on borrowed time; now it was downright theft.

"2100 meters, but rate of descent is slowing."

A low tone, so low it sounded like the ship growling, came from somewhere else in the submarine.

"2150 meters," the phone talker whispered, "and steady."

Camarão held her breath and noticed the others did likewise.

One minute later, the phone talker said, "We're rising! We're rising! 2125 meters...2100."

The lieutenant slapped Camarão's back. "I'm sorry I...I panicked. But thank you, seaman. Well done. What division are you in?"

"I'm a mess cook."

From above came a grinding noise of sliding metal. One level up, they'd managed to move the massive steel cabinet that had fallen and blocked access to the AMR. Down the ladder came several chiefs and officers, Chief Guia in the lead.

Guia looked around the space. "Who's in charge here?"

Everyone pointed at Camarão. "She is," the lieutenant said.

"She jump-started the drain pump with an air compressor," the AMR watch-stander grinned. "If that ain't the kookiest—"

"Hmmpf."

· · ·

After being awake thirty-six hours, Lieutenant Camarão plunked into a chair in her stateroom, exhausted. Now twenty-five years old, she'd advanced to officer rank and earned two promotions. But she'd just guided the sub into port, overseen the reactor shutdown, and then stood duty all night so the other officers could see their families. She had no family to go home to.

Still, she felt some exhilaration, too. After having a cup of tea and changing out of her duty jumpsuit, she would soon don her dress uniform and attend the ceremony where she'd be promoted to lieutenant commander.

Captain Guia darkened her stateroom door. "Come with me, Camarão."

"The ceremony's not for another hour." Camarão bent to unlace her boots.

"You're not going to be a lieutenant commander. Come with me, now."

Camarão looked up with weary eyes at the woman who'd taken her from her parents, raised her in a sewer, made her life hellish, and punished her time and again. "No. You're not taking this away. I've made something of myself. I've earned this. I'm worthy, now."

Guia's bald head glistened in the stateroom lighting. "Hmmpf. Yeah, you are. But you're still coming with me."

"No, Guia. You can't make me." She sized up her long-time oppressor. The woman had to be in her mid- to late-forties. "I can kick your ass."

Guia leaned down, her face harder than usual. "You want to be free of me?"

Camarão swished her hand. "Oh, don't even try dangling that in front of me. I'll never be free of you. That's obvious."

With a crooked grin, Guia straightened and said, "Today's different. You will come with me. You must obey the orders of a superior officer. No need to change for this. Those clothes are fine."

"Superior officer," Camarão grumbled. She loathed Guia, but knew the Navy's punishments for failing to follow orders, or worse, for kicking a captain's rear end. Sighing, she stood. "Lead on. What is it this time? Climb Mount Everest with a piano on my back? Earn the Millennium Prize for cracking an unsolvable math problem? Beat a grandmaster at three-dimensional chess?"

"You'll *wish* it were merely one of those," Guia said, saluting the amidships watch as they left HMMS Machico and entered the underwater tunnel to Áquaforte.

Where's she taking me? Camarão felt very under-dressed in her duty work clothes, trailing behind Guia in her full-dress white uniform. From the underwater submarine depot, they rode an elevator up, even past the surface level to the tower that projected above the surface.

The elevator stopped and the doors opened. Without a word, Guia led her past two well-dressed, and well-armed, guards and through a gold-trimmed door. This repeated at two more doors, both with posted guards and one with a receptionist. The farther they went, the more lavish the décor. Servants hurried about, pushing carts, toting trays, or carrying documents. Camarão felt very out of place in her grubby, sweat-stained jumpsuit.

Guia stopped before another door and turned to Camarão. "Let's have a look at you." She gazed up and down. "Hmmpf. You'll do. Let's go." Without speaking to the guards, or getting a reaction from them, Guia pushed open the door.

Inside, a long red carpet led to a collection of people, all standing.

"Your Majesty!" Camarão gasped and curtseyed low, her eyes cast down. Beside her, Guia also curtseyed.

King Castelo, Monarch of Madiera, stood there, tall and regal, wearing his purple robe and gold braid. "Arise, Renata Novo and Ofélia Machado."

Who? From a near-forgotten memory, Camarão recalled her real name. Apparently, Guia had a real name, too. She stood and faced him.

"Before we get started," the king said, "there are two people who are very anxious to meet you, Renata." He nodded at someone behind her.

She whirled around and saw a man and a woman walking toward her along the red carpet. They smiled at her and looked… familiar…older…

"Mamãe? Papai?" Camarão ran the few steps and hugged them both, her tears mixing with theirs. At length, they let her go and backed away.

"You will see them again, soon," the King said, "but we have a more pressing matter."

Camarão turned toward him. "How may I serve you, Your Majesty?"

"It's the other way around," he said. "Tomorrow morning, I'll abdicate my throne and you'll be crowned Queen of Madiera."

"What?" Her mind raced. This had to be a joke, yet no one laughed. "Forgive me, Your Majesty, I don't understand."

"The past twenty years of your life, under the supervision of your Guia, have all been in preparation for this. I'm sorry for the rough treatment and the deception, but it's how we do things."

"Rough treatment? Deception?" Camarão turned to Guia. "You ripped me away from my parents. You raised me in the Bilge where I ate scraps and rats. You told me I wasn't fit to live with people. What's more, you taught me to distrust *all* leaders. You even told me our King is sub-par and uninspired." In her rising anger, she'd forgotten who else was present. "Oh, I'm so sorry, Your Majesty. Please forgive me."

The King laughed. "Your Guia has taught you well. With her preparation, you stand a good chance of being a fine queen."

"Preparation? Sire, it's been torture. What if I don't *want* to be queen? What if I refuse?"

"It's a strange paradox," the King said, "but not wanting this job actually makes you better suited for it. You may refuse, of course. We can't force you to be the queen. For the past twenty years, we've also been training a backup, not only in case of your refusal, but also in case of accidents."

"Accidents." That triggered memories. "I suppose the time I nearly died aboard a submarine was all staged, then? Just a big studio with props, sets, and actors?"

"No, Cama—, I mean, Renata," Guia said. "That was real. I couldn't be there to protect you from everything. There are risks with this training process."

The King reached out and touched Renata's shoulder. "I know it seems cruel to you now, but this is how we train our leaders in Madeira. Humanity has long sought a method of selecting monarchs who are wise, beneficent, and incorruptible. This is our way. Just today, somewhere in Madiera, two Guias removed two five-year-old boys from their schools. In twenty years, one of those boys will succeed you, should you choose to serve as our queen."

Renata shook her head. "This is too much to take in, Your Majesty. May I have some time alone, please?"

"Certainly, Crown Princess Renata." The King clapped his hands and people began exiting the room.

"Except for Guia. I'd like her to stay."

When all but her teacher had left, Renata stared out the window at the above-water portion of Áquaforte, and the ocean beyond. "I still hate you, Guia, for what you've done."

"Tomorrow, when you are queen, you may have me executed."

"Not exactly the act of a merciful sovereign."

"Not an act you should shy away from, either, when necessary for justice."

Renata let that sink in. "I may hate you, Guia, but you taught me everything I know. I don't mind telling you, I'm scared of being a queen. Can I tote a piano up Everest, instead?"

"All your easy tasks are over now." Guia grinned, then sobered. "I pray you will always feel some fear, some humility, about being our monarch. So long as you respect the position, you won't become arrogant."

"Am I truly ready for this?"

"You're as ready as I could make you." Guia's eyes were moist. "How well do you think I did?"

Surprised at the question, Renata looked at her and laughed. "Hmmpf."

Deep Currents

*T*his *band she'd formed, Harper Greene felt sure, would go* absolutely tidal. Only with difficulty did she restrain her excitement about it during her weekly video-call with her mother.

Weakened by third-stage spinal bone cancer in her mid-sixties, Harper's mom spent her time in the therapeutic fluid tanks of the Watsu Geriatric Center in the aquastate of Pernamia. Only her head showed above water on the video screen, and her mood seemed positive as she recounted the recent tests she'd endured, meals she'd eaten, and Mahjongg games she'd played with other patients at the center. Harper felt thankful her mother had adapted to life in a swimming pool.

Her mom paused. "What's new with you, Harper?"

"Remember me telling you I was holding try-outs for a new band I wanted to manage?"

"I thought that was all you ever did."

Mom said it with a quick grin and twinkling eyes, but the comment still stung. Ever since college, Harper had wanted to manage a rock band, but none of those she'd assembled had ever succeeded. Though most bands formed by themselves first and then sought a manager, Harper believed she could bring the best musicians together for a group with the optimum sound. At forty-one, she'd long wondered if she'd ever find that ultimate combination of talent.

"I'm dolphin-leaping today, Mom. This group has everything. They're young; they're all 'steaders—no landers—and their voices blend like…I can't describe it. I've just got to tell you about them. First, there's Dylann, of course…"

Dylann Wavecrest, Harper's nephew, had exhibited musical talent early in life. He displayed a flair for composing and had taken to playing the hydraulophone, a pipe organ using water rather than air. He dreamed of creating a new sound for the seasteading aquastates, a fresh genre of music suited to oceanic life. He'd given the band its name—Denizens of the Deep.

"…and our aquatar player, who's going to drive girls wild. He's still getting used to the instrument, but he's got a strong, clear tenor. His real name's Gino, but he's chosen a stage name—Zak Manta. Then we got a pretty girl named Sunrize. She's from Mu, naturally, with a name like that, but she's picked the stage name of Krysta. Her soprano floats above the boy's voices without being shrill. She plays the glass armonica, and it sounds positively ethereal. Our fluidrummer is Ngoma, who's still trying to get used to Dylann's rhythms, but he sings with a wide base-to-baritone range, the smoothest voice you ever heard. Honestly, I think this is the group I've been waiting my whole career for. It's going to be so much fun managing them."

Her mom nodded. "I'm happy for you, Harper, and hope this band succeeds. How well do they get along with each other?"

Harper winced, then rubbed her eye to disguise that reaction. "They're young, Mom, all in their late teens or early twenties, and they just met for the first time. You know, sizing each other up, posturing, dealing with sexual tensions. They'll work all that out, believe me. Their music will bind them together."

"It seems you're going from zero children to four rather quickly." Her mom reached off-camera, brought a drink to her lips, and sipped. "That's a lot for any parent."

"I'm not their mother." A decade earlier, Harper's contract marriage had failed, and she'd never had children. She knew her lack of children bothered her mother, but this band couldn't substitute for that. *Still.* "Hmm. I see your point, Mom. Managing a band is a little like raising a family. Do you have any parental advice for me?"

Mom shook her head and chuckled. "When have you ever listened to my advice?"

Is she just poking me to get a reaction? "I'm listening now, Mom. I really want to know."

Mom gazed without saying anything, then moved her face closer to the camera until just her two eyes and nose filled the screen. "Okay, here it is. Being a parent is the world's toughest job. You work twenty-four/seven for zero pay. You agonize over your children's aches; you bleed from their cuts; you weep over their disappointments. You scold them when you're together; you worry when you're apart. Sure, you get to shape the future, but only by giving up yours. Even if you're good, you'll think you're horrible."

She backed away from the camera. "Even if you're the best, Harper, you'll get no credit. They never build statues to commemorate parents."

Her eyes shut, Harper smiled, nodding in rhythm to the music.

"Stop, stop, stop," Dylann shouted, and the others ceased playing. "You're not getting it."

"Been at this for three hours, man." Zak glared at him. "how 'bout a break?"

When her nephew scowled back, Harper intervened. "That's a good idea. Everyone relax for fifteen. Then you can start fresh and rehearse a different song."

"Flukin' Neptune, it's so cold." Krysta rubbed her arms. "Why do we have to practice *here*, anyway?"

The band had set up in a corner of the desalinization plant of Rhapsodia, a seastead in the aquastate of Clarion. Surrounded by metal vats and purification equipment, they had privacy since few workers came their way. "Look, I'm sorry," Harper said, "But this is the only place I could get for free that still had juice for your amps."

"Rotten acoustics," Dylann grumbled. He was the only band member who'd converted to the seasteading religion of Oceanism. He'd undergone the Immersion operation and sported green-dyed skin, surf-styled hair, surgically webbed fingers, and a tattoo of a humpback whale on his forehead.

"This is how it works, guys," Harper said. "You rehearse until you sound good. If people like your songs, they pay to hear you. *Then* we can afford a better rehearsal room."

"You mean when we're rich," Ngoma said.

"And famous," Krysta said.

"And loved by all." Zak smiled at Krysta, who stuck out her tongue.

Harper laughed, shaking her head. "No sense dreaming about that. Focus on making your songs sound better."

"That'll take a while, Aunt Harper." Dylann looked up from the electronic pad he used for composing. "They're not getting my vision."

"When we're famous, we'll get to choose our own outfits," Krysta said, looking up and smiling at something she alone saw. "I want an old-timey costume with frilly sleeves." She swept her hand across the length of the glass armonica, a set of nested, rotating glass goblets she played with moistened fingers. Benjamin Franklin had invented it, but hers was amped. "What do you think?" She looked at Ngoma.

Ignoring her, Ngoma laid his drumsticks down. "Gonna buy the biggest apartment in Rhapsodia, and my own sub."

Harper smiled at the youthful enthusiasm and wild imaginations of these four kids huddled in a water purification plant. She also saw their nearer term, more intimate interests. Zak sought to get in Krysta's jeans. She had no interest in him, but showed a fondness for Ngoma, with his sturdy frame, long dreadlocks, and mixed African-Hispanic features. *Good luck with that, girl. He's gay.* To complete the impossible triangle, Ngoma showed an attraction for the handsome Zak that would never be reciprocated. And her nephew Dylann sat apart, aloof, lost in his music. His creative mind churned out songs more real to him than any live person.

She sighed. *If only they could see themselves as I hear them. A little rough now, but with practice, they'll sound like pure platinum. If I can keep them together.*

"If you're done spending money we haven't earned yet," Dylann stood up, "I wanna talk about the music. You know, that noise we're here to make?" He turned to Krysta. "You're singing too loud. The whole idea is to blend with us."

Krysta sneered at him but kept silent.

"And Zak, you're gonna break that thing if you keep flailing at it. Strum *gently*."

Zak pretended to kick the aquatar. "I want my guitar back. This thing feels wrong." His aquatar looked much like an electric guitar, but the strings stretched inside a flexible membrane filled with water. To play it, he pressed against the membrane with his left hand and strummed it with his right.

Dylann threw his head back and closed his eyes, then stared at Zak. "No. All our instruments use water. That's the whole point. This isn't rock. This is *Liquisic*, the sound that's gonna *replace* rock. Music for the seasteading world. We're the only ones doing it." He looked at Ngoma. "Or *will* be, if our fluidrummer can hook onto a syncopated six-eight rhythm. This isn't four-four time. It rolls along, like water. Get the flow, man?"

Ngoma glowered at him, picked up his drumsticks, and beat out a six-eight rhythm, advancing each downbeat. His fluidrum gave off its characteristic muffled, echoing reverberation with every note.

"See? You *can* get it," Dylann nodded with the beat. "That's the wave I'm angling for."

Ngoma concluded his beat with a crash of the water-cymbals. He leaned forward in his chair. "Harper, when we gonna get paid?"

"Didn't I tell you?" she asked. "Right after Friday night's gig at the Gnarly Narwhal."

A chorus of groans answered her.

"There *again*?" Krysta asked. "We should branch out, ya know, go on tour."

"Not how this biz works, Denizens." Harper tapped her e-pad. "You establish a local rep first. Let word spread, get good buzz, hit every club in this 'stead. After that, we can afford studio time and record an album. *Then* we go on tour."

Zak mumbled something, and Harper thought it sounded like, "Then we fire our manager."

Maybe they all hate me, but someone has to be the adult in the room. "Okay, break's over," she said. "Why don't you practice one of your upbeat numbers?"

Instead, Dylann had them rehearse the forlorn song, 'Compass Rose,' with its plaintive lyrics:

"'Cross the four compass points she has tattered our love;
To the four winds, my Compass Rose scattered our love."

The music died down, and one of the techs spoke into his mic. "Sorry, Denizens, but we're picking up some screechy feedback. Not from you; it's our equipment. Give us a few minutes to track it down. Hang loose in there."

Harper saw Ngoma, Krysta, and Dylann lean back in their chairs, while Zak sat down to drink some water. They'd long ago worked through their ill-fated infatuations and settled into a general dislike of each other moderated by a love of their success. Harper entered the recording room, anxious to convey the good news. Holding up her e-pad, she said, "*This Minute* just reviewed Saturday's concert. Listen:

"The music of Denizens of the Deep," Harper read, "gleams like an enticing anglerfish lure across the abyss of the 'steading music scene. They completely swept the crowd in the Thomas Andrews Arena in Titania last Saturday night, while thousands of fans screamed for more.

"From their opening number, 'Beyond All Charts' to such briny hits as 'Plenty of Fish in the Sea,' 'Her Aqua Eyes,' and 'Dancin' on the Seabed,' this foursome held the audience spellbound. Their chart-topping encore song, 'She Left Me for a Merman (Don't Want No More of Her, Man)' stirred the crowd to a frenzy.

"Their voices mix, flow, and weave in a way that makes four harmonies sound like intertwined melodies. With the irrepressible Ngoma Camacho, hyper-talented Dylann Wavecrest, super-stud Zak Manta, and tantalizing Krysta (who's started her own fashion craze), no other group can touch this foursome or their unique and watery sound. They call their music *Liquisic*; we call it mind-blowing; you'll call it your new fave.

"Don't miss the Denizens of the Deep when their current tour reaches your 'stead. This Saturday, they'll be at…etc., etc." Harper tapped the file closed. "Welcome to the big-time, gang."

"Hmm. Intertwined melodies. Watery sound," Dylann smiled. "That writer gets it. That's Liquisic. It's contrapuntal."

"Contra-what?" Ngoma squinted at him. He'd begun wearing gold watches, bracelets, earrings, and neck chains. Harper thought gold looked good on him.

"Contrapuntal," Dylann faced Ngoma. "Four voices, four instruments, none dominating the others. Each line is nothing much until combined with the others."

"Wouldn't kill you to let me solo," Krysta said, popping some Rainbow Gum in her mouth. Like a girl half her age, she often plucked it from her mouth to observe its random color changes.

Dylann played a jarring discord on his hydraulophone. "No solos. Don't you get the metaphor? We're an ecosystem, like the ocean. All elements are necessary, none more important than the others."

"Just a couple flukin' solos," Krysta raised her voice and leaned forward on her instrument. "Holy Neptune, am I asking too much?"

"Settle down, guys. We'll work this out." Harper made a calming motion with her hands palm-down. *Flotz. I'm talking just like Mom breaking up quarrels between me and my sister.* "Later. Now's not the time." *Krysta's got a point. Have to talk to Dylann in private.*

Zak stood up. "I'm going out for some air. I'm turning my phone on; call me when they fix their feedback problem."

Harper knew he was going out for more than fresh air. She'd spoken to him in private about his growing addiction to gass, the euphoric and illegal drug produced from the sargassum plant. "Please stay, Zak. They'll have it fixed any minute now."

He whirled, his eyes blazing, and walked over to look down on Harper. "You're not my mother. You're just our manager, and maybe not that for much longer. What I do, and who I sleep with, in my off-time is my business."

Shocked that he'd bring that up, she stood to face him, though still shorter than he was. She'd politely and privately warned him about his habit of picking an attractive female fan after each concert to take to his room. He'd had to pay for several abortions and had to settle a rape accusation. One day, Harper had warned him, sex would get him in trouble. "Do you really want to go there, Zak? Here and now, in front of everyone?"

"Yeah, let's have it out. Right now."

"No, we're not discussing your private life in public." Harper swept her hand to include the audio technicians behind the studio window, all of whom looked suddenly busy.

"Why not? You're trying to *run* my private life."

"Yours too?" Ngoma stood, his neck chains rattling. "She tried to tell me how to spend my money."

She'd taken Ngoma aside several times to ask why he and his partner kept trashing hotel rooms and racking up huge repair bills. "What do you care?" He'd asked. "It's only money. *My* money." She'd suggested he retain a financial advisor and offered to recommend one, but he'd refused.

"We don't need a manager who nags and tells us how to live our lives." Zak stood, looming over her, and Ngoma came over to stand beside him.

Harper glanced at the other two to gauge their opinions. Krysta waited, but showed no emotion. Her gum changed from green to red. Dylann, her own nephew, hunched forward typing musical notes into his e-pad.

What did mom tell me? They never build statues of parents? Never mind a statue; my band is ready to burn me in effigy or stick pins in a voodoo doll.

The voice of one of the techs came over the speaker. "All right, Denizens. Fixed it. You can record whenever you're ready."

"Thank you," Harper called to her. "Give us a moment. Please mute this room until I come out."

Then she set her jaw, turned to face the group, and rapped on Dylann's e-pad until he looked up. "Listen up, all of you. Fire me if you want to, but hear me out first. I created this band. Each of you was nothing before I brought you together. Now look at what you've done in one year. Seventy-two sold out concerts in twenty-seven seasteads. Adoring reviews. This third album. You have the world at your feet." She paused for effect, and to catch her breath, then resumed in a softer voice. "When you perform together, it's magic. Your music ripples out to touch everyone's heart. But when each show's over, you're like frenzied sharks, attacking me and each other. And who's the one—the *only* one—trying to keep you together? Me."

She looked at Dylann, Krysta, Zak, and Ngoma in turn. "You want the music, the acclaim, the fans, and the money to continue? Consider keeping me around. In the meantime, just do your magic and record 'On Course to You.'" She walked out of the recording room.

Entering the backstage lounge, Harper found the band dressed for the concert and seated in their accustomed pre-show alignment— facing away from each other like the four stems of a plus sign. She'd been the one to suggest that arrangement two years earlier, to avoid arguments before going onstage.

Ngoma's gold glittered, including shiny strands in his chest-length dreadlocks. Oddly, he wore fewer chains and bracelets today than on previous nights. Zak sported his trademark tight jeans and the red silk shirt he typically tore off in the final number. He looked calm, not agitated or scowling. As usual, Dylann wore faded jeans and a ratty gray sweatshirt and sat hunched over his e-pad. Krysta sat resplendent in her mock-colonial frilly outfit, though no woman from the 1700s would have dared such a low-cut front or such a high hemline below. The retro 'Krysta' look had wowed fashion shows in Paris and Altair.

"Good, you're all together," Harper motioned for them to move their chairs so they faced her. "Warm-up band's into their final number, and you'll be introduced after they're done. We agreed you'd open with 'Divin' into Love,' right? That should get the audience's fins flapping. And Zak, don't forget, it's 'Thank you, Kubla Dome.' That's *Kubla Dome.' Great Neptune, please don't mispronounce it or thank the wrong 'stead again.* She paused and smiled. "Guys, this is your biggest venue yet. You're gonna be great and...Krysta, what are you doing?"

The glass armonica player sat typing on her e-pad. She made a final tap on the keypad and looked up, grinning. "I'm quitting. That was my agent. The TideRiders need a new lead singer, and I accepted. Hear that, Dylann? *Lead singer.*" She stood and strode toward her adjoining dressing room. "I'll just change and go. See ya."

Stunned, Harper needed several seconds to recover. "Krysta, there are twenty-five thousand screaming fans out there, waiting for all four Denizens. You can't quit now. You signed a contract."

Krysta shrugged. "Breaking it." She shut the door behind her.

Harper stared, fish-mouthed, at the door.

"I was gonna say this afterward," Zak stood up, "but might as well do it now. I'm quitting, too. Retiring, starting a family."

Both Ngoma and Dylann laughed as if he'd told a good joke, and even Harper found the family comment implausible.

"Seriously, guys." Zak looked serene and sincere, and somehow more mature. "I've fallen in love."

This brought on fresh bouts of laughter from the other boys, and Zak talked right over them.

"We're going to get married, keep the baby, and settle down. I ain't travelling all over anymore." He turned toward his own private dressing room.

"Wait, Zak." Harper saw one hope of staving off disaster. "Maybe the audio tech guys can dub in Krysta's voice and the armonica. We'll make some excuse for her absence—a cold, maybe. But we can't go out there with just two. Please stay with us, just tonight. You can break your contract afterward."

Zak opened the door and looked back over his shoulder. "No, Harper. I'm done."

"Ngoma, talk some sense into Zak," Harper reached out to him. "You know the value of money. Tell him he can't walk away from his cut. He can't deny his new family 1.3 million digibucks."

In the doorway, Zak didn't appear inclined to listen.

Ngoma shook his head. "I'm quitting too."

"What?"

The fluidrummer sighed, hung his head, and then looked up at her. "Before this band, I was a poor kid from Spectruma. No job, no prospects. But, poor as I was, I didn't owe nobody nothin'. Now I'm drowning in debt. Filing for bankruptcy. Longer I stay a Denizen, the worse it gets." He stood. "Yeah, I *do* know the value of money. I'm better off without it." He didn't bother with his dressing room. He took the door leading out.

With tears coming on, Harper looked at Dylann. "What are we going to do?"

Dylann rose and put a webbed hand on her shoulder. "Probably best this way, Aunt Harper. They never got what I was trying to do. Don't worry about me. I've got more music inside me" —he tapped his temple— "than the Denizens could ever record. I been talking with the Orca Syndicate. They wanna hire me to write liquisic for them. Won't have to perform at all. They'll have fifteen bands singing my songs. It's a dream opportunity. I can't turn 'em down."

He rose and hugged her. "Good-bye, Aunt Harper. Thanks for everything."

Five minutes later, Harper sat on the couch, alone, crying.

Just outside the room, she heard the stage manager's voice. "Okay, Denizens, you're onnn..." His voice trailed off when he poked his head in. His eyes met Harper's. "Where'd they go?"

With tears running down her face, she spread her hands out, palms up. "'Cross the four compass points...to the four winds..."

This time, Harper skipped the small talk. As soon as the image of her mother appeared on the videophone screen—her face wet and glistening from a recent total immersion in the therapeutic tank—Harper began talking through her sobs.

"The band broke up, Mom. They all quit." Her tears stung, but she let them roll down. Years seemed to melt away as if she cried to her mother about skinning a knee or losing a boyfriend.

"I'm sorry, Angelfish."

Mom hadn't called her that for three decades. "It's just like you warned me, Mom. Managing a band *is* like parenting, or like it must be." She wiped her eyes.

"They changed, did they? Left you and went out on their own? How unusual."

Harper picked up the irony in her tone but was in no mood for mind games. "It's the *way* they quit. Just left me having to cancel the concert and all their bookings, and make the embarrassing press announcements."

"They spared you the long good-byes. Good. I always hated those."

"Mom, you're not helping."

"Believe it or not, I am." A soft chime sounded and her mom looked away.

"Am I interrupting anything, Mom? I'm sorry."

"It's time for my mahjongg group. They'll wait. Listen, Harper, you're just wasting a good cry."

"You don't understand. I worked *so hard.*" Harper's lower lip quivered and she smacked her palm with a fist. "I did everything I could to keep that band together."

"Really?" Her mom's mouth twitched, as if she wanted to smile but thought better of it. "Why?"

Harper stared at her, dumbstruck. "Because that's a manager's job. Just like a parent's job is to keep a family together."

"Is that what you think? You didn't get that from me. Harper, you set yourself up for disappointment. The job of a parent is to produce independent adults. Sounds to me like you succeeded."

Harper shook her head. "That's where your comparison breaks down. A manager *is* supposed to keep her band together. And I failed."

Her mom crossed her arms. "The jobs don't seem that different to me. Few bands stick together for decades. Those kids never got along, yet you kept the band going for three years. Could anyone else have done better? I think you're selling yourself short."

"Then why do I feel like they broke my heart?"

"Oh, my daughter, this was never about your feelings, never about you at all." She tilted her head. "Did Dylann and the others learn something? Did your school of little fish grow up?"

Harper thought about that and wiped her tears away again. "I guess so. Maybe they're all getting what they wanted." She felt an odd stirring then, a connection to something like a deep ocean current, an ageless and cyclic current that flowed through human generations.

"Well, then," her mother smiled. "Time you move on to whatever's next for you. You did well, and I'm proud of you."

Something taut inside Harper loosened then, and she felt a

warm sensation grow within, while her misery ebbed away. "Maybe I wasn't so bad after all."

Her mom's eyes twinkled. "That's my Angelfish." She leaned closer to the screen. "But you still don't get a statue."

Eyes of Blue

ike my ancestors, I'd set out to kill a whale. That's illegal,
L of course, but it had been a family tradition for three
generations to violate those laws, and yours truly, Toru Mizumoto,
wasn't about to defy tradition. Aboard my one-man submarine, I
watched the sonar and kept track of my pod. It numbered five Sei
whales, all headed southwest through Mu toward their mating and
breeding area. Though I owned the entire pod, I was only interested in
its oldest member, a female named Sei-rah Conner.

Don't blame me for her name; whoever owned the pod when
she was born had the naming rights. Sei-rah swam at the rear of the
group, her strokes and her voice still strong. With a different pod
owner, she might live for several more years. That wasn't my plan.

The pod lumbered along at eight knots, the two calves
frolicking, the two adult females trying to restrain and protect them,
and the bull moving all around the pod, alert for threats.

Whales knew nothing of aquastates, but I'd had to request
and receive permission to cross the Mu border. Most oceanic nations
recognized whale migration patterns and moved their farming nets
out of the way to form an open channel. Some countries didn't though,
forcing pod owners to guide their whales the long way around. Luckily
for me, Mu had a migration channel.

If you're a typical, law-abiding pod owner, you wait patiently for a member of the pod to die, either naturally or in combat with an orca or giant squid. Once the whale dies, you deploy robotic subs to encase the carcass in a giant bag of tough plastic to protect it from sharks. You tow your catch to the nearest seastead with a slaughterhouse where they appraise it. You sell the carcass and either return to your pod or use your money to buy a higher-value pod. That's what good whalers do, but some of us don't wait around for whales to die on their own.

Bit by bit, I'd maneuvered into attack position. For luck, I reached over and patted the small *butsudan* I kept aboard. Most people kept such family shrines in their homes, but my sub was more of a home than my seastead apartment could ever be. A rectangular cabinet carved from whalebone, my *butsudan* contained objects commemorating my ancestors going back dozens of generations, long before the family moved to Kaiyō Kokka, back to when they lived in Japan. I felt proud to be the latest in a long line of whalers.

The job had been quite different for my long-ago ancestors in the era of sails and harpoons. They'd killed up on the surface, where the whales went to breathe. My ancestors faced harsh weather and fierce whales to bring home their catch. But they hadn't had to contend with other humans.

I accelerated to get lower, just beneath Sei-rah, but not close enough to trigger any alerts from the Cetacean Protection Organization Monitor trailing off to the beast's right, a little behind me. It had taken all day for me to reach the right alignment of whale, monitor, and me. Things were almost perfect for what I had to do.

You can explain to people about the inefficiency of eating meat, how it takes ten kilos of plankton to produce one kilo of whale filets, and how much better it would be to just eat the plankton. They won't care. "Shut up and pass the whale steak," they'd say. But the same people who feel no qualms about letting someone else slaughter cows, well, those same people have a thing about harming whales.

In the years when my great-grandfather and grandfather had hunted, the International Whaling Commission harassed them. The

IWC had rejected arguments that whaling was a traditional part of Japanese culture and had imposed severe restrictions because some whale species were endangered. Once seasteading became widespread, many feared humanity's migration to the sea would drive whales extinct. Instead, the opposite happened. As soon as people could own pods, whales flourished. Wild animal species sometimes do go extinct, but no *owned* species with economic value ever has.

Still, people think whales are different, so we have the Cetacean Protection Organization. The CPO made it illegal to kill a whale, though if one died naturally, you could tow it to the slaughterhouse. The trick, therefore, was to make an intentional death look natural.

From my onboard 3D printer, I extracted a small, dart-shaped object, about ten centimeters long. I pushed its arming button and placed it, point down and propeller up, into the trash ejector alongside some garbage.

The CPO knew about law-flouting whalers like me, and took extensive measures to stop us. To accompany every pod of whales, whether owned or not, the CPO sent a monitor, an unmanned vehicle with sophisticated AI. Using visual and acoustic sensors, the monitor tracked the movements and actions of whales and of pod-owning whalers. After the death of any whale, the monitor examined the body, and only after it backed away could the pod owner encase the carcass and tow it away. Even then, if the monitor's AI suspected foul play, the vehicle would surface and radio all nearby seasteads, citing its observations. All slaughterhouses in all seasteads would then refuse payment and the offending whaler would face fines and imprisonment.

The CPO also inspected all pod owners' subs before they got underway. The female CPO inspector who'd examined mine had scanned all my computer files and did a thorough search of my sub, but gave only a brief glance inside my *butsudan*. Within the shrine I'd hidden a flash chip with all the files needed to 3D print my killer dart. In this way, my ancestors had assisted me even after death, and for that I gave thanks.

That is, I thanked ancestors on my father's side, not my mother's. Her family came from Karakuwa, and for this I felt shame. Centuries ago, according to local legend, a ship from that town encountered a fierce storm and almost capsized. A pair of whales was supposed to have nestled up to both sides of the ship and guided it into port. Ever since then, the townsfolk of Karakuwa looked kindly upon whales, and neither hunted nor ate them. No meal prepared by my mother ever included whale meat, and she didn't eat it when my father made it. This I never understood.

The time had arrived. I maneuvered slowly to the left, then up alongside Sei-rah, the huge whale's bulk blocking the monitor's view of me. I pressed the button to operate the trash ejector. Upon sensing seawater, my 3D printed dart was programmed to activate, swim out, and seek the distinctive sounds of Sei-Rah, whose voice I'd programmed it to find. It would motor toward that sound and enter the mouth, where it would slip between the baleen plates, the bristly screen inside the mouth that sieved plankton. Then sharp miniature cutters would spin and chew through flesh toward the beast's brain. There it would wreak havoc, lacerating brain matter in every lobe of that organ. Finally, my little dart would tear its way to the stomach where digestive acid would dissolve it, eliminating all trace of my involvement.

After releasing my deadly dart, I angled down and away from Sei-rah, back into the monitor's view. I then meandered around the pod, continuing a cruising pattern I'd established days earlier.

Although I loathed the monitor and the CPO with a deep-seated hatred, I had to respect both. Whaling had never been a risk-free business. My ancestors had overcome their obstacles; the monitor was mine to deal with. Either I was clever enough to fool it, or I'd go to jail.

Off to my right loomed a long, surface-to-bottom wall of netting, marking the boundary of the vast algae farms of Mu. My sonar showed a blip, a harvester sub gathering a swath of algae. I sniffed with derision. Such a boring job, no challenge or danger.

Half an hour after I released my dart, Sei-rah shuddered and cried out in tones my sub's computer associated with cetacean pain. The pod reacted, the others slowing and the bull rushing to her side. Her vast body shook one more time and her flukes and fins ceased moving. No further sounds emerged. The bull nudged her, waited, and then moved on, prodding the rest of the group forward. Whether his quick-tempo *eew-eew-eew* sounds were a command to continue the migration or a funeral dirge, my computer couldn't say.

I sent an acoustic signal to the CPO monitor that I'd noticed a death within the pod, but it had already moved in toward Sei-rah as soon as the bull departed. Inert, the whale's body slowly floated toward the surface while the unmanned vehicle swam around it, examining it from every aspect.

Sweat broke out on my brow, and I chewed my lower lip, hoping the monitor would not detect my involvement with Sei-rah's demise. A familiar churning in my gut began. Of all the steps in my high-risk, high-reward occupation, this aggravated me the most. Whether I reaped an enormous profit or went to prison lay in the circuits of an uncaring software program. How I wished the CPO could have afforded *manned* monitor vessels. I could have coaxed, wheedled, flattered, bribed, or blackmailed a human. Nothing but trickery worked against an AI, and often not even that.

Some pod owners experience more whale deaths than others, and the CPO watches them more closely. I was one of those who merited a lot of suspicion and careful scrutiny. But suspicion doesn't prove guilt; they have to catch you doing something illegal.

The agonizing minutes crept along as the monitor explored the immense carcass. I held my breath when it scrutinized the whale's gigantic mouth. Had my dart betrayed me by leaving some sign at its entry point? Maybe the monitor's acoustic sensors would detect suspicious holes in the creature's brain or tunnels carved though the flesh. I stroked the smooth white side of the *butsudan* for luck, imploring my ancestors to exert their supernatural influence over the monitor's cold and logical processors.

Following what seemed a lifetime of fretful waiting, I saw the monitor back away from the remains of Sei-rah. It sent the acoustic message I'd been hoping for, and it appeared on my screen: "Whale inspection complete. No anomalies detected. Scavenging authorized."

With a smile of gratitude for the intervention of my ancestors and a deep sigh of relief, I got to work. I deployed six UUVs to encase the carcass in a huge plastic envelope and to attach the tow cables.

Along with my fully authorized catch, I set course for Le Plongeo, largest seastead in Mu. I had, once again, proven myself worthy of the Mizumoto name and brought honor upon it. In tricking the CPO, I'd furthered a long heritage of successful whaling.

A month later, back in my sub, I still felt proud, and with even more reason. Fortune had not only smiled at me; she'd given me a hug. At Le Plongeo, I found the price of whale meat had risen due to the accidental spoilage of a vast supply half the world away in the Thulean Republic. That meant my rather average twenty-three metric ton Sei whale carcass netted twice the price I expected.

Even better, another whaler needed to sell her pod fast, just at the moment I was ready to buy. She'd simply retired. Whether from frustration, or boredom, or shame brought on by paying too much attention to anti-whaling protesters, she didn't say, and I didn't ask.

Her pod consisted of a single whale, a big old blue. Owning a blue had been a dream of mine, a goal I'd thought unattainable. They're so rarely for sale, and even then, only at monstrous prices. No one in my family line had ever owned, or even attacked, a blue whale, so in this way, I'd already achieved greatness and honor beyond that of my ancestors.

The CPO database showed my new whale migrating north through Mendocino, and there I found it, migrating toward its winter breeding area in Aleut. On first sighting it, I gasped. Having dealt only with the smaller species, I was astonished and humbled by this largest of all creatures in Earth's history. Named Azraq, he left me in abject awe. Measuring thirty meters in length and likely topping 170 metric tons, Azraq flicked his vast flukes slowly and moved with majestic grace. The fluid undulations of his tail had a hypnotic quality that seemed somehow at odds with the immense muscular power working to propel his titanic mass.

Azraq was around ninety-five years old, the previous pod owner had told me. Once unheard of, such longevity had become more common for all whale species. All pod owners protected their whales by fending off predators and by steering pods away from harmful surface ship propellers. This helped extend whale lifetimes, and Azraq had certainly benefited from his owner's care. His advanced age was another stroke of good fortune for me. He might die at any moment, and if not, it should take only minor action from me to deliver the fatal blow.

A CPO monitor already motored near my whale when I arrived, of course, and it dogged me closer than any previous monitor had. After all, Azraq was his own pod, which simplified the monitor's job. However, having a monitor always at my side greatly complicated my task.

For one thing, I'd be unable to use a 3D printed dart this time. I couldn't hide behind the whale's bulk even for an instant to launch the dart, and despite the dart's minute size, the monitor might well detect it. Still, I hadn't become a preeminent whale-killer by stocking only one arrow in my quiver.

To kill Azraq, the least risky method was the saser. Yes, I'm referring to that secret military weapon developed by the Nazcator Navy, the acoustic version of a laser. Through a few unsavory connections, I'd purchased one from a black-market arms dealer and installed it in my mini-sub. That buy had nearly bankrupted me, and the subsequent acquisition of Azraq himself had left me without any savings or assets beyond my sub. I'd bet everything on this whale, but bringing in his carcass would set me up for life. I could retire, start a family, and begin raising the next generation of Mizumoto whalers.

How did my saser equipment miss being spotted by the in-port CPO inspector? Not for lack of trying on his part, that's for sure.

He opened every locker, unscrewed every panel cover, and beamed his flashlight into every crevice. He even inspected my *butsudan*, and would have discovered my flash chip had I hidden it there this time. But I hadn't, knowing even then I'd be unable to use the dart.

"What's in there?" He had pointed to a circular, bolted-on tank cover.

"Sanitary tank," I'd replied, keeping my face impassive. He certainly would have known that; my sub was a standard Harrison Model W-6, and the sanitary tank was always located there.

The submarine designers who'd first termed these containers *sanitary tanks* must have had a sick sense of humor, for these are the tanks the toilet empties into. A submarine's sewer.

He gazed at me, his eyes narrowing slightly, as if assessing the probability that I'd hide something illegal in a place he really didn't want to open, let alone stick his head into. I saw it in his eyes first, the eyes being the windows to the soul. They shifted slightly, then widened, and only then did his skeptical expression soften. "All right, Mr. Mizumoto," he said. "You're clear to go."

I'd previously mounted my saser within the sanitary tank, and what a disgusting, putrid-smelling task that had been. Even recalling that day now makes me shudder and gag.

Operating the saser required a brief opening of the sanitary tank cover, and I waited until the last moment to do that. I'd been motoring along with Azraq for a few days, not only to learn his habits, but also to establish a routine for myself so the monitor wouldn't get suspicious, and to ensure I didn't kill my whale so early that it aroused those same suspicions. Even with a clip pinching my nostrils shut and ventilations fans set on high, I hated opening that tank long enough to remove the saser remote controller and to shut the tank cover on the flat portion of the connecting wires. With the tank lid mostly shut, that cut down on much of the stench, but not all of it.

I'd done some calculations on how to use this weapon, but didn't have complete confidence in them. Aiming a saser is tricky, and

I'd never used it on a blue whale before, so wasn't sure about the power level setting. After all, at maximum intensity, it could cut through a metal submarine hull. My best option seemed to be a shot straight into the gullet. If I sped far enough ahead of a school of krill, then I'd have my opportunity when Azraq opened his vast maw to feed. Assuming my settings were right, I'd shake up some vital organs such as the heart or brain. At worst, I'd hit the lower jaw through which the beast heard sound. Without being able to hear, it would starve in a few days, perhaps a week.

In any of these cases, the CPO monitor would be unable to attribute any of these injuries to me. A saser is a focused-beam weapon, so the monitor would never detect my shot, unless I foolishly aimed the saser at the monitor itself. I had briefly considered doing just that, so great was my hatred for the CPO. But I'd rejected that notion; the organization would recover its vehicle and find evidence pointing to me. No, the whale had to be my target.

Having already established a pattern of sprinting ahead of the whale for long periods, I knew that maneuver would not put the monitor on any heightened alert.

As I drifted alongside Azraq, I detected a large school of krill ahead and just to the left, and knew now was the time. My hand tightened on the throttle control. I casually glanced to the side, and saw Azraq's eye.

Something about the eye made me pause. No, more than pause, it made me freeze. I stared through the porthole at it as it stared back at me, and I could not look away. That eye, much larger than either of mine, yet so clownishly small for a whale, nevertheless drew me into a strange trance.

Surrounded by wrinkled skin, that eye looked so old, so infinitely wise, so human, and yet so alien. I should not assign human emotion cues to a whale, but the eye looked neither fearful nor angry. Just knowing.

He *knew.*

Somehow, Azraq knew I would kill him. Yet I saw no hint of accusation or blame in his gaze. After all, he was a killer too, massacring thousands of lives with each mouthful. No, this was one predator staring at another, scrutinizing, acknowledging, appraising.

No longer was he a mere beast I owned. Soon we weren't even two equals eyeing each other across a gulf of size and evolutionary time. Instead, Azraq gazed deep, deep into me, into my soul, while revealing nothing of himself to me.

He knew I would kill him, knew I'd killed other whales and knew my ancestors had, too. Azraq *knew* me, with a kind of knowing that transcended all dimensions of that word. I didn't just sense this or imagine it. It was just…true.

Generations of family tradition and long experience told me to tilt the throttle handle and send a blast from the saser. But that eye confused my thoughts and stayed my hand.

Immobilized by his stare, I felt a creeping foreboding, a chilly and increasing terror. I bit my lip. Sweat ran down my face, and I found myself trembling. My stomach roiled with an acidic dread that left me gasping for breath.

The eye loomed larger and larger in my mind, magnifying into godlike omniscience. It saw my thoughts, saw every bad deed I'd ever done, saw through to my very essence. It peered back through time to my father and his ancestors, and to my mother and hers.

At that moment, I realized a new and frightful truth. That eye would never leave me. No matter where I went, no matter where Azraq went, he'd watch me. His eye would watch me, and judge me, even after the whale's death. Probably even after mine. There are depths of fear that a human can feel, and his own death is only partway down the scale. It's a lower abyss of terror to know for certain you'll be watched for all eternity.

. . .

One more row and that should finish up the *hijiki*. Then I'll empty the vats and shift over to harvesting my acreage of *nori*. It's been a good season for my crops, though I'm thinking of shifting a few hectares from *kombu* to the more profitable *wakame*.

Yes, I'm a seaweed farmer now, and have been for the past six months. My expansive farm lies to the southwest of Kaiyō Kokka, and I go home every night. I sold my whaling sub, and sold old Azraq, too. He died two months later, but I don't regret the sale. There's more to farming than I ever realized, and I do not miss the CPO monitors.

My memory of Azraq's eye has faded, and with it much of the associated fear. Still, it's a good thing kelp has no eyes.

I'm married now, and happily so. My wife would like children, and I would too. I will raise them to shun whale meat, as I have done for the past half year.

Some traditionalists might say, "Toru Mizumoto has dishonored his ancestors." This is not true. I constructed a new *butsudan*, one made of wood, and I keep it in our apartment. I make all appropriate offerings and pay humble respect.

After all, those on my mother's side were my ancestors, too.

The Prophesy Problem

The religion I founded, **Ford Broadwater sighed,** *is imploding.* Over the years, he'd become adept at gauging others' feelings, and now he sensed the mood of the church elders turning against him. They'd become angry and called for a vote. They wanted to see the boy. Despite Ford's power as high priest, he couldn't prevent their vote.

But he could not reveal the savior to them. Not yet.

The religion's senior leaders sat before him in the Council Chamber, arrayed according to their ranks. Over the decades, Ford had fought to keep the faith true to his original vision, but now at age eighty-three, some of his will to fight had ebbed. He'd come to hate these Pod of Priests meetings and the constant work of persuading and cajoling. Now their vote threatened to wash away the edifice he'd built.

Fifty-five years earlier, Ford had experienced a vision; the god Oceanus had commanded him to found Oceanism. The vision had revealed five prophesies, one being that humankind would reach its true and perfect state when people could breathe seawater. The first person to be born breathing seawater would be a holy demi-god who would lead all Oceanists to their true destiny.

That birth had occurred fifteen years ago and now many priests demanded to see and hear from this savior. But they didn't know the boy like Ford did, and he couldn't show them the teenager yet. But he was running out of persuasive reasons to deny people the savior he had promised.

Warm seawater filled the room to the half meter mark, and by custom, everyone wore bathing suits. The sea of faces resembled a dappled, sunlit sea, for each priest's skin had been dyed in some shade of green or blue. This practice served to give Oceanists a new identity, separate from their origins. Ford had been born a black man, but his blue skin rendered any lingering racial tensions moot. He sat before a large projection screen. Five pentapriests sat in a front row that curved around him. Two semicircular rows around that group contained the twenty-five oceanpriests, and beyond them, five rows of the 125 seapriests. Ford knew that 625 gulfpriests viewed the meeting remotely, but they could not vote. All multiples of five, the sacred number of Oceanism.

In the council's first meetings here, Ford had discovered a beneficial property of an oval room partly filled with water. All sound, however soft, travelled to his focal spot. Now he eavesdropped on the priests' hushed mutterings with growing concern.

"—won't show us the boy because he's not really the One."

"The high priest shouldn't have secluded the kid in the first place."

"—proves Broadwater is unstable, too senile to lead the church."

"How can we force him out?"

"It's time for Oceanism to split into different sects."

That last notion disturbed Ford most of all. He couldn't bear to see the faith fragmented.

Voting commenced on the resolution before them, whether to force Broadwater to reveal the savior within the next five days. By ritual, the seapriests voted first, by pressing buttons on the computers before them. The large screen behind Ford displayed this subtotal—82 for and 43 against. Ford had expected this large initial majority to go against him, despite the imploring pre-vote speech he'd given. In the online reactions to his recent broadcast sermons, Ford had sensed increasing unrest from the seapriests and the Panthallasic School, the name for Oceanism's half-billion adherents around the world.

The lopsided vote did not unduly upset him. He felt confident that higher level priests saw things his way, and their votes counted more. When the twenty-five cceanpriests finished voting, the weighted result got displayed—121 for and 79 against.

This caused Ford some concern. His opposition's subtotal fell just twenty votes short of the majority needed to pass. Now, four or all five pentapriests would have to vote *for*. Still, he felt some confidence he'd get that many votes. He gazed at each of them, looking for clues about their inclinations, and seeing none.

Turning to look at the results, Ford's shoulders slumped and his heart sank as he stared at the screen. Two pentapriests had voted against him. He'd lost. The murmuring volume increased among the seapriests. As a formality, Ford added his vote and waited for the excited mutterings to die down.

He keyed his microphone and cleared his throat. "The Pod has decided. The resolution has passed," he said, then sighed. "I will reveal the savior to you within five days."

Cheering erupted, mostly among the lower-level priests. *Oceanus, what am I to do?* He needed to gather his thoughts.

"Pentapriests," he addressed them. "I call on you to lead the remainder of this meeting, please. Summon me in my meditation chamber if I'm needed." Dejected, he walked out of the council meeting.

Ford sat suspended in his meditation chamber, a three-meter diameter acrylic sphere. Only a telescoping strut connected it to the seastead above. Thus separated, Ford could not hear the throbbing engines of Hydropolis, headquarters of Oceanism, and the world's only free-roaming aquastate. Utterly alone in the abyssal emptiness, the only sounds Ford heard were the soft flowing of water around his sphere and the distant chitters, crackles, and groans of sea life. He'd turned off exterior lighting and could see nothing at this depth. No daylight penetrated here.

Here, he sought communion with Oceanus, to regain the revelatory trance that had started it all. Though he'd never recaptured that rapturous feeling, that nirvana-like enlightenment, he hoped the water god would answer his plea this time. With the religion facing its greatest threat, Ford sorely needed Oceanus' guidance. He tried emptying his mind of everything except the problem at hand. Perhaps here, close to Oceanus' abode, a solution would emerge. But all he sensed were silence and blackness.

Everything hinged on the boy now. That awful boy. The Pod of Priests had forced Ford's hand and he must produce their savior, whether the boy was ready or not. And he most definitely was *not* ready. Ford had raised the boy himself, with assistance from the kid's parents. He'd inculcated the youth in the ways of Oceanism and had done his best to prepare the boy for his role as savior.

This vote put Ford in a terrible dilemma. If he did not present the savior in five days, the Pod would likely vote him out of his high priest office. Worse, they might split the church into two or more sects. Historically, whenever that happened to a religion, the separation weakened the faith, and pitted faction against faction. The fragments might someday reconcile, but they would never rejoin.

If Ford did present this juvenile delinquent to the Pod, or even to the Panthalassic School, Oceanus only knew what the young fool might say. At the very least, he would behave unlike a savior, and cause people to consider Ford a false prophet. Though Ford could not predict the likely consequences, he at least knew they would be disruptive, and probably disastrous, for the church.

Oceanus, what must I do? Which course must I choose? Please tell me, I beg you. I have never needed your guidance more than I do now.

Nothing appeared out of the blackness. No sounds, other than background biologics, reached him. No answers to his questions entered his mind. He let the minutes pass, hoping and praying. *To commune with Oceanus, perhaps I must go deeper, and for that, I need a sub.*

In the peace of the depths, his mind wandered. As often in these meditations, he recalled once again the moment of the religion's founding. Everyone knew about it, for he'd documented the event in the *Tide*, the sacred text of Oceanism, in Flow 3, Eddies 1 through 25. He'd been the repair technician assigned to take his one-man sub and re-weld a support strut at Templemere, then the sole seastead in Kernaria. During the descent, his ballast system failed and the sub entered an uncontrolled dive. For reasons beyond his understating, he fell into a dreamlike trance. A flood of information entered his mind from a source he didn't comprehend. Like a computer data download, he received the entire religion of Oceanism, its practices, beliefs, prophecies, and the text of the *Tide*. One message ran like a strong current through the vast deluge of data—the god Oceanus had created life in Thalassa's oceans, and that god wanted humanity to return.

When Ford came to his senses, he noted with utter shock that his mini-sub had drifted far below the sub's rated crush depth. The metal hull could not possibly withstand the immense water pressure, and yet it had. Moreover, he found the ballast system once more operational, repaired by some miracle. He returned to the seastead and dedicated his life to the new religion of Oceanism.

Now, seated in his meditation chamber, Ford smiled as he recalled those early days after his vision. His struggle had been to write down everything as fast as he could, all the while hoping he wouldn't forget any of it. But the revelation had been so clear, so coherent, and had cemented itself in his mind as if repeated to him over a lifetime, that he was confident he'd remembered it all.

Including the prophesies. Oceanus had given him five prophesies. First, one day Oceanus would exact terrible revenge for the Seastead Tragedy, the nuclear destruction of PaCitadel. That had, more or less, happened. The United States, and all land nations, had suffered and fallen into decline as many of their citizens had moved to the sea. Not just random citizens, but their adventurous, risk-taking, hard-working ones, the very people needed to keep a country vibrant and strong.

The second prophesy specified that Oceanism would relocate its governing priesthood to a mobile aquastate, one that traveled all the world's oceans. At the time, no such seastead existed, and even now, Hydropolis remained the only such roving aquastate in the world, and it served as a perfect home for Oceanism.

In like manner, the third prophesy had also proved true. It held that Oceanism would spread to every aquastate. Today, it remained the major religion in most sea-based nations, and had made significant inroads in the theistic aquastates of Umat Almuhit, Kumari Kandam, Avemh Yem, and Ichthysia, and even boasted adherents in some land nations.

The religion's fourth prophesy, that an Oceanist would locate the Alpha Vent, the origin point of all life on Thalassa, had yet to come true. The search continued, however.

The fifth prophesy had been clear enough, that humanity would reach its true and perfect state when people could breathe seawater. The first person born breathing seawater would be a demi-god who would lead all Oceanists to their true destiny.

For years, Oceanists had struggled to make this prophesy true. Engineers had developed the artificial gills known as Diving Gill Membrane Apparatus (DIGMA), a system much improved over scuba, but this was a mechanical device. A few scientists had implanted working gills in certain humans, calling them *aquans*. However, the procedure only worked on very few people, those with accommodating DNA whose body didn't reject the implant. Aquans could not pass on their water-breathing ability to their children. But the prophesy had stated only the first person *born* breathing seawater would be the awaited demigod, the savior.

Many dozens of hopeful couples had consented to subject their fetuses to undergo experimental genetic engineering in hopes of parenting the savior. As failed attempts and heartbreaking infant deaths grew more numerous, doubt spread that it was even possible. Most aquastates passed laws forbidding further attempts. Ford himself wondered if he'd remembered the prophesy incorrectly.

Then, at last, success. A genetically engineered boy in Ville D'eau, Altair was born breathing water, and survived. Ford recalled his joy at hearing the news. He'd travelled to Altair to see the infant demigod breathing water without effort. He'd arranged for the baby and his parents to be brought to Hydropolis. There he'd raised the lad, restricting access to him, ensuring the boy would receive the proper indoctrination and not be subject to contrary influences.

Fourteen years had passed, and the boy had become the most rebellious, disruptive, and insubordinate juvenile imaginable. In no way was this miscreant, this reprobate ready to be revealed to the other priests, let alone the Panthalassic School.

"Oceanus," Ford spoke to the black waters surrounding him. "Give me guidance. The priests have voted; by our rules, I must reveal the savior, but if I do, I fear the faith will be destroyed. What must I do now?"

He listened, and waited. No answer . The ocean remained silent. After more than half a century's lapse in communication, another man might have questioned the existence of the deity. But so strong and intense had the flash of revelation been, Ford could never doubt Oceanus' presence. He might question the god's methods, but never Oceanus' reality. The long and continued silence could only mean one thing— Oceanus trusted him, as high priest, to make the right and holy choice.

But in this matter of the prophesied boy, what could he do?

Koralle Shore sat in her quarters, crying. As one of the pentapriests she'd been in the council chamber and witnessed Ford's defeat. His strongest supporter and ally, she hated to see the vote turn against him. She cried, thinking what this must be doing to him.

Her instinct had been to go to him, to comfort him and help in any way she could. But he'd rushed to his meditation chamber, and she knew better than to bother the high priest there.

She dabbed at her eyes. Was he crying now, too, in his lonely chamber? Did his tears match hers, drop for drop? No, she smiled. Not Ford. He'd be deep in thought, working out the logic of what to do. She did the crying for him.

That had been their way from the beginning, from the moment he founded Oceanism. Ford did the planning and strategizing, maintained the public face of the faith. Behind the scenes, Koralle did the supporting, the caring, and the suffering. She did it to spare him from it.

She'd shielded him from something else as well, a troublesome secret she'd kept for fifty-five years and intended to keep until her death.

Those many years ago, both Ford Broadwater and Koralle Shore had different names, before they'd taken their new Oceanism names. Ford had been a repairman and Koralle worked as a quality assurance rep, a mini-sub inspector. Her company had assigned her to investigate the malfunction Ford had reported with his sub's ballast system.

She'd listened to Ford's description of the event. His account defied the laws of physics. Submersible structures do not drift far below design crush depth and suffer no implosion, no hull plate deformation, and no residual stress in the metal.

But the way he talked; she sensed a fire that spoke from his soul. She saw in his eyes a truth he believed, a truth she felt she must believe, a truth for all to believe.

When she examined his mini-sub and reviewed its electronic logs, they showed no fault in the ballast system. Neither the depth gauge logs nor the hull strain gauge data showed a descent anywhere near crush depth, let alone below it.

Faced with this discrepancy, a lesser quality assurance inspector would have believed the sub's instruments, declared Ford's story false, and put that in her report. Ford's company would have disciplined him, perhaps even fired him.

Instead, Koralle thought more deeply. She believed Ford. A sea-god had spoken to him and by a miracle saved him from being crushed by sea pressure. Her problem was to determine why the sub's electronic logs were wrong. Obviously, Oceanus had altered the logs. If the god could perform one miracle, why not two?

But why would Oceanus do that? Why change the logs to show nothing had happened? It dawned on Koralle that Oceanus meant it as a test for her, a test of *her* faith. To Ford, Oceanus had granted the visions, the complete truth of Oceanism and the path he must follow. For Koralle, Oceanus had devised a way to measure her trust, an examination of the strength of her belief.

Once she recognized that, she knew she could not fail that test. If Oceanus could change a sub's logs without leaving a trace of tampering, so could she. If Oceanus could corrupt them to show a falsehood as a test for her, she could change them back to their true reading to pass that test.

To this day, fifty-five years later, Ford's submersible and the logs she'd altered counted among Oceanism's most sacred objects. Koralle had never told anyone—not even Ford—about changing the logs to show a miraculous descent below crush depth. What would have been the point of revealing that? Others might see it, not as Oceanus' test of her, but as a fact casting doubt on Oceanism itself.

In this way and in thousands of others, Koralle served as the unseen, emotional underpinning of the church. Ford was its face; she was its heart.

With the current dilemma about the savior, Ford must think of a way to resolve it. Koralle must grieve and weep for him, for them all. She knew she shouldered an emotional burden far heavier than most people could bear, but Oceanus had dictated this role for her, and she would obey. Moreover, she would never, ever reveal the deep secret of Oceanism's founding miracle.

. . .

Outside the aquarium door, Ford drew several deep breaths, steeling himself. *I'm getting too old for this.* He pressed his hand to the scanner and the door swung open.

Inside the large square room, a transparent-walled, floor-to-ceiling aquarium dominated the center, permitting Ford and very few other authorized people to walk in the narrow passageway around it.

Within the aquarium floated Zale Tradewind, the fourteen-year-old savior of Oceanism. He hovered there, facing a wall screen and watching an old children's televisions show, one from the limited library of shows Ford had approved. Zale wore red swimming trunks that stood out against skin dyed in a blue-and-green wavy pattern. His forehead bore a tan tattoo of a starfish, matching Ford's own tattoo.

The boy turned and frowned. "Go away. I don't want to talk to you. Ever." He went back to his show.

Hydrophones in the aquarium picked up Zale's liquid voice and processors converted it into speech Ford could understand.

"Things have changed," Ford said. "The Pod has voted and—"

"I don't care." The youth put his hands over his ears.

Things had not always been this way. Ford well recalled the day he'd received the marvelous news that a water-breathing child had survived birth and appeared otherwise normal. Genetic researchers had tried and failed so often, and so many faithful Oceanist parents had suffered crushing disappointments, that Ford had wondered if the prophesy would ever come true.

But the first part had, and Ford quickly declared that day a religious holiday, and the place of Zale's birth, in Ville D'eau, Altair, one of Oceanism's sacred sites. He'd brought the infant and his parents to the Oceanism Center in Hydropolis and sequestered the baby away. For fourteen years, he and the parents had raised the boy, educated him, and tried to prepare him for his role. Ford had taught him every detail of Oceanism.

For the boy's Immersion process, Ford had not waited until Zale reached the traditional age of fifteen. When the youth reached five, Ford had directed the dying of skin, webbing of fingers and toes, and inking of the forehead tattoo.

All that time, Zale had seen only his parents, and the occasional doctor, nurse, and aquarium technician, as well as Ford himself. Ford had instructed the others how to behave and what to say around Zale, and sworn them to secrecy about revealing anything about the boy or his upbringing to the outside world. Ford had authorized occasional still images and short videos of the boy to become public, and faithful Oceanists worldwide had treasured these brief glimpses.

Somehow, something had gone wrong. At age eleven, Zale began asking more profound questions about Oceanism, about why he should accept it all on faith, about why he had to be different from everyone else. Ford had done his best to give answers, and had instructed the boy's parents on how they should answer as well. By age twelve, the boy had turned against Ford, and against Oceanism. He barely spoke to his parents. Ford knew it was in the nature of teenagers to rebel, but he believed Zale's behavior far exceeded normal boundary-pushing.

"I know you can hear me." Ford raised his voice and spoke closer to one of the microphones. "I came to tell you the Pod of Priests has voted to—"

"Leave me alone." The boy glared at him. "You ruined my life!"

Ford groaned and rubbed his starfish tattoo. "We've been through this before. I didn't ruin your life. In fact, I wish I could trade places with you. Half a billion people already worship you as a demigod. You'll soon have my job as high priest, head of a huge and growing religious order."

"Yeah?" Zale pointed at him. "I wish we could trade places, too. Then *you* could be the freak, locked up in a prison with no friends. I don't want to be a demigod, or high priest of your stupid religion. I didn't ask for any of this. I just want to be normal and breathe air like everyone else."

"I've already told you," Ford shook his head. "The genetic modifications are too extensive. You'd never survive the surgery necessary to make you an air-breather." *True enough today, but perhaps medical science will permit a successful operation in a few years. No need to tell the kid about that now.*

"Yeah, well, thanks a lot for dooming me to be so flukin' different from everyone else," Zale swished a hand in dismissal, "the only water-breather in the world."

Wearied by the sparring, Ford muttered under his breath, "Not the only one."

"What?" Zale swam over and floated next to the glass where Ford stood. "What did you say?"

Ford shook his head, regretting what he'd revealed. He sighed. "There are others who breathe water." Ford had never seen any benefit in telling his savior about the aquan gill implants or the successful births that followed Zale's.

Zale's eyes widened. "Others like me?"

"No, no," Ford shook his head again. "Not like you. You're the *first born*. That makes you the demigod of prophesy."

The youth rolled his eyes. "I don't care about that stuff. That's all flotz and jetz to me. Where are these water-breathers? When can I meet them?" He splayed his hands against the glass, as if trying to touch Ford.

The boy's unaccustomed interest and eagerness gave Ford an idea. He turned away, as if pondering Zale's questions, then turned back, nodding. "All right. I can arrange for some of the water-breathers to meet you."

Zale's smile was the first Ford had seen on the boy's face for ages. "But first," Ford held up a forefinger, "you need to do something for me."

Sneering and crossing his arms, Zale said, "Lemme guess. I've gotta talk and act like a demigod, right?"

"Right," Ford said, "In a live broadcast to the Pod of Priests, and maybe, if I think you're ready, to the whole Panthalassic School. If I prepare you, will you do it?"

Zale's eyes met his. "Yeah, I will. So long as you let me meet the other water-breathers soon after."

"It's a deal." Ford put his right hand up to the glass, feeling good for the first time since the Pod's vote. He felt blasphemous to be achieving his ends by bribing the lad rather than inspiring him to become a true believer. But he had a deadline.

Placing his left hand against the glass to match Ford's, Zale asked, "When do I talk?"

"In five days," Ford said. "That doesn't give me much time to coach you."

"We're on in ten seconds, High Priest," the camera-woman said.

Ford cleared his throat. He felt the nervous jitter of butterflies in his stomach. At first, that seemed strange, given the thousands of live broadcast sermons he'd made. He couldn't attribute his fear to worry over what Zale might say. The boy had learned quickly and the dress rehearsal had gone flawlessly. Ford soon realized the cause of his apprehension; he was about to give the most momentous announcement in the history of Oceanism.

"Five," said the camera-woman, "four, three..."

The teleprompter was in position. Ford stood in waist-deep water. To his left, the aquarium wall loomed as a blackened barrier, arranged that way by the lighting technicians. Ford gave his beatific smile and tamped down his anxieties. This would be his greatest triumph. The camera-woman held up two fingers, then one, then pointed at him.

"Hail, fellow Oceanists! Greetings to the Pod of Priests and the Panthalassic School. I am High Priest Ford Broadwater. I'm here to make a very special introduction. First, let me remind you that fifty-five years ago, Oceanus revealed a prophesy to me, that one day a human would be born able to breathe water and that this being would be a demigod who would lead all Oceanists to their true destiny.

"As I foresaw, a seawater-breathing baby was born. He is growing into manhood now, and I believe this is the right day to introduce him to all of you. I know you're all anxious to meet him, so allow me to present the One, the demigod foretold by prophesy, the Savior of Oceanism!"

Ford flashed a wide smile, raised his left hand and gestured to the black wall. He saw the camera pan in that direction. Three full seconds passed, and then the aquarium lit up. It was empty, except for a golden, high-backed chair adorned with Oceanism symbols and icons, which appeared to float in the center of the view. To the right, a stream of bubbles ascended from an aerator on the floor, as verification of a liquid medium. In a cloud of bubbles, the boy rose up from below and sat in the chair, cupping his hands over the front of the armrests.

Clad in his red swimsuit, the youth took several breaths before speaking. Ford recalled his squeamish feeling the first time he'd seen the baby breathe water. Though he'd long grown used to the sight, he knew the audience was experiencing that gag-inducing discomfort right now.

"Hail, Oceanists!" the young man said. "I'm Zale Tradewind. May the blessings of Oceanus be upon each of you." He spread his arms, webbed fingers splayed out. Then he turned to his right. "Thank you, High Priest, for giving me this opportunity to speak not only to the Pod of Priests, but to the Panthalassic School."

Ford nodded and smiled, though he knew he was off-camera now. The boy was doing well, repeating the rehearsed movements, speaking the words on the teleprompter, words Ford had written for him.

"I know you have many questions for me," Zale continued, "and in the coming days, months, and years I'll make every effort to answer them all. For now, I have just one message for you."

Huh? Ford flinched and stared. The kid was going off-script.

Zale launched himself out of the chair and straight at the aquarium wall so his face filled the televisions screen. "I'm *not* your savior! I'm just a kid who breathes water and wants to breathe air."

Ford stared in open-mouthed horror as the boy kept ranting. He felt a powerful hammering in his chest, and he clutched at his breast with both hands.

"I want to get out of here. I'm a prisoner being held against my will," Zale railed at the camera. "I call on the Hydropolis Police to rescue me and arrest Ford Broadwater."

"Stop! Stop the broadcast," Ford yelled at the camera-woman.

"We're off the air," the camera-woman said.

"The seven second delay?" Ford asked her. "Please tell me we stopped broadcasting before—"

She shook her head. "I'm sorry, High Priest. I'm pretty sure the first part went out."

Slumping in his seat, Ford fought off a wave of nausea and dizziness. His vision clouded and the massive pounding pain in his chest continued. *I'm having a heart attack.*

He looked up at the aquarium and saw Zale floating in a standing posture, sneering down at him. "Why," Ford croaked. "Why did you do it?"

"You're lucky," Zale spoke with disdain. "All I could do was wreck your reputation. You wrecked my whole life." He spun, turning his back.

"But," Ford could barely get the words out, "I thought you wanted to meet other water-breathers."

"Oh, I will." Zale turned back to face him. "Soon, the police will come and I'll be free to meet whoever I want."

Ford shut his eyes and sought to attain a calm, meditative state, He felt a hand touch his shoulder and he opened his eyes.

A member of the film crew asked, "Are you okay, High Priest?"

"Yes," he lied.

Handling the controls of a one-man submarine for the first time in half a century, Ford marveled how well he'd retained the knowledge and skills to operate it. Like riding a bicycle, the old saying went. He left Hydropolis behind and descended, the water around him turning from bluer to blacker shades as he went.

Once his heartbeat had slowed, Ford had exited the aquarium room through a back door and taken an elevator alone to the nearest mini-sub hangar. He felt no worry about the Hydropolis Police. Church sanctuary laws would hold them up for hours, perhaps days. In the hangar, the submarine technicians had helped him. Being on duty, they had no doubt missed the disastrous broadcast, and probably felt honored to be assisting the high priest into the craft he requested.

A message alert sounded, and Ford glanced at the display. Koralle Shore. He thought of blocking the call, but knew he owed her more than that. He turned on the microphone. "Thank you for all you've done, Koralle. For me, and for Oceanism. Good-bye."

He switched off the transceiver, cutting short her plaintive wail. Then, he began to cry.

Deeper he plunged, into an abyss similar to the one where his journey had started fifty-five years earlier. The depth gauge and hull strain gauges displayed the mounting external sea pressure.

Certain of the deity's existence, Ford intended to venture deep enough this time to communicate with Oceanus and find his answers. As before, the omnipotent water god would prevent any harm to him.

"Oceanus," he howled with tears streaming down. "Why? Why did you let this happen? Was I not a devout and faithful messenger? Was the child not really the One? How could the boy's betrayal today be part of your plan? Help me understand, Oceanus, I beseech you. Please, please answer me."

Twenty-five meters below its rated crush depth, the submarine's hull imploded.

The Whole Fish

This bunch of diplomats stand as much chance of stopping a war, Mazarine Robard-Reefe thought, *as old King Canute did of holding back the tide.* From her seat at one end, Maz scanned the faces of people seated along both sides of the long table.

Two delegations—Robardia on her side, Manganor on the other. Here at this neutral location to talk, as if speeches could hold back missiles or torpedoes. Two rows of polite people, trained in diplomacy and tact and platitudes, each one expressionless, giving nothing away. All except the young man sitting opposite her, the one staring at her, whose name plaque read *E. Astor.* Maz ignored him.

The Grand Meeting Room looked lavish by seastead standards. Carpeted floor, wall-screens shifting from one pleasant ocean view to another, and three flags dangling from poles. Robardia's proud flag honoring both Oceanism and PaCitadel on the left, the money-worshiping flag of Manganor on the right, and the odd, nozzle-depicting flag of their host aquastate, Udintsev, in the middle. Bookshelves stood against walls, but metal bars stretched across each shelf as if protecting the books from earthquakes. Maz had never seen a conference table like this one, with ridges and indentations for cups and plates.

At the far end of the table, where the top diplomats sat, the Udintsev Chancellor of Foreign Affairs walked to the podium to start the conference. At 124 years old, Dmitriy Jones needed a motorized exoskeleton to move his body around, but still spoke with vigor. His Russian got translated into Robardian English through Maz's earbud.

"Welcome, delegates, to the Ekman seastead in Udintsev. We're pleased to host this conference. Recently, the UN conducted radiation measurements and declared the PaCitadel Exclusion Zone safe for re-occupation. That two-thousand-kilometer circle is the last unowned area on Earth. Your two nations," he gestured to each side as arm motors whirred, "Manganor and Robardia, have filed claims. My aquastate is neutral in this dispute, with no stake in the matter other than to facilitate a peaceful outcome beneficial to both sides. By random selection, I invite Manganor to speak first." Amid the humming of motors, he sat in a chair behind the podium and in front of the Udintsev flag.

Left out one detail, Maz thought, the proverbial whale in the pool. At that moment, warships, subs, and attack aircraft patrolled just outside the exclusion zone and all along the Robardia/Manganor border, ready to fight if these last-ditch talks failed.

E. Astor watched her again, his eyebrows moving up and his lips suggesting a smile. Maz looked away. How adolescent, so unlike her idea of diplomatic behavior. She thought of her son, Jord, now fifteen. He'd begged to accompany her on this trip. She'd relented, and now worried about him, alone in their room with nothing to do and nobody his age in the Robardian delegation.

Alessa Quispe, the Manganor Director of State, strode to the podium. Dark-haired and brown-skinned, she wore a grayish brown business jumpsuit. Ugly outfit, Maz thought, matching the manganese nodules her aquastate mined, and from which it took its name. The woman even wore glasses, actual eyeglasses, obsolete now for half a century. Perhaps she thought they made her look distinguished, but instead, the affectation branded her as a fashion castaway.

"Thank you, Mr. Jones," she said. "Delegates, we all know about the vast fields of manganese nodules and other mineral deposits lying on the exclusion zone seabed, no longer contaminated, all ripe for mining. There is no question that Manganor is in the best position to extract these resources. Control of the zone should not be subject to emotional, irrational, outdated claims based on events of a distant past. We must look to the future, to the benefit of humankind."

Her speech wore on, and Maz hated every word. All money, all greed, all business. No soul. No heart. No reverence for the hundreds who'd died there.

Every time Maz glanced across the table, she saw E. Astor eyeing her. He never looked away, as politeness would require. Very indecorous. All the rest, on both sides, sat stone-faced, devoid of expression, impossible to read. They played the diplomacy game like poker, revealing nothing, holding cards tight. Maz got the sense Astor found it all amusing and wanted her to laugh with him. We're at the kid's table, his expression seemed to say. Let the adults babble their self-important nonsense while we tell jokes, stick straws in our noses, and flick food at each other.

What did his scrutiny of her mean? Did he know she lacked diplomatic credentials? A historian, she served as director of the J. Hugh Robard PaCitadel Museum. She recalled what the Robardia team told her when they'd asked her to join them. "Your ancestry helps our case and your testimony could prove crucial. After you speak, leave it to us to negotiate a peaceful solution." Maz knew diplomats sometimes said one thing and meant another, but what game was Astor playing?

The Robardia Seaminister of External Relations walked to the podium next. A green-skinned Oceanist, the Seaminister sported a manta ray forehead tattoo.

"I am Kallan Benthos. My pronoun is thon," the Seaminister began.

Maz couldn't discern the birth gender of the androgyne from thon's features, mannerisms, or voice, but that didn't matter.

"Manganor's claim to the zone rests solely, and merely, on economic factors," thon said. "They want the region for the money it can make them. Our claim goes deeper, has longer and more legal precedent, and is based on prior ownership. Ever since the destruction of PaCitadel, Robardia has honored the memory of J. Hugh Robard. Since the founding of Oceanism, we have faithfully worshipped Oceanus. We seek to consecrate this holy region, not to pillage it for profit. With us today is the sole living descendant of J. Hugh Robard. Maz, would you step up and say a few words?"

Maz blinked and stared for a moment, surprised to be called on so soon. She stood, fumbled with her datapad, and walked the length of the room to the podium. She'd memorized her speech, but felt glad to have the datapad as backup.

Two rows of deadpan faces looked back at her. Those on the Robardian side each in a color pleasing to Oceanus—blue, green, or a mix. Each bore a proper forehead tattoo of a fish, octopus, whale, or starfish. Webbed fingers adorned each hand. Some on the Manganor side hadn't undergone Oceanist immersion. It felt weird to see adults in their natural born skin tone, pale whites, browns, and blacks.

"Thank you, Seaminister Benthos. I am Mazarine Robard-Reefe. My great-grandfather designed, built, and governed PaCitadel, the world's first self-defended seastead and the first stable aquastate. Seventy-six years ago, a jet from the United States dropped a nuclear bomb on it. The shock wave destroyed the structure, causing it to implode, killing everyone inside, and leaving the area too radioactive to inhabit until now."

She paused, collected herself, and resumed. "On that tragic day, J. Hugh's eldest son—my grandfather—was not at PaCitadel. He had gone to French Polynesia to negotiate a trade deal. In one instant, he had no one to negotiate for, no home to go back to, and no family left." Though her voice wavered, she went on, her words gaining in volume and intensity.

"Since the early days of seasteading, we've all lived by the code, 'you own what you can defend.' My great-grandfather owned that sector. He died defending it. I now represent him. All of Robardia represents him. His patch of ocean must now be ours. We claim it, not for a reason so base as money, but for a reason much more profound. We claim it in the name of J. Hugh Robard, and in the holy name of Oceanus. Thank you."

On the Robardia side, some delegates smiled, nodded, or even wiped their eyes. Maz saw murmured whispering on the Manganor side, except for E. Astor, who gave her a slight smile when she took her seat. Maz knew both she and the seaminister had glossed over a religious matter known to everyone present. Following the suicide of Ford Breakwater, Oceanism's founder, the religion suffered a schism and divided into two sects. Robardia had sided with the Orthodox Current which held the savior had not yet arrived. Though not citizens of a theocracy, Managnor's Oceanist population tended toward the Ultradox Current, believing Broadwater was martyred as their true savior. This fueled even more tension between the aquastates.

Her part done, Maz watched while the professionals started real negotiations. Speeches by lesser diplomats continued for hours, but Maz heard only hardened positions, lists of grudges, and accusations of bad behavior. No one sought common ground or offered any olive branches.

The Udintsev Chancellor proposed a half-hour break. Maz's frustration with the lack of progress gave way to pleasant anticipation at the chance to call Jord to check on him.

Before she stood, she felt a tap on her shoulder. "Ms. Robard-Reefe?"

She looked up and turned. The man from across the table stood behind her.

He stuck out his hand. "I'm Eon Astor. May we talk?"

Maz shook his hand but wished he would go away. "I'm busy right now."

"I only need a few minutes. We could talk on the way to wherever you're going."

Some diplomats had left for the bathrooms and others stayed to talk. Many had paired up with their opposite number in the other delegation.

She sized up the man who'd been watching her all morning. Late thirties or early forties—her same age range. Handsome, for an adult without permadyed skin. Dark hair, pleasant smile. He wore a wedding ring, so perhaps he wouldn't hit on her. Just talking to him wouldn't violate protocol, and she might learn something of value about Manganor. "Okay."

Maz led him along the carpeted hallway toward a lounge she'd passed on the way in. Wrap-around windows looked out on the ocean surface, a helipad, solar panels, and wave-powered generators. When she'd flown in the day before, she'd seen how the surface portion of the Ekman seastead formed a fat lens shape, like a human eye looking up. She'd learned cables led down to several submerged levels, each of similar eye shape, with elevators running along the cables. From the lowest level, chains ran down to anchors on the seafloor.

A few other people occupied the lounge, sitting, talking, or eating. Several looked up when a holographic news screen switched to a different story. Maz paused to watch, too.

"…world waits as Manganor and Robardia square off," the news reporter said. A map displayed the straight, north-south boundary between the aquastates with the circular exclusion zone between. Colored dots appeared all along the line and outside the zone. "Their naval fleets face each other across the border. All hopes for preventing a war hinge on discussions now taking place in Udintsev. We'll keep you updated on this story. In other news…"

"Manganor has more and better ships," Eon spoke beside her. "All the war game simulations show us winning."

Maz felt her temper flare, but calmed herself and turned to face him. "Wars aren't fought by simulations," she said. "Sims don't take fighting spirit into account. Your sailors fight for money. Ours fight for Oceanus."

Eon just smirked and pointed to a table some distance away from others, and from the news screen. "Care to sit?"

She didn't, but sat anyway, curious about him.

He leaned across the table, looking at her. "It's up to us to keep war from happening."

Shaking her head, Maz asked, "Do you really believe these delegations can—"

"Not the delegations. Us. You and me."

Maz laughed. "That's insane. We're the lowest level members, at the far end of the conference table from where the top diplomats work." She saw no point in admitting she wasn't a diplomat at all.

He sat back and smiled. "They're working all right, but not at making peace. They prattle and posture. They rattle sabers. The real work happens at our level. If there's some compromise, some way out, it's up to you and me to find it."

She frowned, convinced he had things upside-down. How could the fate of two nations hinge on those with the least experience? "I don't believe you, but for the sake of argument, let's say you're right. What are you proposing?"

He paused, looking as bland as any other diplomat. "Have you heard the parable of the poor sisters and the fish?"

"No." What, she wondered, was he on about?

"Their family's poor, and the two sisters have just one fish. About this long." He held his hands a third of a meter apart. "Each girl wants the fish for herself. They can't decide who should get it, so they agree to cut it in half." He mimed the act of carving an imaginary fish in two.

She saw his direction. "You're suggesting we split the exclusion zone in half." As if that hadn't been considered and rejected already.

"Not at all. After they divide the fish, one sister debones her half, throws the bones away, then cooks and eats the flesh. The other sister debones her half, throws the flesh away, cleans the bones and uses the fish skeleton to comb her hair."

Maz thought she'd have to be pretty desperate to run fish bones through her hair. She pondered the parable while glancing out a window. A Udintsev flag flapped in a strengthening wind, and whitecaps roughened the sea surface. "You're saying there's a way for each side to get what we want."

"Yeah." He nodded. "The whole fish."

She shook her head again. "Impossible. We can't share the zone. Your side wants the whole thing, to mine the seabed. My side wants the whole thing too, but to treat it as a holy site. No way to compromise."

A gentle chime sounded, then an announcement. "All Manganor and Robardia delegates, please return to the Grand Meeting Room for the next session."

"We'd better head back." Eon stood up. "But what if there *is* a way to compromise? Only you and I can find it."

As they walked along a hallway, she said, "Don't think so. There's no way to reconcile this mess. Your fish parable is cute, but it doesn't work in the real world."

He strode ahead, then turned around, blocking her way and forcing her to stop. "Okay, let's talk real world. I'm the grandson of Samantha Dawnstar."

"Dawnstar." Her jaw dropped and her eyes widened. "The pilot who dropped…" She glared at him, balled her fists, and raised her voice. "Your grandmother bombed my great-grandfather, and murdered hundreds of others. And you dare talk to me about making peace!"

He raised both palms toward her. "I understand how you must feel. I'd feel the same way."

She brushed past him, unwilling to listen, ignoring the stares she got from others in the hallway.

"To her dying day," he called after her, "my grandmother regretted what she'd done. Now I have the chance to help correct a horrible wrong."

She stormed into the meeting room and plunked down in her chair, furious at him. With the push of a button, his ancestor had wiped out hundreds of people on PaCitadel, including Maz's ancestor. She couldn't forgive that, let alone compromise with anything he stood for.

When he took his seat opposite her, she didn't look his way, keeping her gaze on the more senior delegates as they argued. With a pang of maternal regret, she realized she'd forgotten to phone her son. Jord should be okay, though. The living quarters set aside for Robardia delegates offered a cafeteria and a lounge with holo games.

For two hours, the high-ranking delegates got nowhere, sticking by their extreme positions, offering no concessions, exploring no areas of potential agreement.

An intrusive, bonging chime sounded and a voice announced, "Current alert. Rig Ekman for moderate current. All occupants brace for tilt."

Maz recalled their pre-arrival briefing. Udintsev officials said the Ekman seastead experienced the world's strongest mid-ocean current, the Antarctic Circumpolar Current. Like a string of connected kites in a breeze, the seastead's levels oriented with the flow and inclined when it grew in strength. Other delegates rolled their eyes, sighed, or frowned.

Dmitriy Jones, the Udintsev chancellor, half-sprinted to the podium, his exoskeleton doing all the work. While panting from the exertion, he said, "My apologies, everyone. Please hold on to the table."

The room leaned. Not much and not fast, but enough to perceive it. The chancellor stood at the high end, and Maz sat at the low end. The flags dangled away from their poles. It amused Maz to see some senior diplomats seizing the table edge as if they dangled from a precipice. They might be used to riding submarines that inclined to change depth, but most seasteads remained stable.

"We're accustomed to this," the chancellor continued. He pressed a button and a holographic image appeared above the table showing a graduated scale and an arrow. "As you can see, our inclinometer shows a slant of only six degrees. Please continue your deliberations. The current should weaken soon and the room will return to level." He resumed his seat in front of his aquastate's flag.

Maz nodded as things clicked in her mind. She understood the carpeted floors, the ridges in the tabletop, the bars across the bookshelves. Even their wide-bottomed drink glasses bore a black line partway down from the top, and servers never filled above that line. The seastead's eye-like shape made sense—it could orient itself with the current. The nozzle shape on the Udintsev flag suggested speedy flow, too. The Ekman seastead, she recalled, had attracted oceanologists, particularly those studying currents.

An hour later, both sides concurred on one thing, the need for a break. Udintsev had set aside separate quarters, including small conference rooms for each delegation. The Robardia team gathered in theirs.

Maz took the opportunity to call her son.

"Hi, Mom."

"How're you doing?"

"Fine."

His standard, one-syllable answer to any question. "Do you need anything?"

"No, I'm fine."

Maz thought she heard a voice in the background. Must likely from a holo game character. If she asked too much, he'd get angry and accuse her of prying. He did need some space to grow up, after all. "Okay. See you at dinner."

"Thanks, Mom. Bye."

She'd gotten nine words out of him this time. Better than average.

Maz slipped into the Robardia conference room and found the strategy session had already started. The Prime Seaminister himself, her aquastate's leader, appeared in a holo video, directing his comments to Kallan Benthos.

"...almost in attack position. Just another hour. Keep them talking, thinking you're really looking for a solution, but don't give up a millimeter. Of course, if they yield the entire zone to us, great, but otherwise just pick some issue—doesn't matter what—and get angry. Accuse them of jeopardizing the talks, and walk out."

Maz's jaw dropped, but no one else looked perturbed. What was going on? What had she missed?

"Call me back then," he continued, "and I'll order the admiral to commence the attack. Understood?"

"Yes, sir," thon said.

With a hollow feeling, Maz realized her leaders had planned for war all along. They regarded these diplomatic talks as a ruse, a chance to learn the military weaknesses of Manganor, not an opportunity to seek peace. And they hadn't told her.

The call ended and the strategy meeting broke up. The mood seemed buoyant. The Robardia diplomats smiled for the first time she'd seen.

Maz looked at Seaminister Benthos. "Excuse me. I have a question."

Thon's smile faded. "Ah, Maz. Sorry we had to keep you in the dark. We needed your testimony to be authentic, not forced. You've done your part, and done it well. Thank you. All you need to do now is sit at the negotiating table as a reminder of how wrong Manganor is, and why they'll lose the coming conflict."

Staring at thon, Maz made no reply. Diplomats, she knew, used deception and manipulation cloaked in straight-faced rationalizations. She thought they used those techniques against adversaries, but it never dawned on her they'd lie to a member of their own team. However just the cause, Robardia had entered into peace talks only as a prelude to war. An unwitting accomplice to the sham, Maz felt her understanding of the world taking a strange tilt, even greater than the slant of the Ekman seastead.

Minutes later, back in the Grand Meeting Room, solemn and unrevealing faces stared across the table. Neither side budged in their stances, nor did either offer anything of value to the other.

After forty-five minutes, the warning chime sounded, and again the voice came from speakers. "Current alert. Rig Ekman for strong current. All occupants, brace for severe tilt."

Maz grabbed the table edge and caught Eon smiling at her. She frowned back, then ignored him.

The Udintsev chancellor stood, and his exoskeleton arms telescoped out, extending to the ceiling. Braced by four metal limbs, he spoke. "My apologies once again. These strong currents rarely last long."

The room tilted further, slanting to a greater extent. The chancellor activated the holographic inclinometer again and the arrow swept past fifteen, then twenty, and finally settled at twenty-two degrees. Pens rolled down the table. Drink glasses tipped over, spilling liquid that ran down over datapads and off the edge onto delegates' clothing.

Some diplomats shrieked. A couple of them stood to wipe off their formal jumpsuits, only to stagger and fall on the inclined floor.

"This is intolerable!" yelled the Robardia seaminister.

"Outrageous!" growled the Manganor director.

"We can't negotiate like this," Kallan said.

"We're done here," Alessa Quispe pointed at Kallan. "Your side caused this."

"You accuse *us*?" thon sneered. "It's Manganor treachery. We're through."

Each side's diplomats made their way to separate side doors, stepping with care to stay upright, everyone ignoring the Udintsev chancellor's raised voice. "Nobody can leave yet. Ships and subs can't undock. Helicopters can't take off until the current subsides. I urge you all to stay and continue your work."

Everyone ignored him and filed out the doors.

Fighting to retain traction on the hall carpet, Maz used her phone to call Jord. "Pack your things. We're leaving as soon as this place levels out."

"Now? We just got here."

"Now. Talks broke off. We're going home."

"Can't we stay a couple more days?"

Why would he ask that? "No." She reached the door to their quarters and used her key card to open it. "Everything fell apart. We're all lea—" She looked around at the empty room. "Where are you?"

"Don't get mad."

"Where?"

"Um. Cafeteria 4-C. I met someone."

She shook her head. Kids. "I'll come get you." She ended the call and made it into the hall without slipping. Jord must've come across some Udintsev kid his own age.

As she crept down the corridors, the tilt lessened, making the walk easier. Cafeteria 4-C, she thought, following the posted sector signs. But that couldn't be right. Sector 4 housed the *Manganor* delegation. What was he doing there? In the hallway, she saw some of the Manganor delegates. They glanced at her with ever-impassive expressions, then headed for their lounge.

Maz paused at the cafeteria entrance. Through a window, she saw Jord. A girl sat across from him and they both laughed at something one of them said. Neither appeared bothered by the room's tilt. Jord showed her his datapad and she smiled at it, then she showed hers to him, watching his face for a reaction.

"She's the daughter of Ambassador Vargas," a voice said in her ear.

Eon. The last person Maz wanted to see.

He went on. "The girl composes music, I'm told, but struggles with lyrics."

Maz wanted to rush in and grab Jord, but he looked happy, and had made so few friends in Robardia. "He writes poetry," she said, thinking only of Jord, not Eon's murdering ancestor.

"Poetry," Eon nodded. "That reminds me of something an American president once said. John Adams, I think. I'm paraphrasing. "I study war—"

"so my sons can study history," Maz finished, "so their sons can study poetry."

"And music," Eon pointed at the young girl.

Maz despised most things American, but as a historian, she'd studied the land of her great-grandfather's birth. "Adams was way too optimistic. Three centuries later, we're still studying war."

"My grandmother told me that quote," Eon said. "She came to realize it would take generations to fix what she'd done, and she wouldn't live to see the harm corrected. She's why I became a diplomat. If you and I fail here, there will be war. When that happens," he nodded in the direction of the teenagers, "kids like those two could pay the price."

Maz shut her eyes, unable to look at Jord's happy smile. She'd known her son could be drafted into the navy, but had only considered it a theoretical possibility. With tears forming, she imagined getting visited by officials telling her about Jord's death. In a war she might have—

The pleasant tones of an announcement chime sounded. "Current alert over. Resume normal operations." By degrees, the slant of the floor decreased to a horizontal state.

"We still have a choice, you and I," Eon said. "We can bend with the current and let the war happen, or we can be famous as the two who did something about it."

She looked at him, still furious with his grandmother, but wondering if small actions could really hold back the mighty tide of history. Glancing at her watch, she noted only seven minutes remained until Robardian ships attained attack positions. "Come with me. We'll negotiate on the way. Let's give each side the whole fish."

She and Eon walked into the Robardia lounge just as the Prime Seaminister appeared by hologram. All eyes turned to them as they entered.

Kallan Benthos growled. "What is *he* doing here?" thon asked.

"This is Eon Astor," Maz said, "of the Manganor delegation. We have a proposal to make."

Alone in her office in the J. Hugh Robard PaCitadel Museum, Maz sat and flipped on the news hologram. "Both aquastates have now fully ratified the Treaty of Ekman, first signed two weeks ago. All military forces have withdrawn from the Robardia/Manganor border and the former exclusion zone. The agreement gives Robardia ownership of the PaCitadel debris field, and unrestricted access to it. Manganor gets ownership and mining rights to the surrounding zone, but will give Robardia ten percent of the profits. Full credit for this historic treaty goes to Alessa Quispe of Manganor and Kallan Benthos of Robardia." The holo showed the two chief diplomats shaking hands.

Maz turned it off. "Well, Eon," she smiled, shaking her head, "So much for the 'we'll be famous' part."

Please leave a review!

If you enjoyed this book, please consider leaving a review.

About the Author:

A former submariner, Steven R. Southard now writes science fiction. His characters grapple with new technologies and embark on strange voyages, often to distant seas. Steve's short stories appear in over a dozen anthologies, including *The Science Fiction Tarot*, *Not Far from Roswell*, and *Re-Terrify*. Fourteen of his stories form the *What Man Hath Wrought* series. He co-edited the anthologies *20,000 Leagues Remembered* and *Extraordinary Visions, Stories Inspired by Jules Verne*.

Coming Soon from Steven R. Southard:

The Hydronaut

They captured her, altered her, and made her breathe water. Now, she's escaped.

If you enjoyed *The Seastead Chronicles*, you may enjoy these other books published by Pole to Pole Publishing.

The Re-Imagined Series

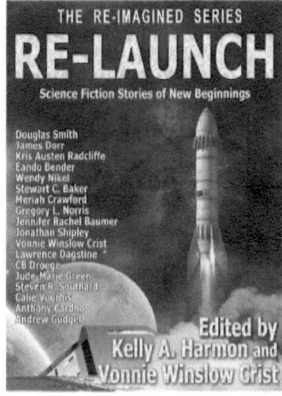  

Re-Launch
Science Fiction Stories of New Beginnings

Re-Launch reminds readers that new beginnings rarely go as planned and danger waits for the unwary on all worlds.

https://poletopolepublishing.com/books/re-launch/

Re-Enchant
Dark Fantasy Stories of Magic and Fae

Re-Enchant takes readers down twisted walkways to discover strange and magical places, people, and creatures.

https://poletopolepublishing.com/books/re-enchant/

Re-Quest
Dark Fantasy Stories about Magic and the Fae

Re-Quest takes readers on fantastical quests filled with adventure, magic, and danger.

https://poletopolepublishing.com/books/re-quest/

The Dark Stories Series

Hides the Dark Tower

Dark Stories #1

https://poletopolepublishing.com/books/hides-the-dark-tower/

In a Cat's Eye

Dark Stories #2

https://poletopolepublishing.com/books/in-a-cats-eye/

Dark Luminous Wings

Dark Stories #3

https://poletopolepublishing.com/books/dark-luminous-wings/